Virtually Yours

Also by Anna Bell

Once Upon a Leap Year

Note to Self

The Man I Didn't Marry

We Just Clicked

If We're Not Married By Thirty

It Started With A Tweet

The Good Girlfriend's Guide to Getting Even

The Bucket List to Mend a Broken Heart

Don't Tell the Brides-to-be

Don't Tell the Boss

Don't Tell the Groom

Virtually Yours

Anna Bell

Bedford Square
Publishers

First published in the UK in 2026 by Bedford Square Publishers Ltd,
London, UK

bedfordsquarepublishers.co.uk
@bedfordsq.publishers

© Anna Bell, 2026

The right of Anna Bell to be identified as the author of this work has been asserted in accordance with the Copyright, Designs and Patents Act 1988. All rights reserved. No part of this book may be reproduced, stored in or introduced into a retrieval system, or transmitted, in any form or by any means (electronic, mechanical, photocopying, recording or otherwise) without the written permission of the publishers.

Any person who does any unauthorised act in relation to this publication
may be liable to criminal prosecution and civil claims for damages.
A CIP catalogue record for this book is available from the British Library.
This is a work of fiction. Names, characters, places, and incidents either
are the product of the author's imagination or are used fictitiously,
and any resemblance to actual persons, living or dead, businesses,
companies, events or locales is entirely coincidental.

ISBN
978-1-83501-400-4 (Paperback)
978-1-83501-401-1 (eBook)

2 4 6 8 10 9 7 5 3 1

Printed and bound in Great Britain by Clays Ltd, Elcograf S.p.A.

The manufacturer's authorised representative in the EU for
product safety is Easy Access System Europe, Mustamäe tee 50,
10621 Tallinn, Estonia

gpsr.requests@easproject.com

Chapter 1

The lift doors of the Empire State Building pinged open and Manhattan in all its majestic glory was laid out in front of me. It might be a truth universally acknowledged that Paris is the city of love, but New York always made my heart beat in a way that Paris never could.

I gasped and Blaine took hold of my hand. A ripple of electricity passed round my entire body.

'I told you this wouldn't be cheesy,' he said. We made our way on to the outdoor platform and looked through the latticed ironwork at the view. The city was glowing with dots of coloured lights, mostly hues of yellow and white, but there were blues and reds all flickering and twinkling. It was like watching an ever-changing sky dance in front of our eyes. Despite the lateness of the hour, the city looked more awake than ever.

'It's beautiful,' I said, 'and you're right. It's not cheesy. It's breathtaking.'

There were a couple of other people in the far corner, but we pretty much had the place to ourselves. And as if the lights and the emptiness didn't make it romantic enough, the sound of soft jazz drifted over to us from the saxophonist playing on the far side.

'Doesn't this just remind you of the scene in *Sleepless in Seattle*?

When Meg Ryan and Tom Hanks finally meet at the end of the movie.' I was trying not to swoon.

Everywhere I went in this city I found myself stepping into the set of a favourite movie.

He shook his head. 'Never seen it.'

'What?' I put my hand to my chest. 'It's a classic.'

'Is it? Nineties rom-com?' There was a surprise in his voice and he almost reminded me of my best friend Kerry. She'd always been distrustful of rom-coms.

'It's more rom than com, to be honest. But nineties movies can be classics. I mean parts of it are a little problematic. They hadn't met in real life and she wrote him a letter begging him to meet her because she feels this connection to him over the radio.'

'You're not selling it.'

'Trust me, the ending sells itself. They're up here alone, at night, with the City dazzling in the background.' I was caught up in the moment. It was like being part of a delicious dream, where I could be Meg Ryan and Blaine could be my Tom Hanks.

'I'm still not buying it. Do you know that they have a lottery where the couple that win can have their wedding here on Valentine's Day?' he said, looking through one of the sets of binoculars.

'Really?'

'Yeah. They don't have weddings here normally, so it's this massive thing. Now that', he said, 'would be romantic.'

I looked around at the view, the sound of jazz drifting round the space, trying not to get even more lost in my fantasy. It only solidified New York in my mind as a city for love.

'You're so lucky. Your city is magical,' I said, its grip on my heart tightening. I took a step closer to the edge, but it disorientated me and it was too quick a movement that made me have the sensation that I was falling. Blaine put his hand out to me.

'You all right?' He was standing so close butterflies started to flutter in my belly.

'Yeah, I think I'll stay away from the edge.'

'Are you scared of heights?'

'Not really. Or at least I never used to be.' Right now I seemed to be scared of everything.

'You don't have to worry about it today,' he said. 'I'm here, and I won't let anything happen to you.'

He put his hand on top of mine and there was the familiar shudder. He took another step closer to me.

With the butterflies growing ever stronger, my already weak legs were getting more unsteady by the second. The feeling was, like meeting Blaine, so unexpected. With everything that had gone on over the last six months, meeting anyone new had been the last thing on my mind. I didn't exactly know what was I was feeling but, unlike most things in my life at the moment, I was excited about it.

We walked around the side of the building, taking in the different views that you could see. I looked out over the Hudson in the direction of Union City in New Jersey, where I'd lived for a year in my twenties doing an internship scheme for British recent graduates. It had felt then that I'd been a stone's throw from the city, but now it looked so far away.

That internship felt like another lifetime. All those years ago I'd travelled there alone, feeling terrified, but that evaporated the instant I'd met Kerry on the scheme and it had been one of the best years of my life.

'This view is incredible,' I said, not wanting to dwell on Kerry. 'There's something about being up here at night.'

'It's the lights,' he said, pointing over to Hoboken, where we'd walked along the riverfront last week. 'Night-time in the city always wins hands down.'

Everywhere I looked across the panoramic views there were different places that I wanted to explore again. It had been far too long since I'd set foot in New York.

'I told you it was worth it, coming here,' he said.

'To see the view, or to spend time with you?' I turned to face him.

Blaine and I had been skirting a fine line between friendship and flirting lately, and it felt like I'd definitively crossed the line.

'I'm hoping both?' His voice was soft.

'Both,' I repeated, nodding my head in confirmation. 'It's been fun.'

'It always is. This backdrop helps, but I think I could hang out anywhere with you and it would be a good time.'

That tingly feeling hit me in the stomach.

'That sounded like a line,' he said, quickly after. 'I didn't mean it to be. It sounds so cheesy. I know this isn't…'

'A date,' I offered, amused by how flustered he'd become.

'Yeah, I know it's not supposed to be, and yet.'

He let the words hang in the air. I knew exactly what he meant. What had started as a random meeting had turned into another chat, and from there a friendship, and now I didn't know what this was. We had an ocean between us and this couldn't work and yet…

'I'm sorry, I shouldn't be saying this, any of this,' he said, with a shake of the head.

'It's okay.' I reached my hand out to his. 'I feel it too. It wasn't what I came here for, but there's something about talking to you. It's as if I've—'

'—known you for ages,' he said. I caught my breath as he took the words out of my mouth.

For a second or two, neither of us spoke. His dark brown eyes seemed to twinkle and dazzle.

'Is this crazy?' I almost whispered.

'Probably,' he said, taking a step closer to me. 'But I can't remember the last time I felt like this about someone I'd only just met.'

'Same,' I said, closing the gap until our faces were inches apart. 'When I'm not with you, I keep thinking about when I'm going to see you next. It's such a cliché.'

My heart was pounding and I was struggling to catch my breath. I wanted to take his hand, to pull him in to me, to kiss him, but it was all too soon: after Jimmy, after losing Kerry. It wasn't the right time.

He reached down and took hold of my hand, the familiar shudder radiated from my hand and tingled round my body. My wrist started to buzz and for a second I thought it was the tingles, before I realised it was my alarm going off on my phone.

'Oh, crap. How is it that time already?' I said, giving his hand a squeeze, before dropping it and silencing the alarm.

'Don't tell me you have to go? Not now. I thought you didn't have to leave until later.'

'It is later. I've got to go to bed. My sister is picking me up early for the wedding tomorrow.'

Blaine groaned. 'Your cousin's wedding?'

'Andrea, yeah. I should have gone to bed hours ago.'

'Five more minutes won't hurt. Stay.'

I smiled. I wished I could. There was a safeness with Blaine that I didn't feel anywhere else.

'I can't.'

He was pleading with his eyes. Those dark brown eyes.

'But I'm not going to see you tomorrow.'

'I'll see you the day after,' I said, trying to break the spell. 'You can help me banish the Sunday scaries?'

'Usual time?'

I nodded my head.

'See you then.'

I took a last look before I swiped out of the app, and flipped up my headset, the world shrinking before my eyes. I blinked as I adjusted to the light. The same four walls that I'd spent too much time staring at came into sharper focus and it hit me in the gut like it always did when I left him.

I hated leaving the Metaverse. The pain wasn't the same there. There, everything seemed possible. Life. Love. Blaine.

I balanced the headset on the coffee table in the grey-walled lounge, wishing that I didn't have to come back to this as my reality.

Chapter 2

I looked around the reception and wondered if weddings had always been this overwhelming. It was a heady mix of it being a family wedding full of elderly relatives whose probing questions I wanted to avoid, and this being the first proper social engagement I'd been to in months.

'Don't you think it's time to get a proper job?' said Hilda, her nose wrinkling.

'I have a proper job.'

I was pinned in the corner by my mum's elderly aunts, the two of them picking over what they saw as poor life choices.

Esme snorted a little. 'Coaches are for football. That's the problem with you young people. I blame the parents. If they were doing their job right, people wouldn't need to be coached out of bed.'

'That's not quite what I do,' I muttered under my breath. I'd spent far too many family gatherings trying to explain to them what I did, only now I didn't have the energy. I'd come to accept that they'd never understand why I'd left what they deemed a suitable career in HR at a big company to work for myself. And, to be honest, with the way I was struggling at the moment, I wondered if they had a point.

'She wouldn't need a proper job if she was with Jimmy. Such a handsome one, that one,' said Esme, patting me on the knee.

'So handsome. He gave me his arm in the church earlier.' Hilda looked smug and Esme's face flashed with jealousy. 'Have you spoken to him yet? He's just over there.'

I followed her pointed finger with my eyes to the far side of the room where my ex-boyfriend Jimmy was talking to a man I didn't know.

'Hmm, not yet,' I said, 'but I'm sure I'll catch up with him later.'

'Don't leave it too long. I saw that girl eyeing him up earlier. The one with the legs.'

Hilda and Esme shared a look between them. They knew exactly who they were talking about, despite the description applying to the entire female congregation of the wedding.

There was a pause in the conversation and I went to stand up to excuse myself, but Hilda gripped my arm, keeping me in place.

'Such an awful business with your friend too,' she said, in almost a whisper.

It was a good job I was still sitting down, the unexpected mention of Kerry winded me.

'She's gone to a better place.' Esme rested her hand on my other arm.

All I could do was nod.

'Hello, everyone,' said my sister Nina, swooping over.

'Ah, Nina. Where's that husband and beautiful baby?' Hilda relinquished her grip from my arm.

'Harry's gone to change Oliver. I'm sure they'll be down later. In the meantime, we're going to borrow this one. If that's okay?'

Nina outstretched her hand and I took it gladly.

'Oh yes, make sure she talks to Jimmy,' said Esme.

'Or that other handsome one. What was his name?'

'Gavin,' swooned Esme.

'Gavin,' nodded Hilda in agreement.

The two women gave contented sighs and Nina dragged me away.

'Thank you for rescuing me,' I said as we weaved our way through the crowd trying not to get stuck with any other relatives.

'You're welcome. They mean well,' Nina said with a sympathetic shrug.

'They do.' I felt guilty. I usually loved speaking to them, but at the moment I didn't want to speak to anyone.

'So did you want to talk to Jimmy?' She raised an eyebrow and I gave her a gentle nudge.

'I couldn't tell them to piss off, but you I can.'

She laughed. 'He looks good in his suit.'

'Nina,' I chided.

'Okay, Chloe Cat, I'll drop it.' She deposited her empty glass on a table and picked up another from a passing waiter. 'I still can't get over how lovely that ceremony was.'

'It was beautiful.'

'Andrea looked stunning.'

'Of course she did.'

'And it was romantic,' she said, clutching her hand to her chest. 'Oh, there's Suz from the hen do,' she said, pointing over to the other side of the room. 'Do you want to come and meet her? She was such fun.'

'I'm fine, you go.'

My sister had done an excellent job extracting me from my great-aunts, but I could do with a minute or two by myself. She looked reluctant, but I shooed her away.

I headed towards the large patio doors of the room that looked firmly shut. What were forecast to be light showers were in fact buckets of pelting rain. I'd heard the wedding plans enough to know that if the weather had played ball, we'd have been stood out on the terrace now, basking in the glow of the late afternoon sun. But looking outside at the dark overcast sky it looked more like a November afternoon rather than June.

I spotted my ex-boyfriend Jimmy. He was still deep in conversation with the stranger. A wave of sadness washed over me. We'd met not long before Andrea and Henry got engaged, and talk of today had been such a big part of our relationship. We'd even booked a room together for tonight when they had announced the date. The universe must have been laughing at us, a fledgling couple booking a hotel nine months in advance. We were so full of optimism that our relationship would last. I'd even booked flights to New York to visit him whilst he was working there over the summer. As if the expense of now having to pay for the fancy country hotel room by myself wasn't bad enough, I also had non-refundable flights to New York that I wasn't going to use.

Jimmy must have caught me staring at him and he raised his hand. I raised mine back and tried a half-hearted smile. I caught sight of Hilda and Esme in the corner watching us like hawks and I turned away.

'There she is,' said Marianne, making her bridesmaid dress swish as she came to a halt in front of me. 'Long time no see.'

She wrapped her arms around me and squeezed me in for a hug.

'You look gorgeous,' I said. 'Being a bridesmaid suits you.'

'Why, thank you. Do you know it's my first time being one and, honestly, I don't love it. I seem to be spending an inordinate amount of time wedged in a toilet cubicle holding Andrea's dress up.'

'It's a fabulous dress, though,' I said, watching the bride across the room almost knock into someone as she went to talk to them.

'It is, but I just wish she'd gone for one of those numbers that had a skirt you could zip off for a slinky evening version. I think I'm going to be black and blue from all the wedging tomorrow.'

Marianne was my cousin Andrea's best friend. The two of them were like chalk and cheese in terms of personality, but the one thing they had in common was the speed at which they talked and verbalised their internal thought process.

'But enough of my moaning. How are you? I saw Jimmy earlier.'

I rolled my lips together. There was a familiar pattern emerging at this wedding.

'Did you? I haven't spoken to him yet.'

'Are things that bad?' She leaned in a little closer, as if she was settling in for gossip.

'No, we're fine. I'm sure we'll chat later on. There are just so many people here.'

'I know. Who knew they knew so many people? Have you met Tom's hot cousin yet? Gavin?'

'I don't think so.'

'Don't tell me he's not your type.' She looked taken a back. 'He would be everyone's type.'

'I'm not interested.'

'Chloe, even I'm interested,' she said with a look of disbelief. 'And I'm very happily married. I should see if I could move some of the seating round for dinner. Andrea would kill me, but it would be worth it.'

'There's no need,' I said, fixing a firm look on my face.

'Maybe a little fling would be just what the doctor ordered. Get you out of that house a bit.'

'I go out. I'm here, aren't I?' I gestured round the room.

'Yeah, but only because Andrea would have killed you if you hadn't been. You've not been to any of our meet-ups or the hen do.'

'I've been busy.'

'Kerry wouldn't have wanted to see you like this.'

My stomach sank. She was right. Kerry wouldn't have wanted to see me like this, but that didn't make it any easier to snap out of it.

'I'm fine. Honestly. I've been hanging out with someone.'

'Like a man, someone?' she said, her jaw dropping and her eyes widening.

'He is a man,' I said, swiping a glass from a passing waiter and taking the tiniest of sips. 'But it's not like that. It's just a friendship.'

I didn't want to tell her that I thought it had the potential to be something more.

'You've practically been a hermit. Did you meet him online?'

'Kind of.' I went to run my hands through my hair, forgetting that Nina had sprayed it with hair spray, and my fingers got sticky.

'I need to hear everything.'

'And you will when there's something to tell,' I said, wiping my hands on my skirt. I didn't want her probing about Blaine so I made a shameless attempt at a change of subject. 'Where's Betty, is she here?'

'No, Jamie's mum said she'd have her for the night. She told us to let our hair down but, if I'm honest, I'm counting down the hours until I can go to bed. I'm exhausted,' she said, stifling a yawn. 'Betty didn't sleep at all last night, or any night, and everyone's trying to have proper adult conversations and I've got to think of clever and witty things to say.'

I might not have a small child, but I understood the pain of small talk when you weren't in the right place.

'It's great you're having a night off, though. How old is she now, eighteen months?'

'She'll be two in September.'

'No!' Time was racing by.

'Do you want to see photos?'

She dug into her tiny purse and pulled out her phone. She talked me through the milestones Betty was hitting and I watched how Marianne's facial expression morphed into one of pride.

'So cute.'

'Takes after her mum,' she said, with a little laugh.

'Naturally,' I agreed.

She slipped her phone away and squeezed my hand.

'It's nice to see you. I've missed hanging out,' she said.

'I know. I'd been meaning to call you. I was thinking that it's almost time for the autumn training programme.'

Marianne took a step back and looked around the room. 'Yes. We're still fine-tuning some details.'

She avoided eye contact as she smoothed out the skirt of her dress, despite the fact that it was intentionally pleated.

'Well, it would be great to get the dates in the diary, you know, so I can keep them free.'

There was nothing worse as a freelancer than when your big clients' schedules clashed.

'Yeah,' she said. 'Um, we should set up a coffee and talk about it.'

She was going to town on the smoothing of her dress and the hairs on the back of my arms started to stand up. Perhaps the worst thing about being a freelancer wasn't a schedule clash, but that one of my biggest clients wasn't going to book me at all.

'I've been working on some new workshop ideas,' I said, the nerves in my voice evident.

She looked up at me again, and patted me on the arm like my elderly aunts. 'We'll go for that coffee.'

A sense of dread washed over me. I'd steadily built up my business with a fair few individual clients, but the big bill-payer was the corporate clients where I delivered regular sessions, like the big multinational company Marianne worked for. She'd got me a gig at her work four years ago, and I'd been delivering sessions there ever since.

'Should I—'

I didn't get a chance to finish the sentence as Andrea came up and practically barged into Marianne.

'Don't tell me you need to pee again,' said Marianne, 'or else I'm going to insist you only drink shots from now on.'

'No, I'm all good,' said Andrea, 'I just came to see this one.'

She leaned over and gave me a squeeze, which was almost impossible, given the full skirt of her dress.

'Thank goodness,' said Marianne, looking grateful for the interruption. 'I'll leave you to it.'

I watched her scuttle away before I turned back to Andrea.

'You look amazing,' I said, trying not to think about the conversation with Marianne. Andrea gave a quick swish of the dress.

'Thank you. I love your skirt. So are you having a good time? I'm worried that people aren't having a good time. Have you had enough to drink? I kept telling them to circulate more drinks.'

I rested my hand on her arm to slow her racing thoughts. 'I am sufficiently hydrated and having fun.'

She visibly relaxed. 'I didn't expect this all to be so stressful.'

'Have *you* had enough to drink? That's the question.'

'I'm waiting until after my speech. I'm going to get emotional as it is. Wine would only make it worse,' she said, grabbing at my hand and giving me a squeeze. 'I'm so glad you came.'

'Me too.'

She squeezed harder, and there they were, the unspoken words.

'And look, here's Jimmy.' She grabbed hold of his wrist as he walked past. 'Have you seen Chloe yet?'

'Ah, only to wave at. Hey you, you okay?' he said, putting his hands into his trouser pockets.

'Yeah, fine. You?'

'Good, thanks.'

Andrea looked between the two of us and, when neither of us spoke, she tapped us both on the shoulder. 'I'm going to leave you to it.'

I'm not sure if she deliberately pushed Jimmy into me with her big dress, but he stumbled a little closer, looking embarrassed.

'You holding up okay?' he asked.

'Yeah,' I said, lying.

'You still have a terrible poker face.'

I smiled.

'It's just a few hours. I can get through it.'

'I'm sure you will. And you're looking... well.'

'Now who's got the bad poker face?'

He laughed. 'Still you. You've done something different to your hair.'

'It's called not having it cut for eight months. It's almost a rewilding experience, although it's not working out so well with the humidity.'

'Yeah, the rain's a right pain in the arse.'

'Isn't it just?'

There was a pause. I looked around the room and made eye contact with my mum and Andrea's mum – my Aunty Sue. Their eyes were glued on us and I knew if I looked the other way Hilda and Esme would be doing the same.

'How's New York?' I asked, trying not to think of all the prying eyes.

'Pretty great. Work's a bit crazy, but that's to be expected.'

'Nice,' I said, trying not to get too jealous or to dwell on the fact that, if things had been different, I was supposed to be going to visit him. Not for the whole of his secondment, but I'd booked flights for a two-week trip.

'Jimmy!' said a man slapping him on the back and holding his hand out for him to shake.

'Colin,' he said, shaking his hand.

'Mate. What's all this I hear about you living in New York and dating some twenty-year-old?'

I felt like I'd been punched in the gut.

'Oh,' said Jimmy. He looked between me and Colin. 'I'm just in New York on a secondment and, um, I'm not dating... she's not twenty.'

He kept looking between the two of us. Eventually Colin's eyes fell on me and it took him a moment or two to focus.

'Ah, you're the ex, aren't you? Kelly?'

'Chloe,' I said.

'Right, gotcha. I, um,' he said. 'I'm going to go get another drink. Jimmy, I'll catch you later.'

He winked as he slapped him on the back again.

'Sorry about him. I didn't mean... I didn't want this to be awkward.'

'No, no,' I said, trying to plant a smile on my face. 'It's fine. We've not been together for a good while. I would have expected you to have moved on.'

He held my gaze before he nodded.

'I haven't really. You know. It's New York. Everyone's on apps and it's uncomplicated.'

I tried not to read into it that he was comparing it with our relationship, which had become too complicated to survive almost overnight.

I couldn't blame him for choosing something easier. What I was doing with Blaine was the same. Uncomplicated. Almost unreal.

'It's fine. We don't have to talk about it.'

'Thank God,' he muttered. 'What were we talking about before he came over?'

'New York and how you were loving it.'

'Oh, yeah. It would be hard not to. Did you manage to get any of your money back on your flights?'

'No, but I'd booked the cheapest option.'

I'd been so excited booking the flights. New York had always owned a bit of my heart since I'd done my internship there.

'Seems a shame to waste them. If you change your mind. I meant what I said about us staying friends.'

I thought of my time with Blaine. The more time I spent exploring New York with him, the more the city was getting under my skin. I shook the thought away.

'I'm sure we can hang out when you're back here.'

'Yeah,' he said, his hands back in his pockets. 'I'm not sure if I'm coming back any time soon. My boss out there, he was kind of talking about making the secondment longer.'

My stomach sank. I don't know whether it was because I was jealous that he got to stay in the city that I loved so much or because we wouldn't get to hang out as friends.

'Oh, that's great,' I said, trying to sound enthusiastic. 'You must be doing really well.'

'Yeah, I guess.'

I took a sip of my drink. Everyone was moving on and it only served to remind me of how I felt like I'd ground to a halt.

'Are you, um… are you still talking to Kerry?' he raised an eyebrow.

'Sometimes. Not as often.' My voice has gone quiet. He was the only person that knew I was doing that.

'And what about the counsellor, have you been back to see her?'

My skin started to prickle. There was something weird about him knowing me better than anyone in the room and yet at the same time he felt like a complete stranger.

'We don't have to talk about this,' I said, going to sip my drink, only to find my glass empty.

'Of course, I'm sorry, Chlo. It's probably the last thing you want to be talking about. What we really should be discussing is the hat-off going on between your mum and Andrea's.'

My heart ached and I smiled. Somehow it felt just as intimate a topic. If we'd been here together, that's exactly what we would have been discussing.

'Clearly, my mum thought she was the de facto mother of the bride.'

'Clearly. I just don't know how they haven't poked anyone's eyes out with the feathers.'

I almost choked on a laugh.

There was a large clang of a bell and the wedding planner over the other side of the room announced it was time for dinner.

'About time,' said Jimmy. 'I have had way too many of these drinks on an empty stomach. It was lovely to chat. Maybe see you on the dance floor later?'

'With your dance moves?' I said, trying to force a smile. In truth, I was hoping to sneak back to my room before the dancing got started.

'Yeah, you're probably right. Perhaps I'll see you at the bar.'

'Yeah,' I said, raising a hand as he headed off towards the dining-room doors.

I hung back, enjoying the quiet moment and taking a few deep breaths.

'Ah, Chloe,' said Andrea. I took a step back so I didn't get whacked.

'I need to go to the toilet before dinner starts and I can't for the life of me see Marianne anywhere. Would you mind?'

'Not at all,' I said, genuinely happy to help.

Despite the ordeal of the cubicle squishing that Marianne had described, it was preferable to having to sit at the table, enduring more looks of pity.

'Thanks so much. You see, you didn't escape the bridesmaid duties after all.'

I smiled weakly back. I tried not to think about how today could have been so different. I could have been messaging Kerry photos of me in my grape-coloured dress and trying to sneak off with Jimmy to our room.

I scrunched my eyes shut. This is why I increasingly wanted to spend time in the Metaverse. There was something so easy and safe about being there, escaping into a bubble where I couldn't get hurt, without the constant reminders of what my life was missing.

Chapter 3

I went to take a step, but I faltered. I shook my head. Even here, I was hesitant.

'Come on,' said Blaine, his voice gentle. 'I won't let you fall, Cat.'

I wondered if it was time to tell him my real name, but there was something appealing about being someone totally different on here. My avatar was already a glossier version of me, surely my name could be too?

He held his hand out and I took it. I felt the tingle in my palm and it rippled around my body. It might be haptic touch, but I liked to think the tingles he caused were real. He led me to the edge of the tower and he leaned up against the ledge of the unglazed window.

'Wow. This view.' I hadn't been prepared for it to take my breath away. Maybe it was him. Maybe it was the moment that we'd found ourselves in.

'See. I told you.' His hands were on his hips and there was a smug smile on his face. I might not know him well, but I knew he liked to be right. And with this, he was most definitely.

'Surely it isn't like this in real life?'

This place seemed almost magical and I couldn't quite believe it could exist in New York.

'It is. You'll have to look it up,' he said. 'And I told you it was impressive.'

Getting my balance, I leaned out over the brick and looked out towards the Hudson. 'It's like someone's ripped up an Italian palazzo and dumped in the middle of the park.'

'I know, right?'

I'd never heard of the Met Cloisters, and I couldn't get my head round how I hadn't. We'd already explored the herb garden at the centre that reminded me of countless cloister gardens I'd seen at European cathedrals, and we'd toured the art-lined walls.

'It's perfect.'

'Yeah,' he said. There was a sadness to his voice at moments like this, and I got it. It was as if, no matter how happy I was, I knew that those moments would always be tinged with sadness.

It's one of the reasons that I liked hanging out with Blaine in the early days, before things became what they are now. Both of us seemed to be escaping from something. He understood me.

We wandered down the stone corridors, stopping every so often to marvel at a stained-glass window or an altar piece.

'Have you been to Italy?' I asked.

There were still chasms in our knowledge of each other. There was something exciting and equally terrifying about the unknown.

'I have,' he said. 'A couple of times. I'd go back in a heartbeat for the food.'

'Little Italy doesn't cut it?'

He laughed. 'Not even close. Those thin pizzas where you can taste the tomato and basil.'

'Stop, you're making me hungry.'

'I'm making myself hungry.'

'I'm sure you can get good pizza there.'

'Yeah, but it's not the same, is it? There's something about being down a backstreet in Naples or on a hillside in Sorrento on a summer's evening. The view of the sea.'

'The smell of the lemon groves. The dappled moonlight on the water. You're making it sound like something out of a romance novel.'

He laughed even harder.

'You can't beat the romance of Italy.'

'I don't know. This New York doesn't seem so bad.'

'This New York,' said Blaine, reaching out and touching the wall, but his hand clearly couldn't make contact. 'It isn't real. But the real one, absolutely.'

'Where would you go for a date, a real one that is?'

'I like to think all the places I've taken you so far. The cherry-blossom walk, the Edge, the path at Hoboken.'

I thought of the cherry-blossom walk at Roosevelt Island he'd taken me on last Sunday after Andrea and Henry's wedding. It had been the perfect relaxing activity after the social overwhelm of the day before.

'That's cheating. New places only.'

'Oh, okay. Let's think. Um, okay. Well, I guess we'd meet at Grand Central. Under the clock, as if you're going for all-out romance, that would tick the box. We'd look up at the painted starry sky and then we'd head to the Oyster Bar for a quick glass of champagne and oysters. Do you like oysters?'

'Depends how they're done. Go on.'

'Okay. Well, we'd have Oysters Rockefeller, as, once you've had them that way, you'll never want them another way. Then we'd head down Fifth Avenue, perhaps go up to a rooftop bar for a cocktail on the way. We'd have worked up a bit of an appetite on the walk, so we'd head to Eataly and pick up some gelato.'

'Now you're talking,' I said, with a sudden craving for it. 'Then what?'

'Perhaps a walk through Washington Square Park, a game of chess.'

'Chess?' I spluttered. 'Not quite sure chess screams romance.'

'Come on, there's got to be that competitive element somewhere. So a game of chess. Gennari's is nearby, we could grab a hero.'

'I have never understood why New Yorkers call a sandwich a hero.'

'Um, because that's what they're called? And a sandwich is what a burger is in.'

I held up my hand. 'Let's quit whilst we're ahead.'

'Good idea. So we'd get a hero, maybe after we'd head to Ghost Donkey for tequila.'

'I can't do tequila,' I shuddered. Like many people, I'd had too many bad experiences with it.

'You think you can't, but I can guarantee this place would change your mind.'

I sighed. 'You're making me want to actually come to New York.'

'You should do.' The excitement in his voice was palpable. 'I can play tour guide for real.'

'You're the second person in as many weeks trying to get me to visit. When I was at the wedding last week, one of my friends who's working out there was trying to get me to go.'

'See, it's a sign.'

It was on the tip of my tongue to tell him about the flights I already had booked. But who was I kidding? It had been a week since I'd been to Andrea's wedding and I was still recovering from the shock of having to be around that many people.

'Imagine us hanging out like this, but for real.'

I sighed again. 'It wouldn't be the same, though. It's like when you watch *Love Is Blind* and they all get on so well in the pods, but then, when they go out in the real world and life happens around them, it rarely works out.'

'Shocking that people dating on a reality-TV programme who, let's face it, were picked by producers, didn't make it. But, you know, I didn't have you down as such a cynic.'

'I didn't use to be.'

'It's a good job you're not in New York. Those blind-dating apps are a thing at the moment.'

'Yeah? You had any luck on them?' We were straying into dangerous territory. We'd never really talked much about our dating life outside of here. Not that I had any dating life outside of here, but I didn't really want to hear about his.

'I think this is the best blind-dating I've ever done.'

'Nicely sidestepped. I hear everyone in New York is on apps.'

'It's true. Eight million people and you can't meet one.'

'Eight million,' I repeated in wonder. New York was one of those places that seemed so small but, at the same time, infinite.

Blaine was quiet for a moment. We'd walked down the end of a corridor and he turned to face me.

'I wish you would come,' he said. His tone had changed. Perhaps the first time it had been a flippant comment, but this time there was a sincerity to his voice.

My mind was racing.

'But I like how things are here. What if we met and it all fizzled out?'

'And what if we met and it didn't?'

My alarm was buzzing. I'd started to hate the noise and the vibration on my arm, but it was getting late. Meeting mid-week after we'd both been at work meant that it was creeping into my sleeping time.

'I have to go. I'm about to turn into a pumpkin. I've got a meeting tomorrow.'

'I wish you didn't have to.'

'I wish I didn't either. See you Friday?'

'Sure. The usual? Thought we could head to Coney Island. Have you been?'

I thought of Kerry and my heart constricted.

'I'd love to go,' I said, not so much lying as avoiding the question.

The whole point of being here is that he didn't have to know the real me. He didn't need to know that I'd visited the real Coney Island with Kerry the year we'd lived there. Or that we'd eaten funnel cakes and drunk ice-cold beers, making our way around the amusements.

'That's settled then.' He held out his palm. I took it and we squeezed each other's hand. 'You promise you'll consider meeting up one day?'

'I'll think about it,' I said, with one last squeeze of the hand I swiped out. I sat down on my sofa, taking a moment. Thoughts swirling round my mind. I wondered if I would ever be brave enough to meet him in person.

Chapter 4

'Try and think it over. What is one of your best attributes that could be seen as a flaw?'

My client, Kiran looked straight ahead at the screen and then shook his head. 'I'm sorry, Chloe, I just can't get my head round this. Can you give me an example?'

I hesitated. Usually I tried to keep the session focused solely on a client, but we'd been talking about this for a little while and it wasn't clicking with him.

'I'm a people pleaser, and I have boundless enthusiasm,' I said, trying to muster the energy to at least make it sound like it could be possible.

I felt like a charlatan. Those personality traits might have been true once upon a time but, as much as I tried to channel that positivity, it didn't come naturally any more. I tried to plant a smile on my face, the type that used to be effortless, only now my cheeks ached. It all felt wrong.

Kiran was staring straight ahead, unmoving. I hoped that the Zoom connection hadn't frozen and I'd have to lie my way through that again.

'I don't understand why they're flaws,' said Kiran. He had a marker pen in his hand and he kept opening and closing the lid, the lid snapping shut each time with a click. If I had the enthusiasm that I claimed I did, I'd be asking him about that lid snapping, exploring why he needed to distract himself, but I'm struggling to keep this session going as it is without taking us off on a tangent.

'It's interesting to consider how things that are your strengths might also be your weakness too.'

It isn't the done thing in coaching to use your own life as an example, but today would have been a perfect illustration of my people pleasing being a flaw. I was supposed to be on my way to meet Marianne for coffee, not having a last-minute coaching session with one of my clients, but Kiran was in a tricky spot. His start-up tech company was in the early stages of being bought out by a huge tech giant and he'd wanted extra sessions, and I didn't want to say no. Although, if I was being honest, today's session wasn't only about people pleasing, but also to do with the fact that Kiran was one of the biggest clients I still had left and I couldn't afford to lose him.

'Okay, I get that being a people pleaser can be a weakness, but how could being enthusiastic be one? Surely being enthusiastic and positive is kind of fundamental to what you do?'

It was true, they were cornerstones of being an executive coach, but right now I only felt like I was masquerading as one.

I nodded. 'Yeah, it is. But believe it or not, not everyone likes it when you're peppy all the time. But let's not get too hung up on me. I'm still waiting to hear yours.'

I was quick to change the subject. Lingering on my enthusiasm only made me think of Kerry. I'd always thought that my people pleasing was my worst habit until Kerry had called me out on my enthusiasm when I was trying to make the best of a crappy night out.

'You, Chloe, are always too upbeat,' she'd said, drink in one hand, the other gesticulating wildly. 'It's like your greatest asset and your greatest curse.'

'Why's it a curse?'

'Because some of us around you are happy wallowing and being miserable, and the constant pep is draining.'

Kerry was an either/or type of drinker, she either loved everyone or she hated everything. The trouble was you never knew which one you'd get.

'Oh, my God, I love it,' I said, clapping my hands together, trying to gloss over her pessimism. 'That's so perfect for when I do "greatest assets are greatest flaw". Too enthusiastic.'

Kerry shook her head at me. 'You see, even when someone's trying to tell you you're a giant pain in the bum, you're seeing the positive in it.'

'And that's why you love me.'

'Yeah, but you make it bloody difficult.'

I could see her lips twitching. It was the closest to a smile that she'd got all night and it was all I'd needed to know that there was still hope for me to salvage that night, and that I'd be able to pull her out of her low mood.

The memory punched me in the gut, hitting differently after everything that had happened.

Kiran had started to flip his pen, as if the faster he was flipping the faster his mind was whirring. I needed to think of more ways to coax the answer out of him, but my mind that used to buzz and fizz in sessions was blank.

'I've got one,' he said, and I silently sighed with relief. 'My worst good flaw is that I have too many brilliant ideas.'

'Nice.' And so modest, I bit my lip. Kiran was one of my favourite clients. He was an entrepreneur that had had moderate success so far with different tech start-ups, but he believed he was destined for bigger things. His delusions of grandeur were not one of his negative flaws. I actually believed him. If he could just put all his energy into his work and focus, he was going to make it big. Maybe it was me that had delusions of grandeur, as I believed that I'd be able to use my skills to get him there. 'And,' I said, with a pause, 'having too many ideas is a problem for you because...'

I left the sentence hanging in the air, an eyebrow raised in expectation, wanting him to connect the dots, and hoping the screen didn't freeze, as it was not a flattering pose.

'Because I don't see an idea through before I'm on to the next one.'

'Okay,' I said. The old me probably would have been screaming 'Bingo!' in my mind. Where did the old me get her energy from? 'That sounds like you need to focus on one idea at a time. How does that sound?'

'Impossible,' he laughed, and I cracked a smile too. 'New ideas are always so much better.'

'The grass is always greener on the other side, but it's not. Your brain tries to seduce you because it's hard work to stick with one idea and see it through.'

He wrinkled up his face. 'But that's just who I am.'

I pursed my lips together. I needed him to make his own breakthrough with this. I was worried I was going to start losing him and I couldn't afford that, either figuratively or literally. I couldn't think what to say. The weight of worry and fear that I wasn't up to this any more was starting to bring me down. That familiar feeling of suffocation and hopelessness started to rage in my mind.

'I'm an enthusiastic person.' I startled myself by saying it out loud when all I was trying to do was calm my intrusive thoughts.

'Yeah,' said Kiran, nodding his head. 'I get that.' He wasn't really looking at me, or noticing the signs that some of my other clients had. The dark circles under my eyes. The hollow, empty look that I caught a glimpse of in the mirror. 'I'm thinking how can I work with having more ideas in the projects I'm already working on?'

He sounded unsure, but he was right on the money and it was enough for me to leap on.

'Let's look at that. How do you think you could incorporate that skill into your project lifecycle?'

He stopped spinning the pen and put it down.

'I guess that it's a good evaluation tool. Seeing if there are ideas that could make the project even better.'

'That sounds like a great way to reflect and improve.'

'You know,' he said, giving a little laugh, 'I nearly came here today wanting to talk to you about working on this idea I had for a new neurotherapy platform using a wearable device, but you're right, stick to this project.'

'So that brings us to a good point then. Shall we spend the rest of the time checking in on what you're working on. Channel some new ideas for those?' I said in relief. The session felt like it was going somewhere purposeful, even if it had taken a while to get us there.

I glanced at my phone, I was due to meet Marianne in half an hour, and I was going to be cutting it fine.

'Okay,' he said, nodding. 'Let's do it.'

I hurried along the high street to the café. The session with Kiran had gone well, but it had also run over a tiny bit and now I was late to meet Marianne.

I pushed the door open, and spotted her over in the corner with Betty in the high chair. Betty was trying to climb out and Marianne was trying to keep her in.

'I'm so sorry I'm late.'

Marianne looked up and smiled.

'Ah, don't worry. You're not too late, we were just very early. Baby sign was cancelled and I naively thought we'd come and have a nice drink whilst we waited.'

Betty started to wail and she threw the biscuit she was holding in her hand. Marianne bent down, trying to retrieve the thrown food, and popping it on an empty plate on the table.

'I'm thinking we might not be able to stay, as she's getting pretty grouchy and might need a nap. Do you want to go for a walk instead?'

'Yeah, that would be great. I'll just order a coffee to go. Do you want one?'

'I'd love one. Oat-milk latte, please.'

It wasn't long before we were walking into one of the parks at the edge of the high street.

'Have you heard from Andrea?' I asked.

'A little. The Maldives look amazing from the pictures she's sent.'

'Yeah, she's sent me a couple too.' I nodded. The photos of crystal-clear waters were so beautiful they looked photoshopped.

'She gets back tomorrow. Can you believe how quickly that's gone?'

'Almost two weeks.'

'Yep, and then she'll be back home. I wonder what she'll do with her time. It feels like she was planning that wedding forever.'

We shared a little look. It wasn't that Andrea had gone full Bridezilla, but she'd had her moments.

Betty started to fuss in the pushchair and Marianne went round the front to adjust the straps.

'Did you hear that hot Gavin hooked up with Susie?'

'Susie that did the mooning on the hen do?' I said.

I hadn't been on the hen do, but I'd heard the stories.

'That's the one. They turned up together at breakfast the next morning too. Caused quite the stir with Sue.'

I laughed, I could well imagine. My Aunty Sue still insisted that Andrea and Henry had separate bedrooms when they stayed at hers last Christmas.

'And how was it with Jimmy?'

I'd known it was only a matter of time until he was brought up.

'It was okay. I found out that he's dating again. A twenty-year-old or something.'

Marianne pulled a face. 'Why do they do it?'

'She's uncomplicated,' I said with a shrug.

'It's because she's young. Everyone gets complicated at some point.' She gave me a look of solidarity, but I knew at the moment I was more complicated than most people.

'I'm happy for him,' I said.

'Of course you are. Because you are infuriatingly too nice.'

'It's not like he's done anything wrong,' I said, shrugging again and she shook her head at me. I knew I should have had more of a reaction to it but, apart from a bit of dented pride, I didn't feel anything other than numb. That was the trouble. Ever since we'd broken up, that's how I'd felt. It was as if my heart had already broken when Kerry died so, when Jimmy and I broke up a couple of months later, my heart had already hardened so that it couldn't fracture any more.

A squirrel ran across the path in front of us and came to a stop on the grass. Marianne went to point it out to Betty, but she was fast asleep already. Marianne bent down and reclined her seat so that she was lying back.

'Well, at least you've got your friend,' she said, with air quotes.

'Who is just a friend.' I took a sip of my coffee, burning my tongue.

'For now,' she muttered. 'So what's he like?'

I opened my mouth and shut it again.

How did I describe someone that I'd never met? His avatar had dark hair, with big brown eyes that you could get lost staring into. But I couldn't have fallen for a CGI-generated man. It was the man behind it. The way that he listened and the way he understood.

'Well, I don't actually know. I sort of haven't met him yet,' I said, caught up in my daze.

'Oh,' she said stepping back, to get a better look at me. 'I thought you said you were hanging out.'

'We are, just not in person.'

She narrowed her eyes. 'I don't get it. Did you meet him on Hinge or an app?'

'Kind of, via the Metaverse. Did I ever tell you about my client, Kiran?'

'Your tech guru?'

'Yeah, that's the one. He develops Metaverse platforms and I couldn't really understand what he was talking about, so he gave me a headset.'

'I used one of those at the kitchen design place to see what our new kitchen was going to be like. Wait...' It was like the cogs were turning slowly and she'd just realised what I'd said. 'You made friends on there?'

She was pulling a face and giving me a look that made me wonder if I had two heads.

'Don't say it like that.'

'Like what? Come on, Chlo, you've got to be careful. So many of these things can be a scam, he'll be after your savings.'

'What savings?' I laughed. I'd had to dip into my modest savings more than I'd wanted to over the last few months. I'd not had the energy to proactively find new clients and instead I'd started doing a couple of days on a coaching platform and, whilst that was easier to manage when I'd been feeling low, it didn't pay well.

'Okay, but this guy could be anyone. He could be catfishing you and be some complete weirdo, and you're living all alone.'

'You have been listening to too many true-crime podcasts. Relax. We haven't shared any personal details. He doesn't even know my real name, or even where I live. And same with me, I don't know those things about him. Plus, it's just a friendly meet-up.'

'But that's how they hook you in.'

Marianne couldn't hide the look on her face.

'Oh, God, now you're giving me that look. It's worse than the pity stare that everyone's been giving me.'

'I don't mean to. You know I'm just...' Her whole face was scrunched up as she searched for the words.

'Worried about me? Look. I can't explain this thing with Blaine, it's like a little escape. That for an hour or so a day I exist in a world where no one is watching me, waiting for signs that I'm going to implode or breakdown. Where no one pities me for what happened to Kerry.'

I braced myself, my muscles tensing, waiting for the onslaught to come, but instead she took hold of my hand and squeezed it gently.

'Just be careful. You don't need any more heartbreak.'

I blinked back a tear. Pleased for the judgement not to come.

'I know and I will.'

We walked for a moment in silence. A Jack Russell ran an excited loop around us, then tore off across the park, much to the dismay of his owner, who was hurrying after him.

'So dare I ask about the company retreat and the coaching?' I said, an uneasy feeling resting in my stomach.

'Oh, yeah. I spoke to my boss.' Her voice had changed. The buzz that had been there initially when probing about Blaine had disappeared. I could hear that it was a no. 'He said that the feedback for the last session hadn't been as positive as the last few and he thought it might be time for a change.'

'But the last session,' I said, a lump catching in my throat. 'It was just after I found out about Kerry and—'

My heart started to race as I was transported back to that moment when her mum had rung to tell me. 'In hindsight I should have cancelled, but I don't think it had really hit me.'

Marianne stopped walking, she kept pushing the pram backwards and forwards with one hand. 'Chloe, I can't imagine what it was like going through that, but I think you need a bit of a break, as you're not yourself. Even now.'

'I'm fine,' I said, wishing that was true.

She sighed. 'You didn't come to Andrea's hen do. You barely stayed for the wedding.'

'So I'm struggling with being out having fun. It doesn't mean to say that I'm struggling with work.' I shoved my hands into the pocket of my dress. I thought of my client Vanessa that had decided not to book another package of sessions only last week. She'd told me that she was cutting back because of the cost of living, but I couldn't help but wonder if Marianne was right; it was impacting my work.

I scrunched my eyes shut. Losing Marianne's company would be a huge blow financially.

'Have they decided what they're going to do instead?'

'Not yet,' she said, shaking her head. 'We've got a meeting about it next month.'

I nodded my head slowly, trying to formulate a plan. 'How about I come in and meet you both? I could give a new workshop I've been working on about self-care.'

Marianne raised an eyebrow.

'I didn't mean that how it sounded,' I said, raking my hand through my hair, with it catching on the scraggy ends. If anyone was in desperate need of self-care, it was me. 'I mean a workshop for managers building up their coaching skills to add coaching to their management toolkit. Give me a date and I'll come in.'

'I'm not sure. Wouldn't it be better for you to have some time out for a bit? Regroup. Come and see us next year when you're fresher and you've got yourself together.'

I knew when I was being fobbed off and I didn't blame Marianne in the slightest, but I also knew how tough it was to get my foot in the door in the first place and how almost impossible it would be to get back in there.

Marianne reached out. 'You've been through a lot and you haven't given yourself time. That's what you need.'

I nodded.

That wasn't what I needed. I needed to make some money. I needed to grow my dwindling client base. I needed to come up with a plan to win them back as clients. But most of all, I needed some oomph. Some fight. Some anything. But I had nothing and instead of doing anything about it, I nodded again. I couldn't believe the person I'd become and I wondered if I'd ever be myself again.

Chapter 5

I was counting down the minutes, feeling like a schoolgirl with a crush. My life in reality might be imploding, but my virtual life was going from strength to strength. I found myself thinking more and more about Blaine. My cheeks aching with all the smiling. I was being ridiculous. But the more I tried to tell myself that it would fizzle out in the real world, the more his words 'but what if it didn't?' played on my mind.

Our friendship had begun to shift into something more and there was a certain amount of inevitability that at some point we'd have to start taking the next steps. I wanted to know everything about him, and the best thing was that it felt like Blaine wanted to know about me too. He listened and it was like he heard what I was trying to say even when I didn't spell it out.

I swiped in, holding my breath until I saw him standing there, waiting.

'Hey,' he said.

'Hey, yourself.'

I wished he could tell by looking at my avatar how much I was smiling normally.

'I've had such a crappy day and you are a sight for sore eyes.'

He walked over to me and my stomach flipped.

'What happened?'

'Work,' he sighed. 'I don't often have to go into the office, but I did today and it's always such a shit show.'

I knew he worked in IT, but that was all I knew. Like everything else in our friendship, we had sketched the lines, and now it was time to start shading in the details.

'Do you want to tell me about it?'

'Not really. You know, all I could think about was seeing you and that kept me going.'

'And the thought of coming here,' I said, motioning to the backdrop of Coney Island.

It was funny, as it was one of those places that seemed relatively unchanged since I'd been there last. New York was an ever-changing landscape that was forever different, but there was a timelessness to Coney Island that made you feel like you could be in the eighties or the nineties, even here in the Metaverse.

'Now this place is only ever as fun as the person you're with.'

My stomach lurched. I'd been here once before with Kerry and we'd acted like kids running on all the rides and losing far too many dollars trying to win oversized cuddly toys on the stalls. It was one of those days that had made my cheeks ache with all the laughing and smiling.

'That sounded like a line again, didn't it?' he said, cursing himself.

'It did,' I said trying to focus on Blaine and not the past. 'You're cheesy.'

'Like the cheesiest. I hope you're not lactose-intolerant.' He groaned. 'I need to think before I speak.'

'I think it's sweet,' I said with a laugh and he joined in.

'See I knew coming here was what I needed, you're cheering me up already. Although it's going to take quite a while to shake my day off completely.'

'Was it that bad?'

'Like you wouldn't believe. The only good thing about being in the office is this Latin-American fusion place, where they do these rice bowls that are awesome.'

'Stop. You're always making me miss New York food. That's the one thing these goggles can't replicate.'

'That's why you should come over.' He laughed. 'That and to see me.'

I found myself nodding.

'What, don't tell me you actually thought about it? I thought there was no hope the way you were talking about it last time.' I could hear the excitement in his voice and it was almost infectious.

'I haven't made up my mind yet, but I've decided not to completely rule it out.'

Blaine did a small fist pump.

'I haven't said yes yet.'

'But you haven't said no,' he said, walking us on to the Wonder Wheel that had been at the centre of countless movie scenes. Blaine walked up and got in one of the static cars on the outer ring. I followed behind him and we sat down. My hand brushed his and the haptic contact made me shudder.

'You know,' said Blaine, as the big wheel immediately started to go, 'Periscope Monkeys are doing a residency in Brooklyn over the summer.'

'They are?'

Periscope Monkeys had always been mine and Kerry's band. She'd dragged me along to see them not long after we'd first met. I hadn't known what to expect of the punk-pop group, but the atmosphere at the gig had been electric. It was thanks to the band that I'd met Blaine too. They'd played a virtual gig in the Metaverse and I'd gone to see them and we'd struck up a conversation and here we were.

'Are you going?' I asked, marvelling at the view from up here. I could see all the famous rides. The chair swings, the carousel, the rollercoasters.

'I'm hoping to see them a few times. You've seen them before, right, other than the gig on here?'

'Once,' I said nodding.

'Best band I've ever seen live.'

'Now that's quite the accolade.'

'Are they not yours?'

'They were good, but it was the first time I'd heard their music.'

The wheel reached the top and from here there was a view of the Atlantic Ocean one way, and the city the other.

'Ah, then you've got to see them now that you're a proper fan. It'll blow your mind. Who's the best band you've ever seen up until now?'

'The Killers, Hyde Park 2017.'

'I saw them once. They were great.'

'And Periscope Monkeys still win?'

'Hands down.' He tilted his head. 'You know all signs are pointing to you coming over. See for yourself.'

'You're not going to let this go, are you?'

'I don't think so,' he said, with a little laugh.

'Have you ever sat in those cars?' I asked, changing the subject. He was tempting me, but there was still a lingering doubt in my mind. I pointed to the cars on the inner track on the wheel that seemed to be swinging wildly all over the place.

I remember seeing them in person with Kerry and even she wasn't brave enough to give them a go.

'Once or twice,' he said, sucking in his breath. 'They're not for the faint-hearted. Even I get freaked out by the—'

The world went black, my stomach jolted like I'd been dropped and it took a moment for my mind to register that I hadn't moved. I flipped the headset over my head, my eyes adjusting to the lighting in my living room. My first thought had been a power cut and that the Wi-Fi router had gone out. But the lights were still on and from here I could see the flashing green lights on the router in the hallway.

I flipped the headset back down. I'd never had any Metaverse platform crash on me when using it before, but I was sure that it was nothing that a power reset couldn't fix.

I thought of Blaine in his apartment or wherever he lived in New York, and I wondered if he was there waiting for me. Would my avatar be frozen on the screen or would he find himself there all alone?

I tried to log back on, but scanning the list of downloaded apps, the one we met on wasn't there. My heart was starting to race a little. How long would Blaine wait for me? What if he thought that I'd left deliberately?

I retyped the app name in the store and it was there, but blanked out. It was one of the most popular platforms. What had happened?

I tore off my headset and hurried over to my laptop, scooping it onto my lap and frantically typing into Google.

Perhaps the app had been the one with a power outage or a server crash or... There was a news article that had been published 20 minutes ago, and I started to feel sick as I read the headline.

Real_World_Dreaming Nightmare Begins

I slid from the edge of the armchair into the actual seat as I scanned the article. Bitcoin fraud. Developer on the run. Site shutting down.

'No, no, no.' I scrunched my eyes shut. I thought again of Blaine and I wondered if he was going through the same as me. Whether he was still trying and failing to get back into the world we'd been in moments before.

I turned to Threads and to Twitter (which I refused to call X), and it was already a trending topic. Journalists were having a field day. The rise and fall of a huge Metaverse platform. They were already wondering if this could be a modern version of the dotcom bubble burst. But I didn't care about any of the hot takes, I cared about Blaine.

In amongst all of the articles were actual people who used it. I scanned through them, not knowing Blaine's real name or what on earth his handle would be, or if he even had a profile. There were loads of disgruntled users, but none of them sounded like him.

I hastily added mine to the stream of tweets, but I barely had any followers and the algorithm would ensure that no one would ever see it.

@ChloeCat27: Blaine?! This might be corny or Coney. But I'm looking for you! Now who sounds cheesy?

'Shit,' I muttered. What was I going to do?

There was only one person I wanted to talk to about all this. I shook my head. I shouldn't speak to Kerry. I'd seen the way that Jimmy had looked at me at the wedding like I'd lost the plot. The problem was she'd always been my first phone call whenever anything went wrong. From the time I locked myself out of our apartment to the time I'd accidentally told my former boss I loved him when I hung up an everyday business call. She always knew what to say.

I picked the headset back up and logged in to find her. Virtual Kerry spotted me walking towards her and she broke out into a smile. Her nose always scrunched when she smiled and the sight of it was almost enough to stop me in my tracks.

'You came,' she said, her voice gravelly.

'I'm still mad, before you ask,' I said, raising a hand.

Kerry was sitting on one of the sofas in the coffee shop, and she swung her legs up, tucking her feet under.

'Do you want to talk about it?' she asked. Her head was tilted as if she was ready. I stared at the brown flecks in her green eyes, the ones that were so wide and almost hypnotic.

When Kiran told me he'd developed a platform where you could create avatars of loved ones who had died, I'd thought it was a ridiculous idea. But then, when he gave me a VR headset to try it, and I uploaded videos of Kerry and it had created an avatar of her, it all made sense. She almost had her voice, and almost had her mannerisms. In the stranglehold of grief, it was enough.

Kerry repeated the question back to me, in exactly the same tone.

Did I want to talk about it? The question rattled around my mind. I wanted to talk about nothing else. It's all I thought about when I woke and went to sleep. Tears started to sting my eyes.

'I just don't understand.' It was barely a whisper out of my mouth, but the months were passing by and I still was no further forward trying to come to terms with it or to make sense of it.

I would never know why she did it. I would never understand. I was going to be stuck in this perpetual state of feeling angrier than I ever thought I could be, whilst at the same time guilty for letting it happen.

'What don't you understand? I want to help.'

I shook my head.

'You're never going to help me with this,' I said, knowing that Jimmy was right, that coming here pretending to talk to her was only prolonging the agony. She couldn't answer the real the questions I wanted to ask.

'Then let me help you with something else. You came here for a reason.'

'I did. Because I needed you.' I tried to blink away a tear.

'I'm right here. What's going on?'

'I've got a problem, that's what going on,' I snapped. I hadn't meant to lash out, but I couldn't help it.

'What's happened?'

I knew I was wasting my time telling her, but wasn't that why I'd come?

'They've shut down the platform that I used to meet Blaine on, and now I can't talk to him.'

She paused for a moment and then nodded. 'You can speak to me instead. I'm sure I'm better company.'

'I'm sure you are.' My heart began to ache. 'But he's the first guy in ages that I've felt that kind of connection with.'

'Connections are important.'

'Aren't they just?' I said, rising to my feet. I started to pace, trying to still my mind, which was buzzing.

Kerry tilted her head to the side, her eyes catching the light. But she didn't say anything.

'How am I supposed to find him?' I muttered.

Kerry's eyes went wide.

'Have you tried social media?'

'Uh-huh.'

I felt foolish admitting that I had, but what had I to go on? Blaine and New York. I didn't even know if Blaine was his real name. Marianne was right. He could be anyone. Any age. Any sex. Anywhere.

'It's useless. I'm never going to find him. I only know his first name, if it even is his first name, and that he lives in New York.'

'You shouldn't give up. You can find everyone these days.'

'But what if he doesn't want to be found?'

There was a pause and the magnitude of the task hit me. I sat down on the couch beside her. 'You realise this is your fault,' I said, pointing a finger in accusation. 'I'd only gone to see Periscope Monkeys because of you.'

I'd been dubious seeing a band in the Metaverse. I thought it would have the same atmosphere of watching a festival on TV when you were sat in your lounge at home. But it wasn't like that, I'd felt part of it, like I was seeing them in the flesh.

'I love Periscope Monkeys.' Her whole face lit up as she spoke.

'I know,' I said, my heart sinking. I'd only gone along to feel closer to her, and that's where I'd met him.

'I would love to see Periscope Monkeys.'

It only made me think of Blaine and the upcoming gigs he was going to.

'You're sad,' she said.

'I just want to find Blaine,' I sighed.

'Then find him.'

'How? We established that it's hard to find him on social media when all we've got to go on is that he calls himself Blaine and he lives in New York.'

'Go to New York,' she said.

I laughed out loud and startled Kerry, who joined in.

'What's funny?' she said, as she stopped laughing.

I stopped too. 'I can't just go to New York. Finding him there would be like finding a needle in haystack. I don't know where he lives.'

'What do you know?'

'I know that he likes to drink two mugs of black coffee before he showers in the morning. That he likes the smell of car wax. That he works near a restaurant that serves Latin-American fusion food. That he once went on holiday to Italy. He lives in New York. He works in IT. And he likes Periscope Monkeys.'

'Then you know plenty.'

I stared hard at Kerry, expecting more, but that was it.

'I know plenty?' I said, repeating it, the sarcasm dripping.

'You know enough.'

I scrunched my eyes shut.

It always felt like a mistake coming to see her. Jimmy's scepticism wasn't misplaced. I had to stop doing this to myself. What I needed to do was tell her all the things I was afraid to say out loud. The things that I came here to say and put off every time. I needed to get the closure that I didn't get a chance to get in the real world. The trouble was I knew it would be the end of this, and deep down I knew I wasn't ready to lose her completely.

'I'm still mad at you,' I said, standing up to leave.

'You can't be mad at me forever,' she called.

I didn't bother to tell her that I could, and I left the app.

'Go to New York,' I muttered shaking my head. That was where this might have headed if Blaine and I had talked about it more, but the idea had been no more than a seed that hadn't properly germinated. It needed to have been cultivated and tended to, with us revealing bits of our true selves to each other, little by little, until it had grown big enough to get me on a plane.

I might as well kiss the idea of Blaine goodbye. Just like that, the last of the good things in my life had gone and now I didn't have a clue what I was going to do.

Chapter 6

My weekends used to be so different from how they are now. Jimmy and I had only dated for ten months, but we'd quickly slipped into a routine of weekends spent at each other's places. We'd nip out for fancy coffee in the morning, where we'd pretend to do the crossword in the paper, only to give up with only one or two answers found. The afternoons would be a late lunch, sometimes on our own, sometimes with Andrea and Henry, who had introduced us. Weekend nights were spent cuddled up on the sofa or going *out* out. Sometimes Kerry would be around, other times my sister Nina would. It was the same, but different, and each week they whizzed by in a blur. But now they rolled on and on.

I'd started to talk to Blaine a few evenings in the week and usually once or twice on the weekend. It broke the monotony. So now, without Jimmy and without chatting to Blaine, I was left feeling lost. Which is how I found myself ironing bedsheets on a Saturday morning, watching *Married at First Sight Australia*.

Virtual Kerry's words kept echoing round my ears. *You know plenty*. I shook my head, trying to shake the thoughts away, but I couldn't. I put the iron down and picked up my phone, typing in 'Blaine' 'New York' 'Periscope Monkeys' out of desperation into Google.

I scanned the results, all of them were for *Periscope Monkeys New*

York with 'Blaine' crossed out. Born and bred in Brooklyn, the boroughs of New York were the band's stomping ground, and there were pages upon pages of results.

I was about to put my phone down, when their own page caught my eye with the information about the weekly residency, which kicked off next weekend. I thought about what Blaine had said about going to see them over the summer and a crazy idea started to take hold. What if I did go over? I had the plane tickets, I could get somewhere cheap to stay.

I clicked on the link to find out more, my heart starting to beat that little more rapidly. I laughed almost manically putting my phone down. I was starting to lose my mind. Even if I did go to the gig in New York and so did Blaine, how would I know who he was?

The doorbell rang and I flinched. I hardly ever got visitors. What if Blaine had been looking for me and he'd tracked me down? I shook the thought away. It was much more likely that it was a delivery of something I'd ordered and forgotten about.

I went to the door, trying to smooth down my messy hair in its bun, knowing that I didn't have enough time to sort out my mismatched tracksuit bottoms and old university hoodie that should have been thrown out a decade ago.

I opened the door and, expecting a package to be on the doorstep, did a double take when I saw my sister.

'Morning,' said Nina, holding my nephew out to me. I took him, even though he wasn't quite the package I was expecting. I just about had time to give him a kiss on the top of his head before he wriggled back towards his mum.

'What are you doing here?' I said, handing Oliver over and stepping aside to let her into the hallway.

'We were just passing and we thought we'd pop in.'

'You were passing here? What, in a time machine, back to a time when people popped in without texting first?'

'Very funny, and yeah, we were heading to IKEA,' said Nina, making faces at Oliver to make him laugh.

'You hate IKEA.'

'Not with this little man. They're very baby-friendly and you can spend hours walking him in a pram there for him to nap without getting soaked round the park.'

'It's not raining.'

One of the good things about my flat was the light; when the sun shone, the place was bathed in a warm glow and today the sun was splitting stones.

'Look, we're here now,' she said, with a huff.

'You're lucky I was in.'

She stared at me, her eyebrows raised. She was right. Where else would I be?

She started to look around the hallway with its bare walls that were painted a grey that reflected my mood.

'I don't know why you don't paint this place, it's so gloomy,' she said, looking the walls up and down. 'How long have you been here now, two years?'

'Almost three, and I keep meaning to,' I said. 'The landlord said I could, but he also said I needed to paint it back if I moved out.'

'And are you moving out any time soon?'

'No plan to,' I said, not wanting to admit that I'd thought, when things were going well with Jimmy, that I'd move in with him at some point. 'But is it really worth all the effort in case I do move?'

'I say yes, because it's soulless in here,' she said, heading down the hallway towards the lounge, which also was in desperate need of an injection of colour.

I wanted to point out that what the flat lacked in colour, it made up for in the fact that it was a maisonette, which meant that I didn't have to negotiate shared corridors, and I had my own private garden. Both had been a blessing in the state I'd been in lately, where I didn't want to see people.

The doorbell rang and I looked between Nina and the door. She gave a little shrug and I opened it up.

'Hey, you,' said Andrea, looking far more bronzed than the last time I saw her. She leaned over and gave me a hug, and I saw Marianne standing behind her.

'What are you two doing here? Don't tell me that you were on your way to IKEA?' I said, giving Marianne a quick hug.

'Why would we be going there?' said Andrea, confused. She was giving Oliver a quick cuddle and cooing over him.

'Oh, I don't know. To create a fictitious reason to drop in and see me?'

'We don't need a fictitious reason,' said Andrea. 'We're worried about you.'

'Oh, God,' I said, looking between the three of them. They all looked earnest and nervous. 'Is this some kind of intervention? You know we're not American, that's not really a thing here. Don't tell me Mum's coming?'

I put my hands on my hips. I could just imagine Mum and Aunty Sue barging in, totally taking charge, enjoying the drama of it all.

'Mum's got a lawn bowls competition,' said Nina.

'Of course she does.' I sighed with relief. My mum lived for drama and she'd be in a right frenzy if she was here.

'Look, we're all a bit concerned. You weren't yourself at the wedding,' said Nina.

'And then Marianne told us about you and this Metaverse man,' said Andrea.

Nina groaned. 'We weren't going to lead with that. Weren't we going to focus on all the other stuff?' She held out her hands, waving them in my direction like I was an exhibit.

'Guys, I appreciate you dropping in, but I'm fine.' I folded my arms over my chest, trying to hide the ketchup stain on my hoodie. 'Honestly. I might be in need of a haircut, but there's nothing wrong. Absolutely nothing.'

'What is that?' asked Marianne, sniffing.

Andrea started to sniff too, her whole face screwing up.

'It smells like burning,' said Nina, protectively holding Oliver to her chest and moving closer to the front door.

'What would be burning? Oh, shit.' I threw open the door to the lounge just as the smoke alarm started to ring out. Oliver started to wail and I heard the front door go.

I hurried into the lounge and lifted the iron that I'd left face down on the sheet, a big brown mark now burned into it.

Andrea had barged in and opened the windows and Marianne started to fan the smoke out with a cushion. My sister, still cradling Oliver outside, poked her head through the open window to see what was going on.

'What the fuck, Chloe?' said Andrea, standing over the ironing board. 'You're ironing your sheets? Who the hell irons their sheets?'

'I think the point we're missing is that she left the iron on the sheet,' shouted Nina over the sound of the alarm.

Marianne choked back a laugh. She turned her attention to the smoke alarm and was wafting it with the cushion and it stopped.

'Chloe, can you understand why we're worried about you?' she said, putting the cushion back down on the sofa. 'Look at this.'

The three of them were staring at me with a mixture of pity and concern and I crossed my arms in a futile attempt to hide the shame.

'I know I wasn't myself at the wedding.' I'd snuck out not long after the first dance. 'But it was the first time I'd been out for a long time. It was just a little overwhelming.'

Andrea's eyes widened.

'Anyone's wedding would have been, not just yours,' I added, to ease the scowl on her face. 'And it was a wonderful ceremony, one of the best I've ever been to.'

Andrea relaxed a little, but I could tell I'd hurt her feelings.

'I'm finding it a bit tricky being round loads of people.'

'Hmm,' said Nina, clenching her teeth.

'What?'

'You're not coming along to anything I invite you to, big or small. I asked you for a coffee this weekend and you said you were busy and here you are, watching *Married at First Sight*.'

'And ironing the sheets,' said Andrea. She was never going to let that bit go. She clearly hadn't tried it, as there is no better feeling than getting into freshly ironed bedsheets.

'Look, what we're trying to say is that we're here for you,' said Marianne.

I kept fending off the texts from all of them, and Mum too.

I looked down at the big burn mark on the sheet and it almost could have been a neon flashing light. They were right. I wasn't coping at all.

'I almost burned down my flat.' Tears started to sting my eyes and Andrea and Marianne flanked me on either side, each putting an arm around me.

'It's okay,' said Andrea, hugging me into her. 'Why don't you go and stay with your mum? You could take some time off work, get yourself sorted.'

I shook my head. 'No, I can't. I really can't.' I wanted to get better, not develop more neuroses.

'You've got to do something,' said Nina, walking back into the room. 'We've got a spare room. Granted it's Oliver's nursery, but I'm sure we could put a mattress in it as he's still in his cot in our room.'

'You just want a live-in babysitter.'

'I do,' she said with a wistful sigh.

'That would be the dream,' said Marianne, nodding her head in agreement.

'I'm not moving in with either of you,' I said, lifting my finger and pointing at them both. 'I'm fine, really.'

'You're not fine, and no one expects you to be,' said Andrea, guiding me down to the sofa. 'But you've got to start getting back to your old self. Marianne told us that her boss wants to use someone else for the training.'

Marianne's cheeks were flushed and she wouldn't look at me.

I'd lost so much: Kerry, Jimmy, Blaine, what felt like my sanity. This had to stop.

'I do know I'm not myself,' I said, touched that they'd all cared enough to come. 'But I will be. I'll coach myself through it. It's what I do for a living, so...'

I sounded so unconvincing. It was no wonder I was barely keeping my existing clients and not attracting any new ones. I took a deep breath. I'd been on autopilot over the last few months and I hadn't realised where I'd ended up, but the smell of burning and the sight of these three had jolted me to my senses.

Marianne was back to the sympathetic head tilt. 'Don't you think you might be better off getting someone else to help you?'

I thought of Kerry and of Blaine. My brain had been so foggy lately, but an idea had started to take hold.

'I need to go to New York,' I blurted out. I'd been running away from what had happened with Kerry and perhaps that's where I'd been going wrong. At best I might find Blaine, and at worst going back to where I met Kerry might offer its own catharsis.

Nina and Andrea exchanged glances.

'That's a terrible idea—' said Andrea.

'That's a brilliant idea,' said Nina, at the same time.

Andrea snapped her head round to Nina. 'You think that's a good idea?'

'You don't?' she said, her brow furrowing. 'I've always said she shouldn't waste those flights.'

'She should be here, where we can keep an eye on her, not running off to New York on her own.'

'But she won't be on her own. She'll be going to stay with Jimmy.' Nina was positively beaming and it took a few moments for her words to sink in.

'Oh no,' I said, shaking my head. I couldn't stay with Jimmy. It was one thing to say you were going to stay friends with an ex, it was quite another to actually put that into practice. Especially not in the postage-stamp-size square footage of a New York apartment. 'I'll just stay in a hotel.'

'I don't think it's a good idea for you to be alone,' said Nina with a tut. 'Look at this place and the wallowing you're doing. How would it be any different there?'

'Plus, have you any idea how expensive the accommodation is now, and food?' said Marianne.

'Hmm,' said Andrea. 'It's so expensive. We considered stopping off there on a honeymoon, but the prices were horrific. Don't you have any other friends from when you worked out there?'

I shook my head. All of us on the internship scheme were British and we'd all returned home, and the few work colleagues I'd kept in contact with had drifted away to more affordable cities.

'No, but look, if you're so worried, I'll make sure I get an Airbnb where the host lives there too. That way I won't be on my own. And it'll be cheaper.' I said, batting away their objections with a wave of my hand.

'I don't know,' said Andrea, before the three of them started to argue amongst themselves as to what the best option was. Nina favoured me staying with Jimmy, Marianne approved of my Airbnb idea, whereas Andrea still thought I'd be better off staying with my mum in England.

'It'll be good for me,' I blurted out, getting sick of them talking about me as if I wasn't there. 'I've been wanting to work on that new workshop about self-coaching. In fact,' I said, thinking on my feet, 'Marianne, I was thinking about presenting it to you and Patrick. I know you said you were going in another direction, but if I perhaps came in and pitched it.'

'I don't know. Patrick was quite adamant.' Marianne shifted on the sofa, patting her skirt down like she had at the wedding, avoiding eye contact.

I thought back to our recent walk, when I should have fought harder.

'Let me come in for a meeting. I promise I'll be prepared.'

There must have been something about the way that I pleaded, and she lifted her gaze to mine. It was my turn to tilt my head.

Marianne sighed and then lifted her phone out of her handbag and swiped across. 'We're meeting on the 18th of August to review ideas. Can you make it?'

That gave me a month, with two of those weeks in New York. That was surely enough time to get myself sorted and put everything together.

I nodded. 'I'll be there.'

'You realise that if you come into the meeting and it goes badly, that it'll be harder for me to convince Patrick to use you in the future?'

'I know,' I said, wondering what I was more nervous about, developing new workshops or the fact that I'd have to sort myself out in that short time.

'So that's settled,' I said. 'I'll get an Airbnb.'

Nina was rocking Oliver back and forth on the spot.

'But you'll at least be in contact with Jimmy?' she said. I could read her like a book. 'You need support out there.'

I laughed, but stopped when the three of them gave me stern looks.

'Fine. I'll let him know that I'm going. We'll meet for a drink or something.'

'Great,' said Nina, picking up her phone and tapping away. 'I'll set us up a group chat.'

'A group chat?'

'Yeah, you can keep us updated, and I'll add in Jimmy. We need someone in the city looking out for you.'

'Does it have to be my ex-boyfriend?' I groaned.

'Unless you know someone else?'

I bit my lip, drawing a blank.

'That's settled then.'

Nina tapped on her phone again causing the rest of our phones to beep in sync.

'There we are: *Chloe in NYC*,' she said. 'We'll expect regular check-ins.'

'Are we really sure about Jimmy being in it?' I groaned. 'Is it even appropriate to put an ex in it?'

'Too late,' said Marianne. 'He's already put a fist-pump emoji in.'

I closed my eyes.

'I think New York is going to be just the tonic for you,' said Nina, putting her phone down and clapping her hands together. Her eyes were twinkling in the same way they did when we were younger watching rom-coms. I knew exactly what she was thinking. 'That city always weaves its magic.'

'It'll have its work cut out for it,' I said.

'It will, but I believe in it, and I believe in you.'

I bit my lip. My sister could be a giant pain in the arse, but she could also be the best.

They were all right. It was time I started to take control again and started to live, and all roads were pointing to the Big Apple. I just hoped I wasn't making a huge mistake.

Chapter 7

I remember when transatlantic flights used to be a thing of excitement. I'd load myself up with snacks and books and even select the movies I was going to watch on the plane in advance. Seven hours would whizz by in what felt like the blink of an eye, and yet here I was staring at the little plane on the map screen and I'm sure it hadn't moved for what felt like hours. We seemed to have been hovering over the middle of the Atlantic Ocean forever.

Stuck on the plane, all I could think about was the time I'd first flown out here for my internship. I'd been a bag of nerves, and then I'd arrived and first met Kerry. She'd been sat on the counter of the breakfast bar of our apartment, her feet perched on the bar stool.

'That suitcase is huge,' she'd said, pointing at it as if I could forget I was carrying it.

'I know, I got carried away.'

Kerry waved my words away.

'I'm just jealous. I could barely get anything in mine.'

My cheeks flushed. She had a warmth in her eyes, brown specks that glowed as she spoke.

'Have you met the others in the corridor?'

'Yes,' I said, trying not to think about how overwhelming it had been. Remembering all those names and where people came from.

'It's like freshers' week at uni,' she said with a shudder. 'But you're the first of our apartment other than me to arrive. I'm Kerry.'

'Chloe.'

'Ah, Chloe,' she said with a nod. 'I read your bio in the pack. So we don't need to do the mindless introductions. Instead we should play Would You Rather? It's a much better way to get to know someone.'

She patted the counter next to her. I felt rebellious climbing up and following her lead by perching my feet on the stool.

'Would you rather have ketchup or mayo?'

'Ketchup, every day.'

'Yes, mayo has the worst consistency and it's so weird how they make it, isn't it?' she said and I found myself nodding, as that was true.

'Okay, would you rather watch *Love Actually* or *It's a Wonderful Life* at Christmas?'

'Oh, um, I've never seen *It's a Wonderful Life* and I'm not a fan of *Love Actually*.'

'How can you not have seen *It's a Wonderful Life*? We have to rectify that.'

It felt strange to think that we were going to be spending Christmas together out here. I still kept pinching myself that this was my life for the next year.

'New York or London?'

'New York,' I said. 'Without a shadow of a doubt.'

Kerry held her hand out to me and I took it and she shook it.

'Chloe, I think this could be the start of a brilliant friendship.'

'*Casablanca*?'

'Ah, this *is* the start of a brilliant friendship. You've confirmed it.'

*

I scrunched my eyes shut, trying to close down the memory before the rest of them started to flood in. The nights out. The days spent watching movies hungover, on the sofa. The countless meals we'd cooked each other. The mindless texts and voice messages we left each other.

I opened my eyes again to see the plane in exactly the same spot. I couldn't help but sigh.

'A watched pot never boils,' said the woman next to me in an East Coast accent.

It took me a couple of seconds to register that she'd spoken to me, and I turned to face her.

'You okay?' She smiled sympathetically as if she already knew I wasn't. 'You've been staring at that plane with such vivid concentration I'm wondering if you're trying to fly the plane by telekinesis or something.'

'That would be a cool trick,' I said, trying to stare harder, just in case.

'Very *Stranger Things*,' she said.

A flight attendant walked through the cabin, carrying a small tray with two glasses of something sparkling, and he stopped at our seats. He turned to the couple in the seats across the aisle from us.

'I hear you're celebrating?' he said to them.

The woman shrieked and grabbed hold of the man sitting next to her.

'We got married on Saturday. We're on our honeymoon.'

'Congratulations,' he said, passing over the flutes, 'from all of us.'

The flight attendant was walking away when the woman next to me leaned across and tapped him on the arm.

'Do you mind? We're also celebrating,' she said, touching my arm and practically dazzling me with the massive rock on her finger.

'Oh, of course,' he said. 'I'll be right back.'

He gave us a huge smile and hurried away.

'And there was me thinking that slumming it in premium economy, I'd get no free champagne,' she said, her eyes wide.

The flight attendant came back with the same tray and two fresh glasses. The woman took both and handed me one.

'Thank you so much. We so appreciate it,' she said, flashing a winning smile.

'Not at all,' he said, hurrying off.

'*Santé*,' she said, chinking her glass to mine, and then she raised it at the newlyweds, who also congratulated us on our imaginary celebration.

'So you never answered the question. If there are no special plane flying powers going on, are you okay?'

I tried to force a small smile on my lips. 'I am, thank you.'

The woman nodded. 'I get it. You're not okay, but you don't want to talk to a stranger on a plane. But look, I've been there on flights when I've been trapped with thoughts and with nowhere to walk it off, so I'm here if you need me.'

'That's kind. Thank you.'

The woman nodded her head as if she was tipping an imaginary hat.

I went back to my plane-watching. It had moved about a millimetre since I'd last looked.

'By the way,' said the woman, and I turned to look at her once more. She winced in apology. 'I promise I'll leave you alone, but my name's Lila. You know, in case you wanted to talk, and this way you weren't talking to a perfect stranger.'

There was something so genuine about the woman's smile.

'Chloe,' I said.

'Chloe. Right, I'll leave you to your plane-watching.'

She mimed zipping her lips and went back to her screen. She'd been flicking through endless numbers of entertainment options and I got the impression she didn't know what she wanted to do with herself either.

'I'm usually very chatty,' I said, still watching the screen. 'It's just I'm not quite myself at the moment.'

Lila looked delighted that I'd talked and she scooped her dark bob up with her hands and let her hair fall.

'Is that why you're going over to New York?'

'Kind of.'

She nodded. 'New York's like that. It's the kind of place you can go for reinvention or resuscitation. I remember when I went back after I'd been in England studying, it felt like a relief. Whilst I loved the friends that I'd made in London and the city was great, it wasn't the same.'

'I lived in New York for a year after I graduated. I think I left part of my heart there.'

'Right?' she said, and then she shrugged. 'Hopefully you can find it and get it back.'

'I hope so,' I said.

She nodded again. 'Oh, I know so. What do you do, Chloe, when you're not getting planes to fly faster with telekinesis?'

'I'm an executive coach. It's kind of—'

'I know what an exec coach is, I've used them. I'm an investment strategist.'

I nodded, pretending I knew as much about her world as she did mine. I knew enough that it was in the financial industry and therefore far from my comfort zone.

'I probably don't look like a good advert for it right now. I should be able to coach myself out of my funk.'

She shrugged. 'Come on, do you think that psychologists don't suffer from depression? Or someone like me hasn't made a bad investment in their personal life? I have a shoe rack full of bad investments. You hoping to find yourself in New York?'

'Myself and this guy,' I said, with a sigh. The words tumbled out before I could stop them.

Now Lila looked like she was really listening. 'Go on.'

'I didn't mean to say that out loud. It's just I can't tell my friends that's why I'm coming and they've put me in a group chat with them and my ex-boyfriend, who's also in New York and—'

'—We're going to circle back to the ex-boyfriend, but right now we're going to start at who this mystery man is that your friends don't know about, and we'll go from there.'

By the time I'd finished filling Lila in on how I'd met and lost contact with Blaine, and how I'd ended up in the world's most awkward group chat, the little plane on the screen was skirting down the North American coast, sitting somewhere above Newfoundland.

'Let me see your list of the places.'

I opened up the notebook in front of me and handed it across.

'It's not very easy to use, so I thought I'd mark them on the map I bought, see if I can—'

'—spot any patterns or districts that he hangs out at a lot to give you a clue where he lives. Very Columbo of you.'

'I was going to say it might make it easier for me to plan routes so I can go to multiple places in one day. But I like your thinking better.'

'Have you got the map on you?'

I started to dig around in the bag under my seat.

The trolley was coming back down the aisle, this time handing out Toblerone ice creams, and I managed to find the map just as the flight attendant passed me mine.

'This is working out to be the best flight ever,' said Lila. 'Much more entertaining than anything on that little screen, and now the amazing snacks.'

She put down her table and I put down mine and I laid the map out as best I could between them. We got to work, me reading out the places and Lila doing her best to find them.

'I'd been hesitant about the idea of Wi-Fi on planes,' said Lila, tapping away to work out what the Latin-American fusion restaurant chain could be. 'But it's come in very handy for this.'

I squinted and looked at the paper map in front of me. There were a lot of marks on it, but I couldn't see one district above all others that won out.

'Okay,' she said, picking up one of the pens. 'If I'm right with the chain, then his office is near one of these five places.'

She marked all of them on the map.

'Oh great, there's one in nearly all of the boroughs.'

'Not Staten Island,' said Lila, pointing.

'Not Staten Island,' I repeated. 'In fact, there isn't anything marked on the map there.'

'Okay, so ruling out.'

I looked at the map again. For such a small geographic space it seemed huge.

'It's hopeless, though. There are so many places, and this feels like borderline stalking.'

'Um, hello,' said Lila, loud enough that she startled the newlyweds, who were sleeping across the aisle. She raised an eyebrow and then lowered her voice. 'He asked you to come and it's not like you haven't tried to find him online. This is the only way. Plus, you had flights booked. I am such a believer that things happen for a reason, and this has got serendipity written all over it.'

'I hope so, as it's going to take a miracle to find him. I could go to all of these places and he could be standing right next to me and I'd never know.'

'Or you could be sitting right next to him, right now,' she said, her eyebrows raising. She cackled. 'Don't worry, you're not, but you're right. That's the worst thing about you blind-dating him in the Metaverse.' She held her hands up, spreading her fingers wide, and turned to me with an almost manic grin. 'I don't know why I didn't think of this before. I've got it.'

'Got what?'

'The idea of how to speed this up. You should look for him on dating apps.'

'But I don't know his name or what he looks like.'

She nodded almost a little too frantically. 'I know, but a lot of the hot right-now apps, according to my girlfriends who use them, take a proper old-fashioned approach. No pictures, limited messages before you meet up. You practically just match on hobbies.'

She picked up my handwritten list.

'If you just put yourself as a chess-playing, art-loving, Periscope Monkeys superfan, I'm sure you'd be matched with him.'

'But what if he's not on apps?'

'Everyone's on apps in New York. Unless there's a ring on that finger, I don't think any New Yorker would come off them, just in case. We're a deeply distrustful bunch.'

I part-laughed, part-groaned. He had mentioned dating apps, and it couldn't be any crazier than flying out to the city, where he lived, trying to track him down via his favourite restaurants.

'Give me your number and I'll message you the details of the app my friends are using.'

Lila reminded me of Andrea, in that when she was mission-focused, nothing was going to stop her. I took her phone and obliged.

'Blaine actually mentioned blind-dating apps.'

Lila put her hands together in prayer. 'There you go. It's a sign.'

I handed her back her phone with my contact added.

'Now I've got your number, we can keep in touch,' she said. 'You can keep me updated on your progress out here and meet for coffee if you like.'

'I'd like that.' My shoulders felt a little lighter at the thought I'd have someone to talk to about it.

'Ah, I've got a better idea,' she said. Her hands were up again. 'You can put me in the group chat. I can be the eyes and ears on the ground for them.'

I laughed, thinking she was joking, but her face was deadpan.

'Oh, you mean it?'

'Yeah, I'm one of those weird people that loves group chats. The in-jokes. The gossip. Add me in.'

I stopped and considered it. It was a great idea.

'And then we can oust Jimmy from the group,' I smiled. The only reason Nina had added him was because she felt they needed someone in the city to be in the group, but now Lila could take on that role.

'Are you kidding? That's half the fun.' She tapped my phone, which was resting on the pull-down table. 'Add me in.'

'I actually can't, as I don't even have administrator rights in a group, which is ridiculous considering it's about me.'

'That's too funny.'

The group chat was insufferable with them constantly checking in on me. Adding in Lila might at least go some way to showing them that I was coping okay without them and therefore they might give me some space.

'I'll message Nina, and get her to add you in.'

Lila relaxed back into her chair and picked up her near-empty champagne flute.

'Thank you for this, Chloe.'

'What, for getting you added to the world's worst WhatsApp group?'

She spluttered a little of the fizz that she was just polishing off. 'No, this whole thing. I was so upset getting on this plane to come home. Ah,' she sighed. 'Don't get me wrong, I'm pleased to get back to Anthony, that's my husband, but being back in London, it made me pine for my London buddies.'

I folded the map up. All this time I'd been talking about me, and I hadn't asked anything about her.

'You didn't tell me what you were up to in England. Were you meeting up with friends from when you were studying?'

'Yeah,' she said, with a wistful huff. 'I spent a semester abroad at Imperial in London. Such a fun semester and I made great friends. One of them just got married and she made me bridesmaid so that I had to come over. Anthony, who is a bigamist – married to his work as well as to me – couldn't get the leave.'

'That's a shame, but it sounds like a nice reason to be over.'

'Oh, it was. It just makes me miss them and the way they all talk so funny. Like you.' She patted me on the arm. 'Now you can take that homesickness feeling away. Is it weird that I get homesick for somewhere I only lived for half a year?'

'That's how I feel about New York.'

She nodded and pointed her finger as if I'd hit the nail right on the head.

'Speaking of which,' she said, nodding over my shoulder as the plane started to dip to the left.

No matter how many times I flew over Manhattan, it couldn't fail to impress. I'd grown up with it as the backdrop to so many TV shows and movies and it always felt comforting. It didn't matter that it never looked the same as a previous visit, that was part of the charm.

I tried to think when I'd last visited. It must be almost eight years since I'd been. Kerry had made frequent trips back at first after our internship, when she'd been trying to make long distance work with her ex, Theo. She'd even spent a summer living with him when she was trying to work out how she'd get a visa, and I'd gone out to visit. Then, when she couldn't find a way to stay, and her and Theo had broken up, the two of us had gone over a couple of times for long weekends to scratch the New York itch.

I thought of the times I'd made this journey with her. She always took the window seat and I knew that we'd be bickering at this point as her big head would have been blocking the view. The memory tightened a grip on my heart. The fun memories were almost more painful than the bad ones as they were a constant reminder of what I'd never have again.

'I've lost you,' said Lila with a nudge. 'Have you gone back to the bad place?'

'Not a bad place, just a bit of a sad one.'

She nodded and the plane righted itself. The 'Fasten seatbelt' sign came on and the newlywed groom woke his sleeping wife.

I focused on Manhattan below, trying to keep the grief from taking hold. The skyline was constantly evolving. No matter what the city threw at it, it kept going and kept thriving, and I hoped that a little bit of that spirit would rub off on me.

Chapter 8

'The tunnel seems to be moving,' said the driver, as we'd left New Jersey. He'd been trying his best to make conversation, and I'd tried my best to be polite whilst shutting it down. Fear was starting to seep into my bones and I couldn't face small talk.

The tunnel was clear, or at least we didn't queue our way through bumper to bumper, as I had on some occasions, and we found ourselves skating through lower Manhattan, where the assault on the senses really took hold. The way that the light shrank and we entered the shadows of the buildings, horns honking, the steam of the sidewalk, the wail of sirens. And the people; there were people everywhere.

I could barely breathe, my throat felt like it was constricting, my chest tight. I had my phone in my hand and it started to beep, but I couldn't look at it. I was too busy staring at New York and wishing I was anywhere but.

This was a terrible idea. The absolute worst. Thoughts swirled round quicker than I could register them, each one making me feel that I'd lost my mind. How did I think I would ever find Blaine here amongst all these millions of people, when I didn't know who he was? Why had I let Nina put Jimmy in the group chat? How was I going to win over Marianne's boss with a session I hadn't even started? Those thoughts were enough to send me into a spiral and that was before I'd even started to think about Kerry. That was the real kicker. This had always been our city, and setting foot in it without her felt like I was trespassing.

The car behind us honked its horn and my driver honked his back. I wanted to get out, but at the same time I wanted to get as far away from here as I could.

My phone beeped again and this time I looked down. It was no surprise that it was from the *Chloe in NYC* group chat.

NINA
Have you landed?

ANDREA
Checked her flight. She arrived two minutes early.

NINA
Let us know when you arrive at the accommodation.

ANDREA
I wish you'd let us track you in real time. Find My Friends is superhandy to stop us worrying.

MARIANNE
I've looked it up and she's a 22-minute taxi ride to her accommodation.

JIMMY
Surely she's not getting a cab, it'll cost her a fortune. I'll send a link to the public transport options. $5 absolute steal.

My lips were twitching, threatening to break into a smile. It was almost suffocating how focused they were on my life, but at the same time it was weirdly comforting to know they were there.

I looked up and we were heading towards a bridge, the traffic moving more freely now. My breathing was less shallow and my heart was hammering less.

> **NINA**
> **WE KNOW YOU'VE READ THE MESSAGES!!!**

I sighed. There was no escaping them, no matter how many physical miles were between us.

> **ME**
> I'm in a cab (sorry, Jimmy). Just heading into Brooklyn now. I'll update at some point later on when I'm at the accommodation.
>
> **ANDREA**
> When you *arrive at your accommodation. There – fixed it for you.

I shook my head and googled: *Do people know if you leave a WhatsApp group?*

As we headed into Brooklyn, the scenery started to change. The buildings were shrinking in height, brownstones started to pop up and trees began to make more of an appearance.

'Park Slope is a real nice place,' said the driver. 'You staying with friends?'

'No,' I said, thinking how much the conversation with Lila had taken out of me.

He nodded and turned the radio up a little higher.

I watched as we headed further and further from Manhattan. No wonder the room was cheap, or at least cheaper than most.

The taxi pulled up to an abrupt halt alongside a row of terraced brownstones, each with their own ornate staircase in the centre sweeping down to the sidewalk. They looked magnificent framed by blue sky and the bright green leaves of the myriad trees that lined the street. The accommodation might be far out of the city, but this street more than made up for it.

The taxi driver tapped his meter and told me the cost. I scrabbled around for my card to pay.

'You'll need to sign,' he said, pointing at the little panel in the back of the cab.

I followed the instructions, trying my best to remember what my signature was and, thanks to the digital pen, it looked nothing like it.

Satisfied I'd paid the fare, the driver was out and opening the boot before I'd had time to put my wallet away. By the time I made it on to the pavement, my suitcase was already at my feet.

'Have a nice day,' he said, scrambling back into the cab, and away he went.

My stomach lurched, the empty hollow feeling growing bigger. I stood next to my oversized case wondering what on earth I was doing.

'Pull yourself together, Chloe,' I said, fighting the urge to call a cab and head straight back to the airport.

I turned to my phone and pulled up the instructions for the apartment I was staying at.

Head under the stairs at number 32 and find the key-lock box.

I did as instructed, heading under the staircase, but there was absolutely no lock box to be seen. I walked back to the front of the house, my hand gripping my suitcase even tighter. It definitely said 32. I checked the map, trying to see if the cab driver had taken me to the wrong address, but my location pin was in exactly the right spot.

I walked back underneath the staircase, looking around the door with the metal grille. It had to be here. I couldn't be looking hard enough. A sickness started to wash over my stomach as I scanned every inch of the archway to no avail.

A man walked past with over-ear headphones and I had to practically grab him to get his attention.

'Sorry to bother you. Do you know if this street is North Park Street?'

'Yep,' he nodded, barely stopping.

'Great, thanks so much,' I muttered at his passing wake, not that he'd hear over the headphones.

I scrolled the email of instructions, looking for something I might've missed and, in the end, there was nothing for it, I'd have to phone the number.

It didn't even ring before I was met with a mechanical voice. *I'm sorry, but the number dialled is no longer in service.*

My stomach sank like a stone in a pond. The hairs on my arms were all standing on end as I checked the number and the area codes and dialled again. It connected to the same message and I scrunched my eyes shut.

'Fuck,' I shouted, startling an old woman who walked by, giving me a wide berth before she shouted back, 'Fuck yourself.'

It was almost enough to make me burst into tears.

I looked up at the brownstone and there was a doorbell at the top of the staircase. I took one look at my big suitcase and the chunky stairs that stood in my way. I couldn't leave my suitcase here unattended.

I started to sweat, dragging the case up, step by step, until I eventually reached the top and rang the bell.

Tears stung my eyes as I waited on the stoop. I shivered, not knowing if it was being in the shade or my body's reaction to what was happening.

'Can I help?' asked a woman answering the door. She reminded me of a schoolmistress, her hair in a tight bun, glasses perched on her nose. She looked me up and down and then took in my large suitcase. 'Oh, for goodness' sake. Not another one. Some scammer is using this address, pretending it's a rental.'

'Scammer?' The word caught in my throat so much that I struggled to breathe.

'I'm sorry to be the bearer of bad news. I'll go find the number the cop told us to ring if it happened again. Apparently, they use a fake address for a week or two, then someone else gets a turn. I was hoping I'd seen the last of you all.'

'But I've paid them,' I spat the words out in shock. 'I've paid them for two weeks of accommodation.'

My head was starting to feel light and I gripped the handle of my case even tighter, to keep me upright.

'Let me guess; they told you if you booked directly, they'd give you a discount.'

'Fifteen per cent,' I squeaked. How could I have been so stupid?

'I'll get you the police number,' she said, shuffling back and shutting the door in my face.

I rubbed at my eyes, the tears starting to fall. I'd been buzzing on the plane, meeting Lila, forming a plan. It had felt as if this trip was meant to be, but now it was turning into a nightmare.

'Here you go,' said the woman, reappearing. She handed me the number and a plastic packet of tissues. 'Happens to the best of us. There's a hotel two blocks on the right. Hope the rest of your trip works out better.'

She retreated inside and shut the door behind her.

I sat down on the stoop, my legs unsteady, and there was only so much propping up my case could do. I ran the card through my hands staring at the number of the police precinct. None of it felt real.

I pulled out my phone to see about an available room in a hotel, scrolling through the different options. There was nothing shy of $350 a night in Brooklyn and a quick search in Manhattan showed it wasn't any cheaper over there.

The tears were flowing now. I couldn't really justify spending that for one night and now the reality was that I was going to have to pay for two weeks of that. I felt sick that I'd spent so much on the taxi.

My phone buzzed and I looked down at the notification. It was from the group chat.

NINA
What's the update?

ANDREA
Is your host nice?

I wiped at my tears. What were they going to say? They'd berate me for being so stupid and getting scammed, but I had to update them, as I knew they wouldn't leave me alone.

ME
Been a bit of a hiccup. Sorting a plan B.

No sooner than I sent the text, my phone rang. Jimmy. I debated not answering it, but I'd reached my limit.

'Hello,' I sniffed into the phone.

'You okay? What's happened?' He was all business. He was always level-headed in a crisis. 'Is the place not nice? Host too creepy?'

'Place non-existent,' I said, with a sigh. 'I've been scammed.'

'Oh, shit!' Jimmy sucked in a breath. 'At least you'll get your money back, Airbnb?'

'Um, well.' I tapped the police card on my knee. 'I sort of paid them directly via bank transfer so I could get a discount.' I said it in a hurry, hoping he'd miss it. I braced myself for the fury.

'Chloe,' he said, with an almost ache in his voice. 'Have you called the police?'

'I've got a number to call. The woman who lives here says I'm not the first to turn up.'

'Oh, shit! What are you going to do?'

I let out a deep breath and him being nice made me sob again. 'I don't know. I spent so much money that I'm not going to get back and then I've looked at hotels and they're so expensive. I figure I'll get one for tonight and then I don't know, look to find another cheap room that's more legit or maybe it'll be cheaper to just buy a flight home.'

I pinched the bridge of my nose, wanting to stem the tide of tears.

'You can't do that. You can't come all this way. Stay with me. I've got room here.'

I shook my head.

'I can't do that.'

'Of course you can. I'm not even paying for it, my work is.'

That wasn't what I meant. We'd hardly spoken since we'd broken up and now he was expecting me to go and stay with him in what was no doubt a tiny apartment.

'I can't.'

'Come and stay for tonight at least and look at other options tomorrow. You've had a long day and I don't think it's a good idea to stay on your own.'

I wanted to protest and tell him that I was fine by myself, but who was I kidding? I wasn't and I didn't have the energy to pretend to be.

'Send me the address you're at and I'll order you a car,' he said.
'It's fine, I'll sort it.'
'I've got it. Text me your address,' he said firmly and it caused me to cry a little more with how good he was being about this.
'Thanks, Jimmy.'
'You're welcome. Now, I better go get tidying. I wasn't expecting company.'

I hung up the phone and rubbed at my eyes, trying not to overthink exactly what I was doing.

The taxi ride didn't take long. Jimmy's apartment was on Wall Street, at the tip of Manhattan. The taxi driver gave me déjà vu setting my oversized suitcase on the kerb in front of me and waving me goodbye. I looked up at the buildings around me. It was so different from the homely feel of the Park Slope. Here it was all skyscrapers kissing the blue sky, with shiny reflective glass that felt corporate and impersonal.

'There she is.' My shoulders sighed with relief at the sound of a familiar voice. I'd only just stopped myself crying, I didn't want to start all over again.

I turned to see Jimmy, a box in his arms and a tote bag full of what looked like groceries under his arm. He looked different standing here, his short-sleeved shirt that I didn't recognise, and his sun-kissed tanned skin.

He balanced the box on my suitcase and he leaned over to hug me. We did that awkward dance of trying to hug: we both went to lean left and we nearly head-butted each other.

'Sorry,' I muttered leaning over his shoulder and patting him on the back, like he was an elderly relative. For two people that had once been so tactile, it felt like we'd forgotten how to touch each other. What I really wanted to do was to cling on to him for dear life, but I didn't think that was the done thing to do with your ex.

'You've had quite the day,' he said.

I shook my head. 'I can't even. I don't want to talk about it.'

'I get that. When you're ready, I'll help you phone the police, then I was thinking you could try your bank too.'

I wrinkled my face up. 'I'll give it a try, but the more I think about it, the more I think it was all my fault for being so stupid.'

He was biting his lip and I'm sure he wanted to say something more, but I was grateful when he didn't.

There was a silence and the heat of the day started to hit me. It was that dry heat that felt like all the air had been sucked out of it. I could feel myself starting to sway with the travel and the shock of the recent events.

He scooped the box off my suitcase and he paused. He held my gaze and smiled. 'Despite the circumstances, it's good to see you.'

'You too,' I said, meaning it, but it didn't stop my churning stomach.

'Something's different,' he said, looking me up and down. 'You've cut your hair.'

I reached my hand up and got a shock at how far it was before my fingers made contact with the ends. The hairdresser had had to take four inches off.

'I needed a fresh start.'

He nodded. 'Yeah,' he said looking up at the building we were standing outside. 'I get that. Do you want to come and see my crib?' he said, in his best American accent, which was truly terrible.

I'd watched *MTV Cribs* far too much back in the day.

'Only if you've got the Cristal in.'

'Ah,' he pointed at me, with a laugh and he pulled up a bottle of fizz from the box. 'Californian, so not quite champagne. The bodega isn't that high-end.'

'Jimmy, I'm shocked that you shopped at a bodega rather than a Trader Joe's.'

'That's what happens when you invite someone to stay last minute and you realise you have nothing in. You would not believe how much these crisps cost me.'

He slipped the bottle back amongst the groceries and, despite the box under his arm and the bag on his shoulder, he went to grab the handle of my suitcase.

'I can manage,' I said, reaching out for it. Our hands brushed against each other and we both let it go like we'd got an electric shock.

'Sorry,' he said, holding up his free hand. 'There's a pretty good lift in the building, so I'm sure you'll be fine.'

He started to walk into the building in front of us and I followed.

'I see you're not talking American just yet. Not talking about your chips or your elevator.'

Talking to Jimmy was making me feel calmer, taking my mind off what had happened.

'Not quite yet.'

At least not everything about him seemed different.

He led me through an impressive lobby with a reception desk, over to a bank of lifts at the back.

We smiled awkwardly at each other waiting for the lift to start, and I wondered how we were going to cope in the confined space of his apartment.

We arrived on the eighth floor in what felt like seconds and it felt like a relief when the lift doors sprang open.

'So,' he said, marching off as if he was relieved to be out. I lagged behind, trying to tug my case along the thick carpet in the corridor.

'This is me,' he pointed at a door before opening it up.

He swung the door open to a small, but perfectly formed, apartment. I followed him inside and set my suitcase down under the coat hook, relieved to be free of it.

'Nice,' I said, nodding and looking round. There was a bathroom to the left and to the right there was a recessed double bed in a nook in the wall that had a curtain to separate it off. Straight in front was a tiny living quarters with a sofa, desk and, as I walked in further round the corner, a kitchenette. It was functional and stylish, with dark blue cupboards and bright white walls.

'This place is great,' I said, taking it all in.

'And the best bit,' said Jimmy walking across to the curtains at the wall.

'Is it another bedroom?' I said, with a nervous laugh.

He laughed back and drew the curtain. I gasped. There was a big building straight in front, but to the left was the East River.

'Oh, that's amazing,' I said, looking towards Brooklyn, where I'd just come from.

'It's pretty cool, even if you have to squint a bit.'

'Still better than your view over the High Street,' I said.

'The only time that was any good was on a Saturday night.'

'Always entertaining.' I nodded at the memory.

We were back there for a split second in my mind, curled up on the sofa spending a night in, then watching the pubs kick out and the trouble kick off.

'So, um, going back to the bed. That nook looked cosy, but...'

'Your face,' he said, laughing. 'Relax, this isn't a Hallmark movie.'

He took the coffee table out of the way and then pulled out a sofa bed that came out as a double bed and it already had sheets on it.

'And for added privacy,' he pulled a curtain round.

'So private.'

'Absolutely, and the nook bed has curtains, so...' He shrugged his shoulders. 'I know it's not ideal.'

I wrapped my arms around me, the air conditioning finally cooling me down.

'It's great, and I'm grateful. I'll hopefully get something sorted tomorrow and I'll be out of your hair.'

He drew back the curtain and perched on the arm of the sofa.

'Stay for the whole time if you need. I'll be at work during the day anyway. Plus, this place might be small, but there are communal lounges and kitchens. There's a laundry in the basement that... well, we'll do laundry one night and you'll see.'

'A laundry room, huh?'

'Needs to be seen to be believed. There's a games room, a business room. There's even a rooftop bar that's got cracking views.'

'No squinting required.'

'No squinting required,' he said with a smile.

I smiled back. No matter how hard he was trying to sell it to me, I couldn't stay here more than tonight. The tension was so thick between us you could cut it with a knife.

'So I should get these groceries away and you'll probably want to shower after the flight.'

'Do I smell that bad?'

'I was too polite to say,' he said, edging away from me. 'There are fresh towels in the bathroom and there might be shampoo.'

'Don't worry, I've got all that kind of stuff.'

'Great, then when you're out, we can work out what to do after. This kitchenette isn't really for much other than microwave popcorn to be honest. But I have done my best to try as many food outlets in the vicinity so we can get a takeaway if you like? Then we can phone the police for you. Get that sorted.'

I nodded. Exhausted and emotional.

I was tired and I was trying not to do the mental maths of working out what time it was back home. What I wanted to do was have a shower and crawl into the bed on that sofa. But Jimmy was right, I needed to get the ball rolling on getting things sorted with the police.

'Go get in that shower. I'll order some food. Thai? The usual things?'

I nodded. 'Extra crab cakes?'

He was tapping away on an app as we spoke.

I headed into the bathroom and flicked on the shower. The water ran and I started to cry. Far from bringing me back to life, so far the city was doing its best to try and break me even further.

Chapter 9

Jet lag always left me feeling the same. Sleep came in waves that knocked me out, making me feel like I'd slept for weeks, only to discover I'd barely closed my eyes for an hour. I spent the night waking and sleeping in short bursts.

Every time I woke up, I had the slight feeling of panic, trying to work out where I was, and each time it took a few moments before the events of yesterday came flooding back to me.

It was ridiculously dark in the lounge. The curtains didn't keep out much noise, but they blocked out light. My watch told me it was just after seven. I might have been grateful to be here last night, but fear started to build in my stomach. I'd seen Jimmy so many times in the morning before, but now it felt different. I shouldn't be here.

I could hear the faint sound of the shower and I wondered if I could pretend to be asleep until he went to work. But what time would that be? I groaned and slipped on a bra and jumper, and pulled the curtain back. I'd only be putting off the inevitable.

I headed into the kitchenette, flicked on a light and started to poke about in the near-dark, looking for capsules for the coffee machine.

'Morning,' said Jimmy, making me jump. He was far chirpier than I remembered him being in the morning.

'Bloody hell, you scared the crap out of me.' I put my hand on my heart to still it, but it was racing. I took in Jimmy standing in front of me. He was already dressed in a tailored suit and crisp white shirt. My belly gave an involuntary flip. I'd forgotten it used to do that at the sight of him dressed up. That was the problem with muscle memory: my body hadn't learned that that was no longer the reaction I should have when I saw him. It was exactly the reason that me being here was a bad idea.

'Did I wake you?' he asked.

'No, I've been awake for a while. My body is all over the place.'

He nodded.

'Yeah, jet lag is a bitch,' he said, opening the main curtains a little, the light flooding in. 'I don't know what your plans are, but I thought I could head into work early, then leave a bit early. Forecast is good today so we could go for drinks at a rooftop bar and head out to dinner.'

'Um,' I said, in that non-committal way. 'You've done me such a huge favour letting me stay here, but hopefully I'll be gone by the time you finish work.'

'I've told you you're welcome to stay here.' I opened my mouth to speak, but he held up his hands. 'At least stay for a couple of days whilst you file the police report and get over the jet lag.'

I thought of the shame of getting scammed and trying to get it sorted. The thoughts started to overwhelm me and that feeling that had led me to Jimmy's in the first place was trying to convince me to stay here.

'Okay, maybe just for another day. But I don't expect you to give up all your time for me too. I know you're busy,' I said, trying to at least create some boundaries. 'Carry on as you would, pretending I'm not here, going on your dates with your twenty-year-olds.'

I was here to find Blaine, after all. Not that I could tell Jimmy that.

'It was one twenty-three-year-old,' he muttered.

'But still,' I said, 'don't be changing plans on my account.'

'Okay then, if you're sure,' he said, running his hands through his hair, which was still wet. 'Wednesday nights I often play pickleball with people from work.'

'There you go. Carry on as normal.'

'So what are your plans?' He headed over to the fridge and got out a bottle of orange juice, raising it up to me as he grabbed a glass out of the cupboard. I nodded and he grabbed a second glass.

'I'm not really sure,' I said, in all honesty. Yesterday had been such a shit show, I didn't know if I was prepared for what New York might throw at me today.

It had all sounded so easy when I was talking to Lila on the plane, but looking out of the window and seeing the tall, imposing building reminded me exactly where I was and that I had a mammoth task in front of me.

'Did you say there were coffee capsules in here somewhere?'

I turned my attention back to the cupboard in the hope that a coffee might revive me.

'Oh, I think I ran out of them. There's probably some instant,' he said, pulling a face.

My stomach lurched at the thought of instant coffee. I was a massive coffee snob. I didn't mean to be, but during the pandemic I'd treated myself to a fancy coffee maker that even ground the beans.

'There's an Australian café in the building next door that has proper coffee.'

'Great! Do they deliver?' I closed the cupboards.

'I was going to head there for breakfast on my way to work. Why don't you come?'

'I probably need to shower. I wouldn't want to delay you.'

'You wouldn't. I can answer emails while I wait. The UK office will have been open for a few hours. Plus, I've got to do my hair,' he said, rubbing his hand through it, water drops flicking off it.

When he said 'do his hair' he meant he'd rub it with a towel and put in a little hair wax. It would take him a minute max.

'I might be a while. I need to wash my hair,' I said, looking at the sunshine and the optimism it brought with the day – and the feeling of fear that didn't want to shift.

'Go get in that shower, and let's go. Believe me, you'll get it when you taste the coffee.'

The coffee shop was, as promised, next door. I hadn't really known what to wear. July back home was supposed to be hot, but often the weather didn't get the memo. Here, the heat was already stifling in the sun, but cold in the shade. I was grateful for my cardigan.

Expecting to get a bit of respite from the heat, we were met with a blast of cold air conditioning crossing the threshold.

'It's freezing.'

'Yeah, layers are your friend.'

I shivered.

'The coffee will warm you.'

'This magic coffee, it's got a lot to do.' But already the smell of it was starting to make me think this was a good idea.

Jimmy ordered us a couple of flat whites and I picked up a tub of yogurt and granola.

'Beautiful day. I wish I didn't have to go to work,' he said heading over to a table. 'You know it rained all last week. You're lucky.'

'Yeah,' I said, looking out at the city that was starting to wake. We'd only been here a few minutes, but it was already starting to get busy both inside and on the street outside. A steady stream of commuters was trickling in and a queue was forming.

'So, what's first? Are you hitting the shops for a little retail therapy?'

'I don't think so. The exchange rate is so rubbish, and there's not a lot I need.'

'Yeah, that's what they all say and then they're laden with Little Brown Bags. My mum and sisters came to visit last month and they spent a whole day in Bloomingdale's. Had their nails and make-up done, everything.' He shuddered.

I thought of Jimmy's mum and his sisters and my heart ached. I hadn't really thought up until now that I wouldn't get to hang out with them again. I'd been too caught up in everything else when we'd broken up, that it was only now that so much time had passed that I was starting to realise what I was missing.

'How are you finding being away from them?'

I was close to my family, but not as close as Jimmy was to his. Their group chat was even busier than the *Chloe in NYC* one.

'It's both easier and harder than I thought it would be. We FaceTime a lot, but I guess,' he hesitated, 'I miss popping round to see them. The weekends can be long here.'

'Weekends can be the worst,' I said, thinking how mine seemed to drag.

He looked at me and it made me shiver. When we'd been together, there would be a way that he'd look into my eyes that made me feel that he could read my mind.

'So, a little bit of sightseeing if you're not shopping,' he said, picking up his coffee and breaking the spell.

'Yeah, and I've got some work to do. I'm planning some new sessions.'

'That's great.' His phone lit up. He picked it up and swiped a notification away. 'I'm glad you're working again.'

'Yeah, so I'll probably just head back to your apartment and get started on that.'

'You're going to work on your first day here?' He looked up from his phone. 'Do you want me to take the day off? My boss is pretty cool and I've got plenty of leave.'

'How? I thought in America you got next to nothing.'

'I've got my UK leave allowance.'

'Smart.'

I curled my fingers around my coffee, warming up my hands.

'I can take the day off, if you need me to.'

'Why would I need you to?' I asked, poking at my yogurt.

He paused and I looked up. His eyes were narrowed.

'Because you'd usually be off walking over the Brooklyn Bridge, trying to catch the sunrise, or queuing to be the first one at the Met.'

'I'm still getting over jet lag.' I took a spoonful of the yogurt, but I wasn't really hungry.

He sighed. 'Okay, well, I'll have my phone on me all day, even in meetings. Drop me a message or call me if you're stuck or—'

'Jimmy. I'm going to be fine. I know I was a mess last night, but it had been a bad day.' I shrugged as if I was shrugging off last night. 'Tell me instead about this pickleball thing. What's that?'

'Pickleball?' said Jimmy, raising his eyebrows. 'Now I know you're changing the subject.'

'I'm interested, really.'

Of course I was lying, and he knew it too, but he still indulged me by explaining the fastest-growing global sport. He gave me a very overenthusiastic spiel, but at the end of it I still couldn't grasp what it was.

'I better get going,' he said, getting up to go. 'I'll see you tonight?'

'You will,' I said. He hesitated and I held up my hands to shoo him away. He still didn't move. 'Don't worry about me, the girls in the group chat will be checking up on me and making sure I'm out and about.'

Jimmy visibly relaxed. At least the group chat was good for something.

'Okay, then. Have a good day.' He left and I gave him a wave as he passed the outside of the window.

Jimmy had been right about the coffee, so I ordered myself another cup and dug my map out of my handbag. I laid it flat on the table and the sight of it today seemed no less daunting than it had on the plane.

I had 13 nights left in Manhattan, which seemed like a healthy number, but at the same time I knew from experience of this city that it would go by in the blink of an eye.

I'd downloaded one of the dating apps that Lila recommended and I took a deep breath before opening it.

'Be brave,' I muttered to myself. I hadn't meant to say it out loud but, as I looked up, embarrassed that someone might think that I was talking to myself, I realised that no one had batted an eyelid. There was someone over the far side conducting what looked like a Zoom call for work, another chatting into a phone she was holding above her head, and other people talking away with AirPods in their ears. I forgot that here I was in good company talking out loud.

'Woah,' said a man, stopping by my table. 'I didn't realise that they still made these things.'

He was squinting with suspicion. I guess he had to be early twenties. I always thought I was still in mine until I met someone in their actual twenties.

'I know, but sometimes you can't beat an actual map. You get to annotate it and—'

'You can do that on digital ones too.'

'But it's not the same.'

'So what are you, some kind of tourist?' He was running his hand over the map, captivated by it.

I nodded. 'Guilty as charged.'

He tapped at one of the starred locations. 'Eataly?' He pointed at where I'd put gelato. 'If you like gelato, you should head down to Figo too. Their vanilla is out of this world.'

For a moment I thought he was going to pick up my pen and mark it for me, but he made do with a double tap like he was marking it digitally. When it didn't work, I picked up my pencil instead and put a little dot and he seemed pleased.

'You've got quite a lot marked out.'

'I know. I'm trying to work out the best way to tackle it.' I felt like I needed to pin it on the wall and get the little bits of string like they would in a crime show.

'This is where I'd start,' he said, pointing up to the Met Cloisters. 'It's a great way to spend a day.'

I was instantly transported back to the time with Blaine, the way he'd stood next to me as we'd watched the light coming through the stained-glass windows. I looked back up at the man and it was such a reminder that Blaine could be anyone. I'd assumed that he was about my age, but he could be younger or older.

'And that,' he said, pointing to my phone and the dating-app home screen, causing me to blush, 'is a very safe bet but, if you're looking for more of a hook-up, I'm on TapDat. I'm going to go buy me a map.' He traced his finger along mine and gave me a little wink. It caused me to blush even more. 'Have a good trip.'

'Thank you,' I called, putting my hands that were freezing from the air con to my cheeks to calm them down.

Thoughts of Blaine at the Cloisters were enough to spur me on to create login details.

Welcome To Blindly Go!
Let's play rapid-fire questions to get to know you and what you're looking for. Ready?

I wasn't ready, but I clicked on it anyway. Did I like cats or dogs? A countdown clock appeared and I knew I'd answer dogs if I was doing this to find my match, but I was doing this to find Blaine. Hadn't he mentioned growing up with a cat? I clicked on cats and hoped for the best.

Next question: Salad main meal or only on the side? Blaine talked a lot about food, but it was always big meat subs or big bowls of rice or noodles. I punted for 'on the side'.

By the time I'd finished answering the rapid-fire questions, I felt I'd earned a lie-down for the rest of the day but, to my mind, I'd managed to sound like Blaine's perfect match.

I was about to put my phone away, triumphant of my taking the first steps, when a message popped into the group chat.

ANDREA
You've got to be up now, lazybones.

I replied straight away.

ME
Up and making a plan for the day.

ANDREA
Keep us posted.

LILA
Don't worry I'll make sure she does something!

I noticed Lila had sent a message directly to me too.

LILA
Morning! You wanna grab lunch? I have thoughts on your hunt!

ME
Hiya! Can we do later in the week? I'm feeling all jet-lagged, going to stay local today.

LILA
I asked you to lunch, not all-night clubbing. Plus, you're literally 15 mins away at best.

She really was like Andrea, plus now that she knew from the group chat I was staying with Jimmy, and therefore even closer, I had even less excuses.

ME
How about tomorrow? I'm setting up my dating profile!

My phone started to ring and I looked at it in horror. I tried to think of a reason I couldn't answer. Short of pretending I was in a cinema, I couldn't think of a single place that I couldn't be on a phone.

'Hi, Lila,' I said, almost like it was a total surprise.

'You can't say let's meet tomorrow, then tell me that you're setting up your profile. I obviously need to vet it for you. I'm giving you two options: lunch or dinner.'

I went to open my mouth, but before I could tell her tomorrow, she said, 'Today.'

I closed my eyes. Lila was taking no prisoners.

'Lunch,' I muttered. At least that way I could crawl back home to bed.

'Good choice. I've got a meeting downtown at three, so I can meet you at two? It's nice out, we could meet in the Village. Weren't there places there that you wanted to get to?'

My ears pricked up at the mention of the Village and my eyes flitted over my map to the area where there were several stars on it.

'The deli.'

'Perfect, message me the address and I'll meet you there at two.'

She hung up without saying goodbye like we were in a movie, and I was left staring at the phone.

'Two o'clock it is,' I muttered to myself, checking the time on my phone before I slipped it back into my bag, along with the map.

I was proud of myself. I'd taken my first steps on my journey to find Blaine; all I had to do now was actually find him.

Chapter 10

'Don't be all British about this,' said Lila, almost elbowing her way to the front of the queue. 'You've got to be decisive.'

The deli was unlike anything I could have imagined. There were as many people behind the counter as on the other side waiting to be served, and both sides were shouting at each other.

'I can be decisive,' I said. I was a strong, independent woman. I'd delivered presentations to full auditoriums. I'd flown to New York on a whim to track down a man I'd never met. I could do this and I could be forthright.

'Who's next?' called one of the voices.

'I would like—' I started but, before I could finish my sentence, a woman had jumped in front of me, reeling off her sandwich choice.

Lila gave me a look, as if I'd gone down a little in her estimation. She was down at the other end of the counter whilst someone added pickles to her order. She'd offered to order my sandwich too, but this to me was like a rite of passage.

I'd let three people pass me, as I tried to work out what I was supposed to be ordering and from whom. Five men were lining the opposite side of the counter, shouting at different people behind them as various bread items were passed along the line at a ferocious pace. Customers in the know shouting orders back.

I was being jostled about, trying to catch what people were ordering, my ears pricking up any time anyone male ordered Blaine's sandwich of choice – a buffalo chicken sandwich.

'If you could eat one lunch, and one lunch only for the rest of your life, what would it be?' I'd asked Blaine when we'd been walking down a waterfront walkway that was a carbon copy of one in Hoboken, with a skyline of Manhattan that had been rotating through day and night, giving the most spectacular of sunrises and sunsets.

'Hands down, a buffalo chicken hero from Gennari's. It's this little deli in the Village and you've never tasted anything like it. Cheddar cheese. Bacon. Avocado. Tomatoes. Switch out the lettuce for bell peppers.'

'Lettuce never elevates a sandwich.'

'I know, too slimy, right? Uh. You're making me want one of these so bad. I'm going to have to order in.'

'I thought you just ate.'

'Trust me, you could eat these round the clock.'

'And for life, apparently.'

'For *life*,' he'd said with emphasis. 'All the time. Breakfast, lunch and dinner.'

'Three of your five a day.'

'You're all set.'

'Ma'am, are you ready?' The voice jolted me back to the deli.

'Gee!' I heard Lila exclaim from the cash register.

I snapped out of the thoughts and stumbled forward.

'Um, yes, I guess I'll have the buffalo chicken hero.'

I shuffled forward and went through the motions, getting the exact same sandwich as Blaine had. No sooner had it been wrapped up than I paid and there I was, out of the queue.

'Finally, I thought I was going to have to cancel my next meeting.' I'd barely paid for it before Lila started power-walking out of the deli. If she hadn't been on a lunch break, I would have wanted to loiter longer, on the off chance I had my Cinderella moment, but instead of a shoe it was a sandwich match I was after.

'I didn't expect it to be so intense.'

She nodded in agreement.

'That is proper old-fashioned. They don't make them like that so much any more. More's the pity.'

I loved walking through the Village, I always had. It was a hotchpotch of brownstones, like the little I'd seen of Park Slope, but there were also apartment blocks and less uniformed architecture. I loved the quirky little shops and cafés that were mostly independent.

It was hot as we headed up towards Washington Square Park and I was looking forward to the shade of the trees. It was busy, but we managed to find a bench near to where people were playing chess like they did in the movies.

'Just in case we see a man under sixty playing,' said Lila as we sat down.

I laughed and we started to unwrap our sandwiches.

'Oh, God,' said Lila, biting into hers and pulling a face. 'That's phenomenal.' She looked down at the wrapper and back at me, almost as if she was surprised that I could have picked a good place. She nodded her head and took another bite. The self-respect I'd lost with my inability to order had been restored.

I took a bite of the sandwich and Blaine and Lila were right, it was good. I don't know if I wanted to eat it for breakfast, lunch and dinner, but it was up there with the best sandwich I'd ever tasted.

'The park's busy today. We've had such lousy weather last week.

At least the city will be quiet this weekend, everyone'll head to the Hamptons.'

'Is that what you've got planned?'

'Me? The beach?' She shook her head. 'I don't do sand.'

Her watch started to buzz on her wrist and she looked at it and tapped it, with a sigh.

'Do you need to get that?'

'No, no,' she said, letting out a deep breath. 'I need boundaries and I need sometimes to take lunch. And to hear about things like this.'

I smiled. She was just as intense as she was on the plane, only now dressed in a skirt, blouse and expensive-looking trainers. It was as if that intensity was being torn between work and the life outside.

'But there is a bar that I like at the pier, that's almost beachlike,' she said, ignoring her watch, which was still lighting up. 'It's a tiki bar.'

'Practically tropical then.'

'We should go,' she said, with the same spontaneity she'd had on the plane. 'You'd like it. I know it's not on the list, but you can't only do items on the map or else if you met Blaine and he asked you what you'd been up to, and you'd only been to his hangouts, he'd think you were a total psycho.'

I almost choked on my sandwich. She had a point.

Lila took another bite and every time she did, her whole face melted as if she was silently moaning. 'Have you been here before? Do I need to play tour guide?'

I shook my head. 'I've been before.'

If I concentrated hard, I could see Kerry and me in our early twenties taking photos under the arch at the entrance to the park. Pulling out our pocket map, trying to work out how to get to Magnolia

Bakery of *Sex and the City* fame. There was no Gennari's for us that day; instead we'd been to Katz's Deli, the scene of Meg Ryan's orgasm in *When Harry Met Sally*. We had literally made an itinerary of cultural references from our favourite movies and TV shows, and we loved every second.

I came to from the memories and turned to see Lila staring at me.

'What?' I said, wiping at my face. 'Have I got sauce round my mouth?'

'No, you had that look again.'

'The telekinesis?' I asked.

Lila nodded. 'No planes to go faster today, so what is it, the chess pieces over there?'

Her face softened into a smile and mine did the same.

'Something like that.'

'Shall I change the subject?'

I blinked back a tear that was threatening to fall. Back home, I kept my mind from wandering to the memories, but here they were popping in at every given moment. 'Please.'

'How about me asking you how it's going staying with the ex?'

I groaned. 'Have you got any more changes of topics up your sleeve?'

'Come on, that's a fair question.'

I took a bite of my sandwich to stall. 'It's just temporary, until I work out somewhere else to stay. Newark's not that far away, right?'

I'd looked this morning, and the more I looked the more I realised I couldn't really afford to stay anywhere.

'Newark is not even an option!' She was so loud that the chess players opposite looked up. 'Is it really that bad with Jimmy? He seems great in the group chat.'

'He is great, that's sort of the problem. It would probably be fine if we'd spent more time together since we'd broken up. But we haven't. We've barely talked.'

Lila shrugged. 'Maybe this is the time to do it.'

'Maybe,' I said, not quite convinced.

Her wrist made the same buzzing noise and, whereas before she saw it as an annoyance, this time she almost leapt at the chance of answering it. Her AirPods were in her ears before she'd left the bench.

'Two minutes,' she mouthed, holding her hand out to indicate it. She walked past the chess players and was instantly talking in work mode.

I kept eating my sandwich, trying not to see ghosts in the park of visits past. A man sat down at the other end of the bench. I grabbed my paper bag and slid it across towards me to make room.

'Gennari's?' said the guy, pointing at my bag.

I turned to look at him. He was probably a little older than me. He was wearing a beat-up leather jacket and faded jeans, and his hair was wildly out of control, but in a styled way.

'Yeah. You know it?' I studied his eyes, trying to see if those were the ones I could recognise. 'Blaine?' I muttered, before I could stop myself.

'I'm sorry?' The guy wrinkled his nose up in confusion.

'Sorry, I'm looking for someone...' Why did I even qualify it? 'What's your go-to at Gennari's?'

'Eggplant Parmigiana.'

My heart sank.

'What you got there?'

'Buffalo chicken. It's got bacon. Cheddar cheese.'

'You lost me at chicken.' He screwed up his face. 'So you're looking for someone? A particular someone or will anyone do?'

'Sorry about that,' said Lila coming back and perching on the bench. She gave the guy a look and he stood back up.

'Enjoy the sub. Hope you find who you're looking for.'

'Oh, God, that was cheesy,' said Lila. 'Can you believe that people fall for that? He had heartbreak written all over him.'

'Yeah, didn't he just?' I watched him walking over to the other side of the park and sitting himself down on a bench next to a pretty girl. He started to talk to her and, as the woman started to laugh, I felt a little less special.

'I'm going to have to head uptown earlier than planned. Are you going to be okay on your own?' she asked. 'I mean, I'm kind of worried having seen how long it took you to order food and then you were falling for a sleaze in the park.'

'I wasn't falling for a sleaze in the park.'

'I beg to differ. Now I've got a couple of minutes before my car comes, show me your dating profile.'

She held out her hand and I hesitated long enough for her to give Nina a run for her money on the eyebrows lodging in the hairline. I dug out the phone and swiped to the right page and she wasted no time reading.

'It was quite involved, setting it up,' I said. 'I had to do a video pan of my face and upload my passport for verification, and then they make you register your date and you have to pick one of their recommended places. Makes me think how unsafe all my other dates over the years have been.'

Lila looked over the phone. 'Yeah, but that's because you can't vet them first. I am loving this profile. You've cribbed my lines from yesterday, chess playing, art loving... and dominoes?'

'I added that. Guilty pleasure.'

'Or pleasure. No need to assign guilt. Own that domino playing.'

She handed me back the phone. 'Let me know when and where you're going, okay? – even if you have registered with the app – and let your sister track your location.'

'You sound just like her. If I didn't know better, I'd swear you'd been talking to her off the group chat.'

Nina had been only too delighted to add Lila in.

'What are you doing for the rest of the day and tonight? Are you seeing Jimmy?'

I shook my head. 'I figure that we're spending enough time on top of each other as it is.'

'Oh, like that, is it?' Her eyes widened.

'I meant his apartment is small, and there's no door, just curtains, except the toilet.'

'I once stayed in a hotel in Switzerland and it had a glass-fronted toilet and shower. I was dating this guy, and let's just say, it removed all mystery from our relationship and killed it off.'

I shuddered. 'Yeah, well, we'll see enough of each other without having to make special plans. Especially if I do stay with him for the whole two weeks.'

'Two weeks is a lifetime in New York minutes.'

'I hope so.' I needed a lifetime if I stood a chance of finding Blaine.

'Well, I'm happy to meet you when I can to help on your search, and to fend off sleazebags. We should go to that beach bar.'

'I need to get over the jet lag first.'

'You do realise that we were on the same flight. It's all in your mind.' Lila batted her hand away again. 'You need to go out. Stay out late. Crash. You'll get over it.'

She pulled up her phone.

'I'm free Saturday for brunch if you fancy that, and Sunday night I could do the bar. Will that give you sufficient time to curb your jet lag?'

'I think it would. But I'm off to see Periscope Monkeys on Sunday. You should get tickets and come.'

She hesitated. 'And go on the hunt for Blaine with you? I'm in.'

She glanced at her wrist where her watch was lighting up.

'My ride's here.' She pulled out her phone and started to tap away. 'Are you sure you're going to stay? My car can drop you off at the subway?'

I shook my head. 'It's fine.'

She stood up, putting her empty sandwich wrapper into the bin, and I stood up to follow her.

She leaned over, gave me a hug, then pulled out of it halfway and held out her phone, snapping a photo of us.

'For the group. I'll call you.'

'Okay,' I said with a wave, and I watched her go.

I sat back down, feeling a little lost and a little lonely.

My phone pinged and I saw the photo Lila had just taken in the group chat.

LILA
Spotted in the wild. Have made sure she is fed and watered.
L

The photo already had three hearts before I'd stopped reading the caption and a tirade of messages of interrogation followed from Nina et al. It was just that little reminder that maybe I wasn't quite as alone as I thought I was.

Chapter 11

I'd heard Jimmy leave at the crack of dawn and, despite being tired, I'd struggled to go back to sleep.

I reached for my phone. It was just after 7.30 am. I didn't have anywhere to be today and I wasn't in a rush to get out of bed. I flicked on the Wi-Fi that I diligently turned off overnight and I skim-read the group chat that was discussing what I should do today, when a notification popped up for the dating app that I was using. I clicked on it immediately.

Ben:
LIKES: Cycling
LIKES: Punk (New-Found Glory, Periscope Monkeys, Sublime)
IDEAL SATURDAY DATE: Art gallery in the Village
HATES: Weekends going so quickly
HATES: The thought of how mayonnaise is made

I snorted out of my nose. I liked the taste of mayonnaise, but he was definitely right, I didn't like to think too deeply on how it was made.

I scrolled down the list. Chess: check. Art: check. Lives in New York: check. There wasn't a lot to go on, but the fact that he made me laugh out loud had to be a good sign. But was it enough to click to say I liked him back?

I sat up a little higher in the bed, pulling the comforter around me. The air con in the apartment was welcome in the sticky heat, but it still took some getting used to.

I sent Lila a text telling her about the dating developments. I watched the ticks hoping they'd go blue, but it remained unread.

I closed my eyes, wondering what I should do. I thought of the countless times I'd phoned Kerry to ask her advice over the years. My heart ached to speak to her again. I'd told myself that I was going to stop talking to her, but I'd brought the headset with me. I got up and dug it out from the case that I'd not unpacked.

Grief was one of those things that hit me in waves. I'd held it together yesterday. I'd concentrated on the mission, but today I felt daunted by the long day ahead with no plans.

I slipped on the headset to the familiar view of the coffee shop and virtual Kerry waiting patiently for me.

'This is all your fault,' I said, staring at the flecks in Kerry's eyes.

She laughed. 'You tell me everything's my fault.'

My chest ached. She had no idea. She was sitting by the window of the coffee shop today. It almost reminded of the one that I'd sat in yesterday with my map spread across the table. There were the same high ceilings and the red-brick wall running the length of it. It somehow made me miss her even more.

'I'm in New York,' I said eventually.

'I love New York.' Her smile widened. 'You're looking for him. You took my advice.'

I was loath to admit I had.

'I haven't found him yet. It's early days.'

'Tell me everything,' she said, leaning forward, her hands on her knees, her head a little cocked.

'I arrived the day before last. I met a nice woman on the plane, Lila, and I met her again for lunch yesterday.'

Kerry's smile didn't falter. In the real world, Kerry would have probed further. She loved nothing more than meeting new people, and she'd have known that any friend of mine would have ultimately become a friend of hers.

'It doesn't feel right without you,' I said, ploughing on. 'I went to Washington Square Park yesterday and it reminded me of the time that you played chess with that old guy.'

I started to laugh at the memory. Kerry sitting down taking it so seriously. Her sleeves rolled up, her brow furrowed in concentration.

'You were convinced you were going to beat him. And how many moves did it take him?'

Kerry opened her mouth and shut it again.

'Three,' I told her, not acknowledging that she couldn't know, as she had no memory of it. 'You'd barely moved a pawn before he had you in checkmate. *The Queen's Gambit* you were not.'

'That was a good TV show.'

'It was.'

'I am not good at chess.'

'You are not,' I said, my heart hurting at the memory of Kerry handing over the five bucks that the guy had bet her. I could still picture her startled eyes. 'He must have hustled tourists all day.'

'I wish I was there to try again.'

'Me too.' I had to stop digging up the past, it made my heart ache too much, but at the same time it was almost addictive.

A silence hung in the air. My heart started to constrict as pain tightened its grip.

'Tell me about New York.'

I wondered if she could sense the pain or if she was programmed to fill the void.

'It hasn't changed. Not really. It's still always the same. I mean, it's louder now, if that's possible. The number of people walking along, holding their phone vertically and talking. And people trying to film content and take pictures. You add all that to the drone of the city, that hum of mechanical whirring and traffic. Plus, there are so many people. It's crazy and confusing. But you'd love it still.'

Her head tilted to the side as if she was taking it all in.

'I would,' she said. 'What else have you seen?'

I shrugged my shoulders. 'That's all I've done. I told the girls that I was going to coach myself and refind my mojo, but it's like everywhere I go, I think of you and I can't get my mind straight. It's too hard.'

'Sometimes life is hard, and sometimes you have to accept that and do it anyway.'

Kerry kept coming out with fortune-cookie advice. The kind of advice that could have been lifted from any number of self-help books. Kerry loved a self-help book. She read them all, so desperate to find answers. Each one would work for a little bit, she'd feel energised and have a new coping strategy, only for it to fade the next time she got pulled under a black cloud. My vision went blurry and I tried to blink back the tears.

'Where are you headed today?' she asked.

'I don't know. I've signed myself up for a dating app. It was Lila's idea. It's a blind-date one, so I don't know who I'm chatting with, but I've set my criteria to appeal to Blaine.'

A scowl knitted her eyebrows together before she broke into the nose scrunch.

'That's a great idea. When's your first date?'

'Good question. I got my first match and now all I have to do is pluck up the courage to like him back and set up a date.'

'That doesn't sound difficult.'

'Difficult, no,' I said, biting my lip. 'Terrifying, yes.'

'Everything can be terrifying if you let it, but that's the secret – make sure that you don't let it.'

I nodded. 'Easier said than done.'

'You've got to try harder,' she said again. 'Go and explore the city. Accept the date. Find Blaine.'

I thought of the session that I was planning for Marianne's company with the framework I was developing that looked at the need to self-coach on a regular basis. Why was it so easy for me to see what everyone else needed to do, but impossible for me to do it myself?

'Hello.'

I froze. The voice from the real world echoing in my ears.

'What's wrong?' asked Kerry.

'I've got to go.'

I didn't even have time for my usual sign-off and I swiped out of the room and took off my headset, but not quick enough for Jimmy not to see.

'Hello,' he said. He looked at me funnily, taking in my headset. He was dressed in shorts and T-shirt and he looked sweaty. 'You're still doing that? Did you borrow it from the games room?'

'No,' I said, a little sheepishly. 'I thought you'd left for work.'

'Ah,' he said. 'I woke up and couldn't sleep, so thought I'd go for a run.'

'You run now?'

'Started to. There's something about running down to Battery Park and catching a glimpse of the Statue of Liberty in the early morning sun.'

He lifted the bottom of his shirt to wipe the sweat on his brow with his T-shirt and I caught a glimpse of his stomach that looked a lot more toned than I remembered.

'I better jump in the shower.'

'Yeah,' I said, feeling my cheeks flush.

'You want to grab breakfast before I go to work again? There's a traditional diner a couple of blocks away. Their food isn't Instagram-worthy, but it tastes amazing.'

I was about to bat it away, a combination of embarrassment about him catching me in my VR headset and my body reacting to him with muscle memory, but my stomach rumbled, giving away how hungry I was.

'Sure,' I said, and he smiled and headed off towards the bathroom.

I put the headset back away into my case, Kerry's words echoing in my ears. I needed to do what was hard.

I pulled up the dating app and clicked on the 'Like' button for Ben and it popped up with different date options. Ben had ticked his availability and, whilst it was tempting to pick later in the week, I knew it was better to meet up as quickly as I could. He could meet tonight at 6 o'clock for an hour. My finger hovered over the 'Accept' button, my stomach lurching. I found my face wrinkling into the type of nose scrunch of Kerry's that I missed so desperately, and I hit 'Accept'.

He'd suggested Midtown and I scrolled down the list of suggested bars and gave a little squeal as the Oyster Bar at Grand Central Station was listed. The very place where Blaine had suggested going on his ultimate date. It ticked so many boxes, it was public, iconic and Blaine approved. Could it also be a sign?

I sent Lila a quick follow-up text to let her know and then I put the phone down. A rush of adrenaline was making me sick to the stomach and I needed to get up and walk off what I'd just done.

The chat with Kerry might have been full of generic, fortune-cookie-style advice, but she was right, I should get out and explore, even if it was hard.

Today's breakfast spot with Jimmy was a complete contrast to the minimalist white glossy coffee shop. He'd picked the epitome of an American diner.

'This place is great,' I said, sliding into a Formica booth opposite him. I picked up the giant menu and unfolded it, marvelling at all the options, wondering what the hell I was going to choose.

A waitress came over and almost immediately poured us coffee. It was from a ubiquitous coffee pot, rather than barista-made, but after the sleep I'd had I'd take anything with caffeine in it.

'What's good here?'

'Most things,' said Jimmy, flicking over a page, then rubbing at his shoulder. 'Ah, I've pulled something at pickleball.'

'You're getting old.'

He raised an eyebrow. 'It's a strenuous sport.'

'Uh-huh.'

'I think you'd like it.'

I picked up my coffee and started to drink it. 'Do you remember the time we played tennis?'

He tilted his head to the side. I watched as the moment came flooding back to him. I did not have good hand–eye co-ordination for racquet sports and the one time we tried to play doubles, I almost knocked Jimmy out when I went to hit a ball and missed.

'Ah!' He folded up his menu and placed it on the table. 'Yeah, perhaps best avoided.'

'But good that you're playing. It sounds very social.'

'It is. I've been trying to force myself to get out and do things. It's easy to come home and hide away.'

I knew he was talking about himself, but I couldn't help thinking it was a subtle dig at what I'd been doing over the last few months.

We both ordered our food and I took a look around the diner. It was funny to me that this place was right in the middle of the Financial District. There was a mix of people, from the suited and booted to others who looked as if they'd walked in off the docks.

'What are you up to tonight? Fancy going to the rooftop bar?'

Jimmy had already made up in his mind that I was staying with him for the entire trip. It was still awkward between us but, at the same time, there was something comforting about staying with him. The feelings of overwhelm and loneliness that had hit me in the taxi felt manageable when I was at his, and the way that he kept talking about loneliness, I couldn't help feeling that maybe I was doing him as much of a favour staying with him as he was letting me stay.

'What is it with these rooftop bars?' I asked.

'They're the best bit about the city. Didn't you go to loads when you lived out here?'

'I couldn't afford to do anything when I lived over here. The monthly stipend we got barely covered the transport and food. I lived off Kraft mac and cheese and hot dogs bought in plastic packs.'

It was funny looking back at my time working my year-long internship programme. It was one of the best times of my life. Kerry and I hit it off immediately. It wasn't just that she was fun or that we had the same sense of humour, which meant she could have me in stitches, it was more that she seemed to see the real me. So many of my friends up until that point had tried to boss me around and I'd followed, but Kerry wasn't like that. She listened to my ideas and she valued what I had to say. When I hung back socially, not wanting to speak up or be the centre of attention, Kerry would always bring me in to make sure I wasn't left out. With Kerry building me up, I'd left my year in New York with a new-found sense of confidence.

The year wasn't all fun, though. The gruelling long hours and tedious work at the insurance company I was working at, followed by a commute and a punishing budget to live on made it challenging. Then there was travelling in every day to a city that you couldn't afford to do anything in, that was torture.

'Then you definitely need to go to one. So tonight?'

I smiled. 'I'm actually heading out tonight. I um...' I was being ridiculous, Jimmy was actively dating, I was a single woman, I could tell him that's what I was doing. 'I'm meeting a fellow executive coach.'

I inwardly sighed at the lie, but the truth would lead to too many questions that I didn't want to answer.

'That's good. It's good to see that you're building it up again. Are you still coaching that guy, the one that made that app?'

I knew that he was skirting round the idea of me talking to Kerry on the app that Kiran had developed, but I didn't want to go into that. 'Yes, he's doing really well with it. There's a big US company trying to buy him out.'

'Wow, really?'

'There's huge potential in his apps,' I said, thinking how I'd been dubious before I'd tried them out. 'But with the takeover, it means that there's lots of coaching to be done.'

Jimmy smiled. 'I'm glad that you managed to carry on with it all. I was worried.'

I didn't tell him about the clients I'd lost. 'I know. Me too. But I'm going to work whilst I'm out here on developing new workshops to roll out.'

He looked impressed and I think it was enough to distract him.

'Okay. Well, maybe we can go out tomorrow night.'

'Yeah, maybe.' I said, accepting that I wasn't going to be looking to stay elsewhere. 'The only real plan I've got is to see Periscope Monkeys on Sunday. Remember that band that Kerry always used to play?'

The waitress put two huge plates in front of us and my stomach growled in appreciation.

'I remember,' he said. 'Where are they playing?'

'In the Village. I'm meeting Lila there. You want to come too?'

'And meet the famous Lila?' he said, digging into his food. 'Absolutely.'

'She's bringing her husband, if you wanted to bring a date,' I added in a panic. If I found Blaine, I didn't want it to look like I was on a double date.

He gave me the look again and shrugged his shoulders.

'Yeah, um, maybe. I still can't believe you made friends with someone on the plane on the way over. I hate people that talk to me on the plane.'

'Do you still have headphones on even if you're not playing anything?'

'Of course. Gives me the ability to selectively hear.'

My food was disappearing at a rapid rate. At least it was good, even if the coffee was bad.

'Imagine all the life stories you've missed out on, not chatting to the person sitting next to you,' I said.

'I'm fine with missing out.' He dipped hash browns into his perfectly runny egg. 'But I'm glad you've found Lila. It's good that you've got an extra person to hang out with.'

'So I don't stay in and hide away?'

He smiled in a way that confirmed he had been making a dig before.

'Are you seeing her today?'

'Nope, I've got the day free.' I held up my hands. 'And before you ask, no, I don't need you to take the day off to babysit me. I'll be perfectly fine.' His face fell a little. 'I'm sorry that sounded really rude. I just meant you've done so much for me already, letting me stay, but I'm going to potter about and do some work.'

'I wouldn't be babysitting you. I'd be spending time with you. That's what friends do, right?'

'Right,' I said, nodding. Friends spent time with each other. It still took some getting used to, us finding our feet as friends after the break-up. It's the kind of lip service that you do when you break up, especially given our friends in common, but putting it into practice was quite another thing.

We ate a little in silence and I let his words sink in.

'Don't forget to phone your bank,' said Jimmy, putting his cutlery neatly on his plate when he'd finished.

'I've got it on my list.'

He raised a stern eyebrow. Jimmy knew I buried my head in the sand when it came to money. 'It's important.'

'I'll do it today, I promise. I can't believe you ate all that food.' I pointed to Jimmy's empty plate.

'The run gave me a good appetite. You should come out with me one morning.'

'I didn't bring my running shoes or a sports bra or anything I could run in,' I said with a small smile. Deliberate exclusions from my suitcase.

'I hear they have shops here.'

'Really?' I said looking round. 'Not in this little city.'

He coughed. 'I promise it'll be fun. There's a Rei up in the Village and I'm pretty sure there's a Target on the same street if you don't want to spend a fortune.'

'For someone who doesn't like shopping, you seem to know where all the shops are.'

'Sports shops are different. I've needed to get bits for pickleball.'

I nodded. Who even was Jimmy in New York? He'd always exercised, but over here he seemed to have taken it to another level. Maybe when we were dating, I'd been holding him back from his inner athlete.

'Right, I've got to go, but try and go somewhere.'

'I will,' I said as he opened up his mouth to say something, 'and I'll phone my bank.'

'Good,' he said, getting up. He got his phone ready to tap and pay.

'I've got this,' I said. 'You got yesterday's.'

He nodded, putting his phone away. 'Call me if you need anything. Enjoy your coaching meet-up.'

I squirmed in my seat.

'I will. See you later on.'

He headed off and I glanced at the large clock mounted on the wall. It was only 8.30 am, I had another ten and a half hours until I met Ben.

Once I paid and left the diner, I stopped on the street, contemplating my next move. What I wanted to do was slink back to the apartment and spend the day watching comfort TV. But Virtual Kerry, and now Jimmy, were right that I had to stop hiding away. With plenty of time and comfy trainers on my feet, I put my New York playlist on, put on my headphones and started walking. I had a map in my bag and places I could try. It was time to properly be here and be brave.

Chapter 12

I'd done Blaine's walking date backwards and ended up finding myself standing at the clock at Grand Central. It was one of those places that, if you blocked everyone else out, you could imagine arriving here at any age throughout the last century, caught up in a magical romance. Watching the hands tick round, and the boards of the trains change, waiting for the arrival of your beau.

I forced myself to look up, not caring that it singled me out as a tourist. There was something about the calming nature of the turquoise sky depicted here with the ornate constellations and stars that made it feel dream-like.

I was supposed to be meeting Ben at 7 o'clock, and I didn't want to be early. I hated to be that person watching both the door and my watch, worried that the person I was to meet wouldn't show. Instead, I was watching the giant clock here. It was 6.55. I wiped my sweaty palms on the skirt of my dress.

With a couple of minutes to spare, I skim-read the latest in the group chat.

ANDREA
Loving the photos, Chlo! I feel like we should have made this a girls' trip. Perhaps we should do this for my 35th?

MARIANNE
Not sure that's a landmark birthday – but defo up for the girls' trip.

NINA
Love this for us! Plus, Chloe Cat, what's your plan for this evening? Are you heading to a swanky rooftop bar?

I knew that they'd probably be in bed now, but I replied anyway. Not wanting them to worry, waking up to a lack of reply.

ME
No rooftops for me. Heading for a quick drink at the Oyster Bar at Grand Central.

I took a quick photo of the big clock for good measure. I'd no sooner posted it than my phone started to vibrate. I'd never had so many phone calls.

'Hey Lila,' I said, answering it.

'Why can't I see you? Is your camera off?'

I took the phone away from my ear and held it out. It looked as if she was still at work and her face lit up when she saw me.

'Ah, you're at the station,' she beamed. 'Not that I was phoning to check up on you and to make sure you hadn't posted a stock photo to the group chat.'

'You blatantly were,' I said, laughing.

'I did solemnly promise your friends I'd look out for you.'

'I'm not sure that's in the t's and c's of the WhatsApp group.'

A train must have arrived because the concourse flooded with people.

'You'd be surprised. So you're really doing it? I'm impressed.'

'Do you think I shouldn't? I can still cancel.' I moved away from the rest of the people standing by the clock. I felt self-conscious that they'd be able to hear.

'No, I think you definitely should. Come on, what's the worst that can happen?'

'I get murdered by my date.'

'I was going to go for a bad oyster but,' she laughed with a shrug, 'you're going to do great.'

'I just keep thinking that if by some miracle he's Blaine, he'll think I'm such a stalker flying out here.'

'You had flights booked, and I'm sure if he'd have been in the same position to find you, he would have done, and you'd have been flattered.'

'Or a little bit terrified.' My mind was trying to go through every possible scenario of how he'd react if I ever did find him.

'Don't get ahead of yourself. Concentrate on meeting this Ben guy first, huh?' she said.

'Okay,' I said, letting out a deep breath. 'It's almost time. Don't work too hard.'

'I won't. Let me know ASAP if it's him.'

'Will do.'

She ended the call and I stared at the blank screen. I was never going to get used to the lack of sign-off. I turned off my music and slipped my headphones back into their case.

My phone had a notification, and it was for another match on the app. I automatically agreed to someone called Ryan. I half wondered if I'd need to bother if Ben turned out to be Blaine...

The big clock struck 7 o'clock, I took that as my cue to head to the Oyster Bar.

I weaved my way round commuters running for their train and

people meeting up for dates and nights out. I tried to keep my breathing measured and steady, but the nerves were starting to build. There was something in this ethos of the app to make people meet quickly. I hadn't had that much time to build it up in my head or to convince myself that this might actually be Blaine, but all that was changing with every step leading me closer to my date.

Of course, in my wildest fantasies and dreams it was him, sitting there in the Oyster Bar, glass of champagne in one hand, oyster shell in the other. Our kindred souls would recognise each other immediately on some cosmic level. And from there we'd follow his path down Fifth Avenue, seeking out the rooftop bars and the tequila spot that didn't seem appropriate to go to on my own.

The door to the bar was open and inside it was a hive of activity. There were rows upon rows of tables that were reminiscent of a canteen, and there was a long bar counter with seats along it. I took a deep breath as I was greeted at the entrance.

'I'm, um, meeting someone,' I said, a little sheepishly.

The woman nodded without batting an eyelid. 'Name?'

'Ben? Table for two.'

'Got it. Follow me.'

She led me across and my heart was in my mouth.

'Here you go,' said the woman, stopping at the end of a long table with a group of four people down at the other end and a man who stood up as I approached.

The woman raised her eyebrow at me as she left and, looking at Ben, I interpreted it as a 'didn't you do well?' gesture.

I got lost immediately in his hazel eyes, and I had to snap myself out of it and take in the rest of him. The tousled blonde hair. The strong chiselled jaw.

'Hi, Cat?' He offered an outstretched hand and I took it, my palm fitting into his large hand. I tore my eyes off his face and down at his arms with the muscles that were doing an excellent job of creating such a firm handshake. He was so good-looking it was as though he'd been designed by a computer.

'Ben,' I said, finding my voice. 'It's lovely to meet you.'

'Oh,' he said. 'English?'

'Guilty.' He was still shaking my hand. Whilst my arm was starting to ache, I couldn't help but let him carry on. I was mesmerised by the bulge of his arm muscles.

He broke out into a smile and that seemed to break the spell. He dropped my hand and gestured for me to sit down.

'What brings you to New York?'

He was making me a little speechless, which was no bad thing as the first thing that wanted to come out of my mouth was 'you hopefully', which might have him running for the hills.

'I worked over here once, for a year, and I've missed it. It was a good time to come back.'

Ben nodded. If he was bothered that I was from out of town, he didn't seem to show it.

A waitress hurried past, but doubled back to us. 'Can I get you guys some drinks to start?'

'Sure, I'll take a craft beer. Whatever IPA you recommend,' said Ben.

'I'll take a lager, not fussy.'

The waitress rattled off what they had and I picked a local one. She headed off to get the drinks and I turned back to Ben.

'I'm just going to grab a snack whilst we're here,' he said, picking up the menu.

'Great. Me too.' I scanned the menu, knowing what I was going to pick. I'd looked online and remembered Blaine's choice. This could be the eureka moment where we order the same appetiser, our eyes meet over the menu and—

'I'm just going to grab the mozzarella sticks,' he said, placing the menu down.

'Mozzarella sticks? You're not getting oysters or any seafood?'

The board behind the bar was chock-a-block with their global seafood haul.

'Do you know,' he leaned forward on the table, 'I can't stand oysters. Or shellfish in general.'

'Not even baked shellfish? I was going to get Oysters Rockefeller.'

'I'm not sure if baked makes it better or worse.' He shuddered and in that shudder any fantasy that this was Blaine packed its bags and went home.

The waitress put our bottles of beer down and I took a large sip, trying to swallow my disappointment along with the beer I'd been given. I was still desperate to taste the oysters that Blaine had suggested, and we ordered our food whilst she hovered at the table.

'So you said you liked Periscope Monkeys,' I said, trying to keep up my enthusiasm and remind myself that it wasn't all bad. I was sitting in a fancy oyster bar in Manhattan on a date with a man who could have doubled as Adonis.

He picked up his beer and swilled a mouthful round like he was tasting vintage wine.

'I do,' he said when he swallowed. 'Love them.'

'Are you going to see them whilst they're doing their residency?'

Ben looked over his shoulder before he leaned back onto the table.

'Do you want to know something weird about me?'

'Weirder than putting an oyster bar as one of the preferred date locations when you don't like seafood?' I said, with a little laugh escaping.

Ben was looking deadpan and I got the impression that he didn't do sarcasm.

'What's weird?' I said, trying to take back my comment.

He looked over his shoulder again and I wondered just how strange this was going to be.

'I don't like live music.' He almost sighed with relief when he'd got it off his chest.

I blinked a couple of times, trying to tell if I'd heard him right.

'Like you don't like live music in big venues like stadiums?'

'Like in dive bars or concerts. I hate that it's loud and there's people. It's often hot and you can't hear them. Half the time they sound nothing like they should.'

My mouth was agape and I had to force myself to close it. I thought of how much music has played a part in my life and how I love nothing more than being in a crowd sharing a moment with hundreds or thousands of people.

'Wow! That's great that you know what you like.'

'Yeah. I used to go when I was younger but now, that's the best thing about getting older, isn't it? You can just say no when you don't want to do something.'

'Can you?' I was laughing again, as the eternal people pleaser.

'Of course,' he said. 'That's why I love this app. It's so great that you can put everything out there. I mean, the chess thing. It's so important to me to find someone who loves chess as much as I do. And the problem I've had on other platforms is that people see the guns,' he said, pointing to his arms, and my eyes instinctively followed. They were great arms. 'And they don't see beyond that. But now here we are, bonding over our love of chess.'

My cheeks started to flush as I wouldn't say I had a love of chess.

'What's your go-to starting move?' he asked, leaning forward.

I tugged at the neck of my dress to create a little air. 'Um, I usually lead with a pawn.'

'Okay,' he said, his hand waving. 'Which one?'

'I don't know, the one in the middle?' I said.

Now it was his turn for his mouth to be agape.

A silence descended on the table and he sat back further in his seat. It gave me the opportunity to properly take in the restaurant. It had vaulted ceilings with crisscrossed, latticed brickwork that was accented with lights. It was truly beautiful.

'I love these bricks. Everywhere you look at this station there's such cool architectural features.'

'You know that's a common misconception. The station refers to the subway at Grand Central, and where the trains are, that's the terminal. It's Grand Central Terminal.'

'Huh.'

'Fun fact, huh? I've got more if you want to hear.'

The waitress popped down our plates of food and, as I dug into the baked oysters, Ben started to give me an informative lesson about Grand Central Terminal. It was interesting, but so different from the dates I'd had with Blaine.

As I ate the food, I couldn't help but think of him, wherever he was. He was 100 per cent right that they were the best oysters I'd ever tasted. The crunch of the breadcrumbs and the squishiness of the oyster, salty from the sea yet sweet from the cheese.

On paper, Ben and Blaine liked all the same things but, in reality, they were like chalk and cheese. It started to hit home how impossible it was going to be to find Blaine. If I thought it was like finding a needle in a haystack, it was as if the haystacks were multiplying.

Chapter 13

The date with beautiful Ben was disappointing, not because we were woefully incompatible, but more because it brought home to roost how impossible it was going to be to find Blaine in this city. I was going to have to seriously up my game. But all that would have to wait as I had a call with Kiran to get through. I had barely thought about work since I'd got here and the days were already racing by.

I'd left before Jimmy this morning, avoiding the need for us to go through what had become a morning routine of him checking that I was okay and offering to take the day off. It had felt good to have had a purpose for getting up. I'd felt like a salmon swimming upstream as I headed in the opposite direction to the sea of commuters, and I found myself near the Natural History Museum on the edge of Central Park.

'Hey, can you hear me?' I said, as the call connected. Turning off the street was such a shock to the system at first. The path was cut between the trees and shrubs that were a colour palette of all the different greens.

'Yeah, I can hear you. How are you? How's New York?'

'Amazing.'

'You in Central Park?'

'I am,' I said, trying to channel the mindfulness teachings and to take in the little details: the flowers that were in bloom, the black lampposts with Victorian-style lamps that reminded me of something out of Narnia, the sound of joggers rhythmically hitting the path as they completed their circuit. 'It's pretty early here still, but it's coming to life. Where are you?'

'I've made it down to the park.'

'Have you actually?' I said, trying to detect any background noise. I sometimes thought Kiran would sleep in his office if he could and we'd started to hold the sessions outside to change his mindset.

'I can put my video on... There.'

I pulled my phone out of my pocket and I watched on the screen as he panned around the park that I usually walked around with him.

'Come on, I've shown you mine. Show me yours.' He laughed and I obliged, switching my camera on and scanning round the park.

'Looks stunning,' he said, as I panned around the vista in front of me. I'd come to one of the forks in the road, but all the routes were tree-lined, not a hint of cityscape in sight.

'Have you been before?'

'I've never been to New York.' I flicked off the camera and put the phone back to my ear.

'I meant Central Park, but you've not been to New York? You're always flying over to the US.'

'I know, but everything I ever go to is on the West Coast. Everyone tells me it's amazing. Is it amazing?'

I thought of my trip so far. Even in my below-par state, it was incredible. 'It's better than you could imagine.'

He sighed. 'I knew it. If I get the time, that will be my first holiday.'

'Like you ever take a holiday.'

I'd known Kiran for almost a year, and I'd never known him to take a proper break. He was always on the go.

'I'll have to find some time.'

'You have to make the time,' I said firmly. 'It's not going to magically appear in your schedule. And knowing you, even if you did block off time, you'd find a side project to fill it with.'

Kiran laughed and it distorted through my speakers. 'You know me too well. It's a shame I wasn't heading to the Tech Futures conference in person next week. I could have stopped off in New York on the way,' he said. 'Have you been doing your best *Man vs Food*?'

'Not perhaps my best effort, but I've been trying,' I said, his words sinking in. 'There's still time for you to change that so you can go in person. I think you're ready for it.'

Kiran was one of the most confident and charming people I'd ever met, yet he hated public speaking. It was one of the things that we'd been working on over the last few months. We'd been identifying areas in his life where he was comfortable and at ease, and trying to channel that feeling into a boardroom or a conference podium. We'd progressed so that he could present virtually, with his camera on yet the window minimised so he couldn't see his audience, but I couldn't get him to make that leap to do it in person.

When I was starting to spiral, I wondered whether, if I was at my best, I'd have got him there already.

'My schedule is so busy at the moment. Let's go back to the portion sizes. I'm guessing they're giant.'

He was changing the subject and this time I wasn't going to let him.

'Portion sizes are always giant.' I took a deep breath. 'But that's not important. Kiran, that conference sounded like such an amazing opportunity. Forget the panel and think about the networking. Haven't you said before that those contacts will be important if you sell the company, that they'd be useful for the next project. What's holding you back?'

The phone line was quiet and I wondered if I'd lost him.

'I know they're important. It's just...' His voice sounded flat and it reminded me so much of my own lately.

'I know, you hate it. But I think that this is your moment. You're right at the top of your game. You should be shining.'

I know I shouldn't have interrupted him, but this is exactly what he needs to hear.

'I just don't think I'm ready. Maybe a few more virtual appearances.'

'Hiding away and presenting isn't the answer. You might have to face facts that you're never going to be ready, but we're just going to have to get you to a stage where it's good enough.' I'd well and truly crossed the line of coaching, but I'd got to know Kiran so well over the last year and I believed in him so much that I just wanted him to take that final leap. 'It's not too late for the conference. You could stop via New York, we could do an in-person session on conference tips. This place,' I said, looking around as I walked past the statue of Alice in Wonderland, 'this place is always inspiring and makes you think you could do anything. Be anyone.'

I closed my eyes, pleased he couldn't see me. I was pleading to him, but I was pleading to the woman I hoped I still was. There was a slight fizz in my belly that I could do this. I'd helped people overcome imposter syndrome and confidence issues. I could do this. I needed to follow my own advice and believe I could.

'I don't know,' he said.

'Can the giant portions tempt you?'

'I'm pretty sure I could just order double portions here.' There was almost a snap to his reply. It wasn't very Kiran and I knew it was a signal to leave it. Coaching on the phone or the internet was always tricky, trying to gauge reactions, so it was better to park that and go back to it later.

'Okay, then, do you want to pick up from where we were the last session, working on current goals? How have you been getting on with that?'

Kiran reported on the last couple of weeks and how he'd been getting on, but I started to sense that every time he mentioned the takeover talks, his tone changed.

'With regard to the buyout talks,' I said, trying to choose my way into the subject carefully. 'You mentioned that they'd want you to stay on and manage the company, which perfectly aligns with your goals of where you wanted to be. But I'm sensing that that might not be the case?'

There was a small sigh on the other end of the phone and I sidestepped a tiny dog on a very long lead as the owner tried to untangle the lead of their other dog that had wrapped itself round a tree.

'It's just that they're wanting to implement changes to how the platform operates and they're going to alter other things too, and I guess I don't know how I'm going to cope with that. Lead a company where I won't agree with all the changes.'

I nodded, remembering a second later that he couldn't see me do it.

'That's the hard bit about being a CEO and, as we've talked about before, that might be something you'll have to get used to, whether you're part of this buyout or not. Your company is growing, and you've noticed how you're needing to delegate more and more. Would it help at some point to work on ways that you can make sure you're managing staff to allow them to make decisions on their own, whilst making sure you are brought into the important decision-making?'

'Yeah, I think it would. Winning friends and influencing people.'

'It's all in the communication skills,' I said, smiling at the dog owner now untangling both leads of the little dogs.

There was a slight pause before a little bit of a laugh escaped. 'All roads lead back to communication skills.'

'They're an important part of your work.'

He laughed again. 'Unfortunately, they are. Right, so should we work on communication skills today, then?'

'That sounds like a great idea,' I said, pleased that he'd led himself back to public speaking. 'Why don't you tell me a story, any story, of the last time you properly laughed. I don't mean had a little chuckle. I mean tears-pouring-down-your-face-type laughing. I'll give you a minute or so to think about it, then pop your camera on and tell me.'

I closed my eyes. I hadn't used this exercise for a while and it, of course, made me think of Kerry. There hadn't been a lot of laughter since she went, and she was the last person to make my belly ache and tears stream down my face.

Late last summer we'd been down in Portsmouth, where she thought she'd seen Ryan Gosling. He'd supposedly been filming in the area and there had been all these sightings of him.

We'd been down having Sunday lunch with Jimmy and his sisters for his birthday, and after lunch we'd headed for a walk along the amusements near the Hovercraft. We'd been playing on the 2p sliders when Kerry was convinced she'd seen him.

'I don't know what's more unbelievable, the fact that he'd be here on his own or the fact that, of all the places to go on his day off, he'd come here.'

She tutted at me, and pulled her tub of coins to her chest, stalking the machines closer to him.

'He looks nothing like him,' I mouthed. The only similarity was the fact they had the same hair colour and they were both male.

She flashed me a wink as she started to play the slots next to him.

'Hi,' said Kerry.

The guy looked at her and smiled, and carried on putting the coins in.

Kerry raised her eyebrows at me, her smile widening. To her, that was proof of who he was.

'I'm sorry,' she said. 'I've just got to tell you this, but *The Notebook* is one of my favourite films of all time.'

I coughed over my side of the room. That was always my favourite.

'And *Drive*. Inspired.'

The guy looked her up and down and shrugged with a nod.

'I know you must get asked this all the time, but can I get a picture? I know it's mega cringe.' They guy was starting to edge ever so slightly back. 'My friend Chloe will take it.'

I got my phone out and the guy reluctantly stood next to Kerry, who was grinning like a Cheshire cat.

The guy went over to other side of the arcade and Kerry squealed as we reviewed the photo.

'Jimmy, look,' she said, calling out to him and his sister Teresa, who'd just walked in. 'You'd never guess who we just met. Ryan Fucking Gosling.'

'What? Were you down at South Parade Pier too?'

'What do you mean?'

'He's there filming, look.'

Teresa pulled out her phone and showed us the picture of actual Ryan Gosling.

'Then who the bloody hell did I have a photo with?'

We all squinted and looked at the photo. Kerry looked crestfallen.

Not-Ryan-Gosling walked out of the arcade, but not without giving Kerry a wink as he went.

At first I thought Kerry was crying, but I soon realised it was the silent laughing that you did before full on belly laughs took over.

I was so lost in the memory that I almost tripped over a dog off the lead.

'I'm ready now,' said Kiran, switching on his camera.

I took a deep breath, trying to put Kerry out of my mind.

'There was this time recently,' he said, 'when I'd been working late the night before, and then I'd had back-to-back meetings all morning and come lunchtime I was exhausted. I could feel my eyes starting to close, but everyone was busy, and I had to look busy.

'Remember how our office is like all glass and the only place where the glass is opaque, is the meeting room?'

I found myself nodding and, realising my camera was off, I flicked it on so he could see his audience.

'So I went inside and lay down underneath the massive table, as it was the only dark bit in the room. I hadn't meant to properly sleep, I just wanted to stave off the worst of the tiredness by resting my eyes. Only I woke up to the sound of voices. Most of the senior staff had come in and they were having a meeting. I was racking my brains, trying to work out how I'd explain it away – could I pretend to be meditating or investigating the power sockets under the table? – but I had no idea how long they'd been in there. So I had to lie as still as possible and wait for the meeting to be finished.'

He was talking and trying not to giggle as he was recounting it, and his laugh was infectious. I had spotted a nearby bench and sat down because I was starting to laugh too.

'Did you get away with it?'

'There was this one point where I thought I was going to get caught. Hayley bent down to go under the table to plug in her laptop and the plugs were pretty close to where my head was. I was sure she'd clocked me. Once the plug was in, she scrambled back up to the table and I could see that she hadn't switched it on, so I flicked the switch really quickly and hoped she hadn't noticed that it suddenly came to life.'

I wiped away a tear of laughter. I could only partially see Kiran walking around the park telling his story, but I imagined his arms flailing about. His voice was getting more and more animated as he went on.

'And it didn't even stop there. The meeting finished and I was stuck. Peter was tapping away on his computer for a while after. It probably wouldn't have been so bad, but I'd drunk this huge mug of coffee earlier on to try and keep myself awake, and not only had it failed to keep my eyes open, but it had also left me absolutely bursting for a wee. I thought I was going to wet myself and I nearly had to break cover, but then by some miracle he left. I had to wait a couple of minutes before I left too, in case he saw me leave. And I can tell you, those few minutes were agony waiting until I could escape.'

I was really laughing now. A few people were giving me puzzled looks as they walked by, but I didn't care.

'I still can't drink a coffee bigger than an espresso now.'

He was properly laughing. It was exactly the type of story and delivery I was after.

'Kiran,' I said, trying to pull myself together. 'What's your body language like now?'

'Huh?'

'I want you to think about your body language. Look at you. You're smiling so much you've got creases at your eyes. Your shoulders look relaxed. You're waving your arms as you talk. You're making eye contact with me, and using your whole face to stress the emotions of the story. How could you channel those feelings when you're presenting next time? Think about this and that storytelling. And whilst I know that you're not going to be framing things in the same way when you're telling a funny story, shall we look at how you could replicate those feelings when you talk and communicate your presentation?'

'Huh,' he said, this time in an almost-sigh.

'We could unpick all that and see how it can apply to the way you work.'

Kiran was nodding. 'Let's do it.'

I let out a deep breath. For the first time in a long while, I felt a little bit like the old me at work. The one that could be in control and could steer the sessions. I looked around at the park and the abundance of green. I wasn't sure if it was that that was inspiring me or if it was my trip. Whatever it was, it felt like it was getting easier, and I couldn't help but have a spring in my step as I carried on round the park.

Chapter 14

I was looking forward to getting back in the saddle with my date with destiny, aka Ryan. He might not have been such an on-paper match as Ben, but we'd seen how that might not be a bad thing. He liked art and live music and worked in tech. We were meeting at a bar in Williamsburg. There were several dots on my map that, in Lila's mind, meant that it was possible that Blaine was Brooklyn-based, so it made sense that I headed over the water to at least see.

'You know I didn't need you to come and pick me up,' I said to Lila as I headed across the lobby of our building to meet her.

'I know I didn't, but I wanted to.' She held her hands out and then gave me a quick hug. 'This is cute.'

I was wearing a little playsuit that made me think I was auditioning for a children's TV presenter role. I did a quick curtsey, because I did feel the tiniest bit cute.

'Does it scream *going to meet my soulmate*?'

'It's giving *I was wearing overalls when I met your grandfather* story potential.'

That was just the look I thought I should be going for.

'This is such a great location. Jimmy's lucked out here.'

'I know.'

'Speaking of which,' she peered over my shoulder, 'I'm not going to meet him, am I?'

I turned her at the elbow and steered her out of the lobby.

'He's playing a pickleball tournament.'

'Oh, God, he's not inflicted by the curse too, is he? Anthony keeps telling me we need to play that. It's like a cult.'

'Yes,' I said, nodding, 'Jimmy keeps trying to recruit me.'

She shuddered. I naturally turned to walk towards the subway.

'Hey, we're going this way,' said Lila.

'Aren't we going to Brooklyn?'

'Yeah, but there are better ways to get there.'

I could see the Brooklyn Bridge in the distance and my body started to go rigid. I took in her comfy trainers and the bottle of water in her hand.

'We're not going to walk over the bridge,' I said, my mouth going dry.

'Um, it's only a half-hour walk you know,' she said, almost laughing. 'But no, have no fear. I'm not going to make you walk in this heat before you have a date. I'm not that mean. Especially when you're soulmate hunting.'

'Ah.' My shoulders started to relax. I could at least pretend that that was exactly my fear.

'I've got a much better way for us to get there.'

She started leading us down towards the water and I spotted signs for the ferry.

'We're going on a public ferry?' I said, and Lila screwed up her face.

'Less of the public,' she said, 'but yes, the only public transport I take. It's New York's best-kept secret. Why be forced to be like a sardine below ground when you can be on the water re-enacting *Titanic*.'

'I'm hoping you mean the "king of the world" bit, rather than the hitting the iceberg and sinking bit.'

'Naturally,' she said, buying us the tickets that came to the princely sum of $9 for the two. 'Just so you know, I'm always Rose.'

The ferry was pulling in and we had to pick up the pace, as people were already getting on by the time we'd got down to the entrance.

'I'm actually really excited about this,' I said, as the line started to move forward.

'I was dubious when they said they were going to create these ferry lines, I didn't think anyone would use them, but they're awesome. Before I wouldn't be bothered to head to Brooklyn on the weekend but now, if the sun is shining, I do.'

We headed on to the ferry and got a good spot on the top deck. I was going to treat it like I was on my own personal sightseeing cruise.

'So, how's it been going over the last couple of days?' asked Lila, sitting down and resting her arm on the railings.

'Yeah, it's been good.' I sat down next to her. 'I had a client meeting round Central Park yesterday which reminded me that I have to work whilst I'm here.'

'In person?'

'No, we did a phone walk. I have this client, Kiran, and we spend most of our sessions walking round parks. It's supposed to lead to divergent thinking.'

Lila's mouth twitched. 'That's proper corporate-speak.'

The ferry was starting to move and, as it glided through the water, I started to get butterflies in my stomach. Lila was right. This was an excellent way to travel on a sunny day.

'I know. But the weird thing is, it works. It helps to get away from the desk.'

'I can see that. So how did you get into coaching in the first place?'

I leaned back in my chair watching the Brooklyn Bridge in front of us slowly getting bigger and bigger.

'I worked as a business partner at a large tech company, and I used to get frustrated at how many bad managers there were out there. They'd be really nice people, but they couldn't lead. I started to run workshops on it and I got to the stage where I really loved it and thought I wanted to do more. I took the plunge and it kind of took off.'

I made it sound so effortless, as if it was as easy as that. But no one really wanted to hear about all the hours I'd put in at first. The late nights. The weekends. The money I had to borrow. The freelance HR work I'd had to pick up to keep myself afloat until I got enough clients to make it financially viable.

'That's so brave. Walking away from a job and setting up by yourself.'

I shrugged my shoulders. 'I don't know if brave's the right word. Stupid might be a better one,' I said with a laugh. 'I never thought I'd fantasise about company benefits and pensions.'

Lila nodded. 'That's how they get you, though, and then you never want to leave. But you left. Working for yourself. Helping people.'

'Trying to help people.' I tucked my hair behind my ears, knowing that I'd be doing it a few minutes later, thanks to the breeze that had whipped up as we glided along the water.

'Still, it's inspiring.'

The skyline of Manhattan was looking remarkable in the sunlight. I watched the distinctive One World Trade Center glint in the sunshine.

'How about you? Do you like your job?'

'As much as the next guy. But I'm lucky. I've got good bosses and good benefits. The healthcare.' Now it was her time to shrug. 'I think it would take a lot to make me move. Complacency. That to me is early middle age.' She was pulling a face as if it was the worst thing to hit us. 'Look at the bridge.'

She pointed in front of us. We skirted round towards a pier.

'Are we getting off here?'

'Next stop,' she said and then she put on a voice. 'There will be a short interruption whilst passengers debark and embark.'

'I still can't get over this ferry,' I said, staring up at the bridge that was tantalisingly close. 'When I was living out here, me and my friend Kerry used to go on the Staten Island Ferry at the weekend. Especially in the winter, when it was so cold out. The ferry was warm inside, and we'd go back and forth a couple of times, each time marvelling at the Statue of Liberty.'

'It is pretty cool.'

'So cool. Even on the billionth trip, you just can't take it for granted.'

'Where were you living when you were out here?'

'Union City.'

'New Jersey? Oh girl, you weren't in New York at all.'

'Come on, it's a train ride and a short one.'

'I'm teasing, and at least it was closer than Newark. Did you have a time?'

The easy thing to do would be to shut down the conversation. To nod and tell her I did and leave it at that. But it was one of the best years of my life, and I couldn't spend my life trying to pretend it wasn't because of the ache in my chest when I thought of it.

'The best,' I said, steeling myself for the pain that was incoming. 'It was hard being here when I couldn't afford anything. It makes me laugh that everyone keeps suggesting that we go to rooftop bars; when I was out here, we couldn't afford to go.'

'The city can be such a temptress.'

I thought of me and Kerry tottering about, walking past the fancy bars, looking longingly at queues at ground level, wishing we could go up.

'One day,' Kerry had said, pointing to the entrance of one of them, 'we'll come back here when we've got money and we'll order appletinis.'

I'd watched a group twenty somethings, dressed like us in their business casual attire, heading into the lift in the lobby. They might have looked like us, but they clearly didn't have the same meagre monthly stipend to live on as we did.

'I can just see us,' I said, playing along with the fantasy. 'We'll be there in our Louboutins, sipping our cocktails.'

'Yes,' she squealed, 'and then some hot Wall Street guys will come over and tell us how fabulous we look.'

'Because of the Louboutins.'

'Oh no, it'll be from our rich-person glow. Then we'll chat to them and dazzle them with our wit and intelligence.'

'You'll charm and dazzle them,' I said, correcting her.

'We both will.' Her voice was stern and she made a point of looking me in the eye as she said it. 'One of these days, Chloe, you're going to realise that you're not just there to make up the numbers.'

'Okay, so we'll both dazzle them and then…'

'And then,' she said taking a sip of her Mike's Hard Lemonade that was wrapped in a brown paper bag from the liquor store, 'we'll revel in the fact that we've made it.'

'Appletinis and a rooftop bar. The new benchmark of success.'

'Exactly,' she said, holding her bottle out for me to chink mine against.

The ferry began to move again, shaking me from my memory.

'We always said that we'd come back and drink appletinis in a rooftop bar one day. That's how we thought we'd know we'd made it.'

'Appletinis?' she shuddered. 'We used to drink those in college. I guess that's the equivalent of an Aperol Spritz today.'

'I guess so.' My first thought was that was a great idea, Kerry loved Aperol Spritzes, and then the reality hit me that we'd never get there together.

'You okay?'

I planted a smile on my face, my cheeks aching at the effort. 'Of course.'

The ferry had started to move again and we were now going underneath the bridge.

Lila hesitated as if she was going to pick more at the loose thread, but she put on a smile to match mine. It was the perfect moment for me to tell Lila about Kerry, but at the same time there was something nice about her not treating me with kid gloves.

'So I should tell you about where we're going. Now, I hope you're hungry as Smorgasburg has every different type of food you can imagine.'

'I can't wait.'

'You know, it's so great having you here. I used to do these kinds of trips all the time with my girlfriends at the weekend, but the last few years it seems too hard to get anything organised.'

'People get busy,' I said, knowing the feeling. I'd been guilty of it too. When I was with Jimmy, I reached out to my friends less. It was something, now that Kerry had gone, that I couldn't help but feel guilty for.

'They do. Kids. Husbands. Moving away.'

Life was constantly changing for everyone.

'I'd almost forgotten what it's like to make spontaneous plans,' she said, 'that don't involve diary matching months in advance. It's refreshing. You're refreshing.' She squeezed me on the arm.

'I don't think I've ever been called refreshing before. Are you sure it's not just because I'm acting out some crazy fantasy that you'd see in a reality TV show?'

'Oh, of course. Are you kidding? This is better than watching *Married at First Sight Australia*.'

I yelped. 'You watch that too?'

'I live for it.'

She started to cackle and went on a rant about her favourite villain in the show, and I got lost in the conversation. To borrow Lila's word, it was refreshing talking about mindless TV and ignoring all the big things.

I got to the bar a little early for my date, and the server seated me at the empty table. The bar was cold and almost soulless. All white shiny surfaces and a chrome finish. It couldn't have been further from the Smorgasburg market I'd spent my afternoon at with Lila. Stalls with colourful canopies and banners and vibrant food, with laid-back beats pumping from speakers and a view of Manhattan in the distance.

I searched the table for the menus, but there was just a QR code and I scanned it on my phone, wanting to see what was on offer. I scanned down the list of drinks, thinking of Lila as I found the Spritz section, the new appletini.

Waiting for my date to arrive before I ordered, I looked around the bar. It was busy as you'd expect on a Saturday night and I took in the other people. I spotted a couple a few tables away who were getting up to leave. The woman was putting on a light jacket and the guy helped her slip it on her shoulders. I watched as she flicked her hair out of the collar and turned to face him.

I couldn't hear what they were saying from where I was sitting, but I watched the body language. Her tilted head and coquettish smile, the way he kept patting her on the arm. It had all the hallmarks of an early date. I was hooked.

They stopped talking and they leaned in for a hug, before she turned to leave. I watched her walk across the bar and she paused to turn and wave at him before she went outside.

My heart was warmed and I watched the woman walking with a spring in her step until she went out of view.

'Hi,' said a voice.

I looked up, startled, at the blue eyes of the man in front of me. It was the man that had just seen off his date.

'Oh, hello,' I said, my cheeks flushing. I was mortified he'd caught me in the act of watching his date, like I was watching *Married at First Sight*. 'I, um...'

I didn't know what to say.

He sat down in the seat opposite me and the smile slid off my face.

'I'm sorry, I didn't mean to be watching. But, um, that seat's taken.'

'It sure is, sweetheart,' he said, his smile lighting up. He had a great smile, but that didn't change the fact that he couldn't sit there.

'I'm waiting for someone.' I tried again, my arms folding themselves.

'Me. You're waiting for me.'

'Don't be cute. I have a date.'

'With Ryan, right? And you're Cat?'

My jaw almost hit the floor, my eyes narrowed as I took him in.

'You're Ryan?'

'Guilty as charged.'

'But you were just with that woman and you guys were so into each other.'

He scanned the QR card with his phone, and I wondered if it was a deliberate attempt not to make eye contact with me.

'Oh, yeah. Hannah. Nice girl. So, what are you having to drink?'

'An elderflower spritz, but hang on,' I said, trying to get my head around this. 'You had a date before this one?'

'Yeah, I usually schedule a few in a row. It's like speed dating.'

I found myself blinking uncontrollably as I tried to process the information.

'Speed dating? Um, doesn't that only work if the other person knows about it too?'

He shrugged his shoulders.

'Look, none of us are new to this. It's a numbers game. I've averaged that one in three dates leads to something a little more, so this way I'm staying ahead of the game.'

My drink arrived along with Ryan's bottle of beer. He'd bought me a drink, which was at least something.

'But that girl, Hannah, she seemed really into you.'

'And I'll see her again,' he said, drinking his beer. 'So tell me about yourself.'

He leaned forward and rested his chin on his hands. Under normal circumstances, I would have thought he was interested in me, but I was really unsure. I thought of Blaine and how he made me feel in the Metaverse. Was he just going through the motions, telling me what I wanted to hear? Was he logging off from me and finding someone else to talk to after?

'Um, well, I...' I stopped. 'Ryan, I don't think this is going to work out.'

'Stay and drink your drink at least. It's on me,' he said, leaning back again. 'I'm not meeting the next date for another half an hour.'

'Another half an hour? You weren't kidding about the speed dating.'

He shrugged his shoulders and I rose to my feet.

'It was ni—' I was going to say that it was nice to meet him, but I stopped myself, as it wasn't. 'Just one thing before I go. Do you, um, like Periscope Monkeys?'

'Periscope what now?' he said, completely not fazed that I was getting up to leave.

My heart sank in relief. At least he wasn't Blaine. I couldn't have handled that if I'd discovered I'd been hanging out with such a narcissistic arsehole.

'Never mind.'

He reached over and took the drink he'd bought me that I'd not even sipped. His phone was already open and I could see he was messaging Hannah.

I headed back to Jimmy's apartment, knowing that he was going to be out. It meant I could curl up on the sofa and watch TV. I opened the door and put my stuff down on the suitcase that was doubling as a table.

'Hey,' called Jimmy, startling me, coming round the corner from the mini-kitchen.

'Hey, I thought you were out tonight.' I hadn't expected to feel so pleased to see a friendly face after that awful date with Ryan.

'I am, but we're not meeting until ten,' he said. He was dressed in tracksuit bottoms and a T-shirt. He didn't look ready at all.

'Until ten? Bloody hell, you're going out at bedtime?'

He shrugged. 'Sienna and her friends don't go out until after ten o'clock, at the earliest.'

He was holding a beer in his hand and he offered it to me. I nodded and he disappeared into the fridge to get another.

'I know I used to do that, but I can't imagine doing it now.'

'I know,' he laughed. 'The other weekend I went to bed and set my alarm to go out with them.'

I snorted with laughter, sitting down on the sofa, quite content that my evening was ending rather than beginning.

'If I'd done that, I'd not have got up. Once my bra's off and the PJs are on...'

'Oh, I remember,' he said, and he perched on the arm of the sofa. 'You're welcome to join us, your bra's still on.'

'Ha, yes, well, no, thank you,' I said, sinking further into the couch. 'I don't think I'd want to crash your date.'

'It's not a date. It's just hanging out with mates, most of them play pickleball too.'

Lila had planted the seed of the cultlike nature of pickleball and her argument grew stronger the more I heard about it.

'I'm fine here. I'm just going to make the most of this giant TV and comfy chair. I've walked about a million miles since I got here.'

'Hmm, you fancy walking more? I thought it might be nice to head over the water tomorrow, to Hoboken?'

'Hoboken?'

'Yeah, it's opposite Midtown. It's got this walk that's supposed to be really impressive and—'

'The riverfront walk?'

'Oh, yeah, of course I forgot, that was your neck of the woods.'

I thought of Blaine and how we'd walked there in the Metaverse.

'One of my work colleagues was saying that the views are incredible, and apparently there's a Frank Sinatra walking tour. I thought it would be nice to spend some time together. I haven't seen a lot of you this week.'

I didn't want to point out that that had been quite deliberate on my part. I might have decided to stay whilst I was over, but I hadn't wanted to impose. There was part of me that thought that I should think of an excuse as to why I couldn't go, but we'd almost managed a week under the same roof. That had to show that perhaps friendship wasn't out of the realms of possibility.

'Yeah, that sounds like a nice way to spend the day.'

'Perfect.'

He finished off his bottle of beer.

'I should really jump in the shower or else I'm never going to make it out.' He stood up and hesitated before he went. 'I could cancel tonight if you want. We could hang out.'

'Oh, no,' I said, waving my hand to knock the idea away. 'Go have fun being young.'

He groaned. 'I don't feel young.'

'Stop your whining, Grandad.'

'You going to be okay?' he asked.

'I feel like I need to be wearing a T-shirt that says I'll be fine,' I said, putting on a brave face. 'We'll hang out tomorrow.'

'Looking forward to it,' he said, finally heading off to the bathroom. I tried to ignore the niggle that as soon as he left the room, a feeling of loneliness took hold. I steeled my heart and picked up my phone. I had messages from Lila asking about the date. I smiled. She wasn't going to believe what had happened. I laughed to myself as I typed it out. It might have been the shortest and worst date I'd ever been on, but at least it had been memorable. If nothing else, at least the trip was reminding me that, in a city that haunted me so much, I could still make new memories.

Chapter 15

Stepping off the PATH into Hoboken felt a little like coming home. The view of the city was different from how it had been in Union City. It wasn't as far up the river as where my apartment had been, but there was still that crushing familiarity. Here, we were more in line with Midtown and the skyline, which you felt you could reach out and touch across the river beyond, was flatter, with high-rises flanking it on either side.

'Takes your breath away, doesn't it?' said Jimmy, standing beside me. He'd been looking at Google Maps, trying to get his bearings, and it had taken him a second to look up and appreciate where he was.

'I know. It's funny, as yesterday I saw Manhattan from the East River, but it's so different this side.'

We'd got up early to avoid the heat, and Hoboken was having a sleepy Sunday morning start, with only a few people out and about, and there was a gentle stream of traffic building.

'So I think the walking tour starts in the town,' I said, pointing away from the river towards the main street.

'I thought we could walk along the river first,' he said, pointing to a walkway in front of us.

I recognised it immediately from the time that I'd walked it virtually with Blaine.

The path was sheltered on one side by trees, and the river butting up to it on the other side. Despite the buildings and the spectre of New York looming from the other side of the Hudson, it felt peaceful.

There was a coffee van at the end of the pier and neither of us talked as we approached it. We got our takeaways and then headed up the river.

'Did you walk this when you lived here?' he asked. 'It would have been close, right?'

'No, and I wish I had. We only came here for the bars and shopping, or window shopping, as it's mainly upmarket boutiques.' I thought of the many times I'd walked down the high street. 'When my mum came to visit, she bought me a blouse from one of the little shops. It has a big bow at the front and it was made from that crepe type of cotton.'

'I remember that,' he said.

'You do?'

'Yeah, I've definitely seen you wear it.'

'Ah, I don't think I've worn it since Andrea and Henry's engagement drinks,' I nodded. It felt like the type of occasion that warranted special clothes. 'I can't believe you remember.'

'Well, it was memorable with it being so see-through.'

'See-through?'

'Yeah, under the lights in the bar.' He pulled a face. 'You didn't know?'

'No,' I said, trying to remember if I'd ever worn it to work, and cringing that back in the day I probably had.

'Well, if it makes you feel any better, it was one of my favourite outfits of yours.'

I stuttered a laugh. 'I don't think that makes it much better. I thought your favourite outfit was that hideous Union Jack dress that I wore as fancy dress.'

'Don't mention the Geri Halliwell dress,' he said, trying not to smile. 'And that wasn't my favourite. It was close.'

'Well, I'm sorry if I don't take fashion advice from someone who lives in variations of Portsmouth football shirts from different vintages.'

He looked down at his button-up polo shirt. It started to dawn on me that that's what was different about Jimmy.

'The football shirts have gone,' I said with an almost-shriek.

'Not gone, just retired. Thought I'd try out a new look,' he said with a shrug.

It was a good look on him and just another reminder that he was no longer the Jimmy that I'd been with.

'You've still got the baseball cap, though.'

'Still got the cap,' he said. 'Only now it's to hide the fact I'm receding.'

He pulled the baseball cap off his head and ran his hand through his hair and my fingers instinctively skirted along the edges of his hairline.

'It's only a little,' I said, tracing the line, before I caught Jimmy's eyes and my brain caught up with what I was doing. I dropped my hand and he put his hat firmly down on his head again.

We walked along a little way.

'Is that the Chrysler Building?' I squinted at it, wondering if I needed glasses.

'Yeah, I think so. That sun is blinding.'

'I know.'

'And there, behind it, that's the Empire State.' He stopped and pointed.

I nodded. It was back to that familiar pattern of staying on safe ground. Picking out the landmarks, avoiding talking about the past.

'Stand there a second,' said Jimmy, pulling his phone out of his back pocket.

I did as I was told and he snapped a quick photo.

'For the group chat,' he said, swiping.

'Ah, the group chat.'

'They mean well,' said Jimmy.

'I take it you saw Andrea berating the fact that I hadn't posted enough yesterday.'

'Uh-huh, hence the photo,' he said. 'You're welcome.'

A man was jogging towards us and I took in all the details about him. His baseball cap backwards on his head, earbuds in his ears, the Nike swish on his shorts and top, the expensive-looking running trainers on his feet. I wondered if it was Blaine and thought again of the impossibility of finding him, of hoping that if it was him that there would be some sign or something that would…

It happened so quickly, before I even got a chance to finish my thought process. He'd started to stumble and I watched the panic take over his face as his arms windmilled, trying to save himself before he finally tumbled down to the ground.

'Shit!' said Jimmy, he did a light jog over to the guy and offered a hand. 'Are you all right, mate?'

I approached him slowly, wondering if this was the cosmic sign from the universe.

'I am now,' he said, taking Jimmy's hand, a smile forming over his face. 'That accent of yours.'

'I can't take credit for where I was born.'

'Stop,' said the runner, putting his hand over his chest. 'You're too much.'

He turned and looked at me as if noticing me for the first time.

'Are you okay? Did you hurt yourself?' I said.

'Oh,' he said, a look of disappointment crossing over his face. 'No, it's more my pride that's hurt. And my heart.'

He looked at Jimmy. Jimmy gave him a little shrug, that unspoken conversation passing between them.

The runner dusted himself down and gave Jimmy one last wistful look and headed off at a pace.

'You've still got the magic,' I said.

'If only the women of New York felt the same.'

'What about Sienna?' I raised an eyebrow.

He nodded. 'Ah, Sienna. Yeah.'

He hadn't mentioned her much since I'd arrived, but he had gone out with her last night.

'Am I going to meet her when I'm over?'

He put his hands in his pockets. His gaze was straight ahead.

'Do you want to meet her?'

I didn't, but at the same time I didn't want him to think I still had feelings for him.

'Yeah, you should bring her to Periscope Monkeys. I think there are still tickets.'

'I could, but I'm not sure she'd like them. She's into cute metal.'

'What the hell is that?'

'Haven't got a clue.'

'The joy of youth.' I let out a deep breath, thinking of what I was like at her age. 'I wish I could be that age again.'

Jimmy turned and looked at me. 'Do you? I'd hate to be twenty-year-old me again.' He shivered and shook it out. 'I hated that part where I didn't really know who I was.'

I'd met Jimmy when we were in our early thirties and, whilst I didn't feel like a fully-formed person when I hit 30, I at least had stopped trying so hard to be someone that I wasn't.

'I don't think from your stories we would have got on well when we were younger,' I said, thinking over the times he told me of the drunken antics of him and his friends.

'Yeah, I think sometimes timing has a lot to do with things.'

The words hung in the air and I could feel his gaze on me whilst I was staring straight ahead.

'So, Sienna,' I said, steering the conversation back.

'I'm sure you can meet her if you like.' He went to drink more of his coffee, but it was empty. 'You finished?'

He gestured at my cup and I shook my head, as he went and threw his in the nearby bin.

We didn't talk for a while as we stepped around cyclists and runners, the odd family wrangling their kids.

'I feel like we need a soundtrack for this walk,' said Jimmy, reaching into his pocket and pulling out a box with earbuds. He passed one over to me. 'Here.' He put the other in his ear and pulled out his phone and started scrolling.

'This feels like we're on a school trip in the late nineties.'

'Although we'd be walking along like this,' he said, butting up against my shoulder.

'And then one of us would move too suddenly and rip the other's ear piece out.'

'Oh, to be wireless,' he said. 'So what are you in the mood to listen to?'

'I kind of think that we should be listening to Frank Sinatra seeing as we're doing his walking tour.'

'We're not, technically. We haven't started that just yet.' He scrolled some more and selected a song. 'This one always sounds good in the sunshine.'

The opening beats started and I immediately had the urge to start dancing.

'Are you going to do the dance?' I said, my shoulders automatically moving.

'What dance?' Jimmy looked at me as the words started to 'Come and Get Your Love'.

'You know, the opening of the *Guardians of the Galaxy* movie,' I said. The more the song played, the more I wanted to channel my inner Chris Pratt, surely everyone had one? 'Chris Pratt has got the headphones on and he's dancing along by himself, with the moves.'

I moved my shoulders a little to try and recreate the scene, and Jimmy's face lit up.

'I don't know what you're doing,' he said.

'What? We watched this movie together. It's the one with the racoon and the spaceship?'

'Maybe I fell asleep.'

'This was the opening few minutes.'

'Perhaps if you did more of the dancing, I'd remember,' he said.

I looked over my shoulder to see if anyone was paying attention before I carried on.

'You have to remember.' I looked at him in disbelief and he shrugged.

'I probably blocked it out. Superheroes aren't my bag, you know that. I know they're right up your street. Saving the day and all that.'

I knew he didn't mean anything, but his words stung. I didn't always save the day, no matter how hard I tried.

I stopped dancing.

'Hey why did you stop? You've just got to the good bit.'

I shot him a look with daggers in my eyes. 'You do remember! Why did you let me do that?'

He pushed both eyebrows up.

'Because it was like seeing the old you for a split second.'

I stopped still. He was right. I wouldn't have blinked about dancing in public or making a fool out of myself, but I couldn't remember the last time I'd done it.

'Your face. Speaking of iconic dances,' he said, giving me another nudge, 'I hear there's this dance that's on the internet, Tom Holland doing a Rihanna song, and I'm not sure I know how that goes, fancy recreating that?'

'Very funny,' I said, pushing him a little, and he began to laugh.

'Yeah, well. To be honest, I'd forgotten the song was in the film until you started to dance.'

'That's the only reason I know the song.'

'What are you talking about? It's an absolute classic.'

I shrugged my shoulders back.

'Classic rock. Come on!' He scrolled on his phone and selected another song. 'You know this one?'

It took a while for the slow beat to kick in and the melody to go over the top, but as soon as Elton John started to sing, it clicked into place.

'"Benny and the Jets",' I said.

'See? There's hope after all,' sighed Jimmy with relief. 'Our time together wasn't wasted.'

'Yeah, well this was in the bar scene in *27 Dresses*.'

Jimmy looked like he was going to pick me up and dump me into the river.

'I was always playing this kind of music and you only know it from films?'

He got cross and put on another song.

'*Coyote Ugly*,' I said as Def Leppard's 'Pour Some Sugar' started to play.

He shook his head.

'And there was me thinking that I'd given you a musical education when we'd been together.'

I knew he was joking and usually I'd let a dig at my inferior music taste go, but a rage started to bubble inside me.

'I've had a musical education,' I snapped. I didn't know where it was coming from. The pent-up frustration that I'd usually swallow down, the people pleasing, accepting of all other world views as being superior to my own, was too much. It was as if my stomach was full and I wasn't going to take any more. 'It's not my fault that good songs end up in movies or that my mum brought me up on a diet of boy bands, and you were much more likely to hear Take That and New Kids on the Block playing in my house than you were Fleetwood Mac. We can't all be the cool kid.'

A light breeze blew my hair into my face and I struggled to tuck it behind my ears so that I didn't swallow it.

'I'm not the cool kid,' Jimmy tried to butt in, but I was on a roll.

'Perhaps it's you that needs a musical education. Have you ever thought that? That you pick all the obvious songs, so obvious that they're in hit movies. But you wouldn't know obscure genius if it slapped you round the face.'

Jimmy opened his mouth to say something and then stopped.

'What?' I snapped, the anger pulsing round my brains. It wasn't just Jimmy who did this to me. I let everyone. I was so eager to please people and to think that their opinion was more valid than my own. Kerry was the worst at that. She always seemed to tell me what she thought I should know. I'd looked up to her so much and she was always my first phone call when I wanted advice. When Kerry would come round when Jimmy was over and the two of them would chat music and control the playlists. They'd often intrinsically know a shorthand for things I'd never heard of. 'Say it if you're going to say it.'

That confidence that he wore so well had seemed to evaporate.

'I never knew you had it in you to be so feisty.'

'Maybe you're just bringing out the worst in me.'

I closed my eyes. The words were out before I could stop them. We'd never been one of those fiery couples that fought and even when we broke up, it had never got nasty. I opened my eyes, expecting him to have put up his defences, but instead he simply shrugged it away.

'Maybe I do, and maybe that's not a bad thing. It's not like it's made me feel great, you being like this, but I'm glad you told me.'

He held out his phone to me.

'What am I supposed to do with that?' I said, losing the battle with the hair, slipping my hair band off my wrist and scraping it back into as slicked-back a messy bun as I could make it.

'You're supposed to give me a musical education in pop.'

'Now you're being sarcastic.' I started to walk a little quicker, definitely not taking the phone.

'No, I'm trying to be humble. Realising that I've sounded like a dick, so play me your favourites.'

I looked at him, his face unreadable. Once upon a time I would have known what he was thinking by looking at him, and I wondered at what point in our decline I'd stopped recognising the signs. But he was holding out his phone and he wasn't taking it back. I sighed and snatched it from him. There was no need for me to snatch, it was overly dramatic, but I'd backed myself into a corner.

I stared at his Spotify, Def Leppard getting perilously near the end of the song. What the hell would I pick? What was an obscure song that's pop-based but kind of cool and that he wouldn't know?

I stared out across the water at the towering buildings in the distance and it hit me.

I hit 'Play' and the drums started to play. Jimmy looked at me, squinting as if he was trying to place it. The song was slow and Harry Styles started to sing but, if he recognised it, he didn't say.

He tilted his head, reminding me of a dog trying to hold its ear up to hear better, its eyes narrowing. I'd forgotten this song and how good it is.

'I don't think I've ever heard this. Who is it?'

'Harry Styles, "Ever Since New York",' I said, and he screwed up his face.

'Harry Styles?' There was a hint of surprise in his voice, but not detestation.

'You like it?'

'It's not half bad. You know,' he shoved his hands in his pockets, 'if it came on the radio, I wouldn't turn it off.'

'Wow, high praise indeed.' I found myself smiling, walking along in silence. Even smiling like this felt unnatural, my muscles aching, unused to it. But I'd missed how that felt. Slow steps.

'The views are amazing when you get to that pier,' said Jimmy.

I nodded, remembering the time I'd walked here with Blaine in the Metaverse.

'You've been here before?' I said. I'd thought he'd said last night that he hadn't.

'No, but according to Google Maps.'

'Ah, Google Maps, practically like having been here. We could have skipped straight ahead to the Frank Sinatra walking tour.'

'And what, miss out on my musical education?'

Just for that, I cued up Westlife's version of 'Uptown Girl' as the next song on his app.

The path split and to the right was a wooden walkway that hovered above the river towards an island-shaped pier. I found myself slowing as we got to it.

'Ah, Chloe!' he shouted, before he started to sing along.

'I'm sticking with the New York theme. Seems appropriate.'

Jimmy went to step on to the bridge to the pier and I hesitated, turning to look over my shoulder.

'Should we go and head back, get a coffee? See a major Sinatra destination?'

The walkway was only a metre or so above the water, if that. I could see the water through the gaps between the wooden planks.

'Come on, we're going this way. I bet the views from over there look incredible.'

His voice was authoritative and I looked up to the natural viewing point, where even from here I could see people standing to get their skyline shots.

'But I feel like—'

'—Walk over the bridge,' he said, his voice stern but soft. 'You'll be perfectly safe on it.'

The water down below was dark and cold-looking. All I could think about was Kerry. The shock of how cold that water would be if I fell in. The shock of how cold the water must have been when she died.

'I can't.'

'You can.' He reached over and took my hand. I wanted to recoil. I didn't want anyone to touch me. 'We're walking this way.'

He took a step forward, slow and deliberate, and I found myself following.

'Give me the phone,' he said, putting on a song. 'My favourite Harry Styles song.'

I stared at him, as 'Golden' started to play, my fingers loosening on the rail.

'Yeah, I have one too. Don't think you've got a monopoly on Harry. Plus, you know I could hear your music too when you played it in your flat?'

I laughed and I started to walk, slowly at first, my hand hovering over the rail.

The water kept lapping against the posts, the sound of the waves still unnerving me.

'You're doing really well. We're almost there and I promise the views will be worth it.'

I thought of the kind of approach I'd use for my clients who were scared. One small step at a time. Celebrate the little wins. I looked over my shoulder at how far I'd already come and I started to increase my pace.

'You did it,' said Jimmy when we made it to the pier. He leaned over, gave me a hug and my lips brushed his cheeks as I went to kiss him and then stopped myself short. In the rush of the moment I'd forgotten he was no longer mine to kiss.

We stepped back out of the hug, a little embarrassed, and I wonder if he felt it too.

'I did do it, didn't I?'

It was an irrational fear to have, and yet I wondered if I'd always have it now. 'And look at those views,' he said, pointing.

I turned and gasped. They had been amazing in the Metaverse, but that was nothing compared with what was in front of me now. Midtown was perfectly framed, the sun dappling light on the Hudson River.

'Fuck, that's beautiful,' I said.

'See, it's always worth walking over the bridge, no matter how bad it seems.'

'Oh, that was cheesy.'

'Yeah,' he said. 'Because I'm not the one that does the pep talks.'

I pushed the hair off my face and took in the view once more. 'Thank you.'

'For the pep talk?'

'For making me come out of the apartment.'

He smiled, seeming genuinely pleased.

'You want to carry on walking?'

'I think I want to stay here for a minute, if that's okay?' I asked, looking back at the bridge, at how far I'd come.

'Of course. There's no rush.' He looked down at his phone again and I wondered if he was going to change the song. 'Nina's replied. She wants a photo of the two of us.'

'I bet she does,' I muttered.

Jimmy shrugged his shoulders and held his hand aloft and I found myself leaning in for the photo. He put his other arm round my shoulders. My body tensed and my heart started to beat that bit quicker.

For someone who had been so quick to take the original photo, he seemed to take an age to take this one.

'There,' he said, showing me the results. He'd somehow managed to get both of our faces in and the skyline beyond. It looked incredible.

'The girls will like that,' I said, knowing what they'd no doubt be discussing amongst themselves outside the group chat. They'd have a field day with our body language.

'You know,' he said, scrolling on his phone, 'what we should be listening to is Periscope Monkeys, get ourselves in the mood for the gig.'

I'd been so focused on how I was going to get through a day with Jimmy, just the two of us, I'd almost forgotten about the gig tonight. The nerves that seemed to have been kept at bay under the surface were starting to intensify. Tonight I might be the closest to Blaine that I'd been since I arrived and, for the first time, I had a strong feeling of hope that I could actually find him.

Chapter 16

Not since I'd tried to get into nightclubs underage in my teens had I felt such trepidation walking up to a bar. The nerves took me right back to being a 17-year-old with a friend's provisional driving licence, hoping the bouncer wouldn't look too hard at the ID.

All the other times this week when I'd gone to Blaine's favourite places, or gone on the blind dates, I'd known the chances of running into him were slim, but there was a fair chance he was going to be here tonight.

I rubbed my sweaty palms on to my denim shorts, tugging them down as they were skimpily short. I would have been happier in jeans, but it was far too hot to entertain the idea. Jimmy and I had been for a drink beforehand and Lila had come to meet us. But not even the Dutch courage I'd drunk was calming my nerves.

The venue where we were going to see the band came into view. It looked like it had once been a factory. All burgundy brick, yet blacked-out windows. There was already a queue outside.

'I'm going to wait for Sienna out here,' said Jimmy, stepping back.

'Sienna,' repeated Lila.

'Okay, see you in there,' I said, guiding Lila away to the back of the queue.

'You know, I'm only just noticing how cute those heels are.'

I may have headed to Target on Friday to get some clothes, just in case the inspiration took me to run with Jimmy one morning, and I'd spotted a pair of PVC heels that I'd never in my normal life entertain the thought of wearing.

'I thought they'd be practical, you know, stop my feet getting wet if people spill drinks.'

'I like your thinking, plus they make your legs look like they go on forever. Blaine is in for a treat when you find him.'

'*If* I find him,' I said with a groan.

'Come on, you need to send positive vibes out to get positive results back.'

Lila pulled out her phone and gave it a quick check before sighing.

'Is that your husband?'

'He's still on the call.'

'I can't believe he's got to work on a Sunday night.'

'Uh-huh, it's often the same. Once the market opens in Japan,' she gave a little eye roll. 'But he'll be here. He promised.'

Lila looked over to Jimmy, who was scrolling on his phone on the corner of the street.

'What do we think to Sienna then? I take it she's the young one?'

'Yep. I told him he should bring her.'

Lila pulled a face with pursed lips before she said her name out loud. 'Sienna,' she said, saying the name all seductively. 'Come on, that's a hot girl name. Does it not bother you?'

I tried to put a little smile on my face to pretend it didn't, but any of my friends back home would have seen straight through me. 'We broke up months ago now, he's free to date whoever he wants.'

'I'm married, but yet every time I go back home and see my high-school boyfriend with his troll-like wife, I still get a bit prickly with jealousy. What once was mine will always be mine.'

I laughed. Lila saw the world so differently.

'I just want him to be happy.'

'Oh, now I know you're lying.'

The queue shuffled forward and after my ticket was scanned and my bag searched, we found ourselves inside. There was an acoustic-guitar player on stage, sitting on a bar stool, and he was attracting a good crowd, whilst the bar was already two people deep.

'It's busy,' said Lila, rubbing her hands together. 'What's the plan? Are we going to divide and conquer?'

She was peering all around, looking men up and down. 'Have you got anything more for me to go on than some chess-playing computer nerd, as right now I'm seeing a lot of that?'

A man walked past who was covered head to toe in tattoos. Lila held her hand out and stopped him.

'Excuse me, me and my friends were just trying to settle an argument, have you seen Periscope Monkeys live before?'

'I have,' he said with a nod.

'Great, and I don't suppose you saw them when they performed in the Metaverse a couple of months back? Little bit of a long shot.'

He shook his head. 'No, sorry.'

'Ah, then you can't help.'

Lila turned back and gave me a winning smile.

'See, that took all of twenty seconds and gave us a no.'

I was transfixed.

'You came pretty much straight out with it.'

'What's the point of pussyfooting around, plus I hid it in a nice little story, just in case we found him. That way we could ask him what he thought: better live or virtual?'

'And what would be your next question, whether he'd been to the Cloisters?'

'I hadn't got that far,' she said, resting her hands on her hips and surveying the room for more options. 'But probably something along the lines of where would they recommend you go for a day trip? Short of calling everyone Blaine, I don't see we have a lot of options.'

I thought it was genius, and I wished I had an ounce of her courage.

'Excuse me,' she said, talking to someone else.

I turned around, seeing if I could spot someone who looked approachable, when Jimmy walked in.

I stuck my hand up to wave and he put his hand up, then turned to his side and touched the shoulder of the woman next to him. She looked over to me and followed him over.

'Hey,' I said.

'Chloe, this is Sienna. Sienna, Chloe.'

'Hi,' I said, holding my hand out. Sienna, hot girl name, hot girl in real life, took hold of my hand and shook it, her smile wide, but with no warmth behind it.

'So lovely to meet you. Jimmy has been talking about you non-stop all week.'

'I wouldn't say non-stop,' he said, putting his hands in the pockets of his shorts.

She gave him a look that suggested she thought otherwise. 'He told me all about that housing scam.'

Every time I was reminded about it, I felt sick to my stomach.

'Anyone could have fallen for it,' said Jimmy.

'It's one of the oldest tricks in the book,' she said, as if she would never have been so stupid. 'You're just lucky that you had Jimmy here to be your knight in shining armour.'

'Yeah, well, it was supposed to be a stopgap; I need to sort something out for the rest of my trip.'

'Nonsense! I've hardly noticed you're there. Apart from the bowls being put in the wrong bit of the dishwasher.'

'They're supposed to go on the top rack,' I said, my buttons well and truly pushed.

Jimmy bit his lip. He was winding me up. Whenever he came to mine, I always had to rearrange the dishwasher before I ran it, and I'm pretty sure he did the same at his flat.

'Where's Lila?' he asked, probably because he knew he was going to lose the argument.

'Should my ears be burning?' she said, linking her arm through mine. She whispered in my ear, 'No biters yet.'

'Lila, this is Sienna.'

'Ah!' She dropped my arm and put her hands up. 'So lovely to meet you.'

She gave me a look and mouthed the word 'hot'.

'Does anyone want drinks?' asked Jimmy.

'Desperately,' said Sienna.

'I'll get them. What does everyone want?'

He took our orders and Sienna went to help.

'Told you she'd be hot. How old do you think she is? Twenty-two, twenty-three?'

'I think she's twenty-three. But seeing as that's how old I think I am, to me she looks about seventeen.'

Lila laughed. 'Right, we should get down to business whilst the coast is clear.'

'Lila, I'm not you. I just can't go up to a random stranger and start interrogating them.'

'Sure you can. Just think of it like you're at a networking event. Channel your inner networker.'

She'd glided off before I could stop her. She was right, though. It was networking, only with louder background noise and a potentially cold drink, rather than lukewarm wine.

I turned to look at the person standing next to me.

She was a tall woman with tattoo sleeves down her arm and hair that was down to her bum on one side, and completely shaved on the other.

'I, um, love your hair,' I said, when the woman caught me staring.

She touched it with a hint of self-consciousness and she walked off. A man took her place and he started to tap his foot as he watched the guy on the stage.

'Excuse me,' I said, in quite frankly the poshest telephone voice I'd ever done.

'Yeah,' he said, turning to look at me. He had dark eyes and a crooked smile. 'Can you say that again?'

'Um, excuse me.'

'Ah,' he said, with a little smile. 'I'm sorry, that just sounded so good when you said it. British?'

I nodded and he smiled wider.

'You live here?'

'Just visiting.'

'Shame,' he said, his dark eyes focusing on mine causing a shiver to go down my spine.

'You live here?'

'For my sins.'

'Are you a big fan of Periscope Monkeys?'

The noise was getting louder as the place was filling up and I found myself taking a step closer to him.

'Isn't everyone here?'

'I guess so. Have you seen them before?'

'Once or twice. You?'

'Once years ago and then kind of once recently.'

'Kind of?' He raised an eyebrow.

'I saw them in the Metaverse,' I said, no longer caring. If I was going to find Blaine, I couldn't beat about the bush.

'Oh, in April? Me too.'

My heart started to beat that little bit quicker. I tried to search his eyes.

'I borrowed a headset from a friend for the night,' he said. 'I couldn't get on with it at all. I'd rather just stream the album.'

My stomach lurched. So close.

'Metaverse not for you?'

'No,' he shook his head. 'I felt like my dad when I tried it, bemoaning the tech.'

He laughed and I tried to laugh back, but I didn't know how long I could keep building myself up, only to be knocked down every time.

The moment had passed and I wondered if he sensed it too.

'I'm going to find my friends. Have a good night!'

'Yeah, you too,' I muttered weakly. I sighed deeply and turned to find Lila standing grinning at me.

'Chloe, I want you to meet someone,' she said, her eyes wide. 'This is Theo. He works in IT and he goes to virtual gigs and he—'

I don't know if she stopped talking or if I'd stopped listening, because my eyes had locked on to Theo's and every muscle in my body had gone rigid.

'Chloe, are you okay?' She took hold of my arm and gave me a gentle stroke. 'You've gone so pale.'

'Chloe?' he said, his shock mirroring mine.

My legs started to go and my throat started to constrict.

'Is it me? It's so hot in here,' I said, tugging at my shirt. Blinking rapidly. I had to get out of there. My head was starting to spin.

I turned and knocked straight into Jimmy and he dropped the plastic glasses he'd been carrying. They fell to the floor and I felt the splash of cold liquid down my legs.

Sienna screamed. 'My dress. It's vintage.'

I looked between Jimmy and her.

'Jimmy, my dress,' she was almost screaming.

'I'm sorry' was all I could manage before I bolted for the door. I still couldn't breathe.

The heat of the street hit me when I got outside and yet I couldn't stop shivering. I bent over double, trying to force air into my lungs and trying to stop myself being sick.

'What the hell was that about?' said Lila, rubbing at my back. 'Are you okay?'

I took a deep breath, satisfied that I wasn't going to be sick, and stood upright, closing my eyes. I could still see the look he gave me, the look that he'd seen a ghost and that's how I felt seeing him.

'That was Kerry's ex-boyfriend. Kerry's my best friend.' My eyes stung and I shut them tight. 'She *was* my best friend.'

A tear trickled down my cheek.

'That's the sad place you keep drifting to.'

I nodded.

'Do you want to talk about it?'

'I never want to talk about it,' I said, the tears rolling thick and fast now.

'Sometimes that's why you have to.'

I nodded and she led me down the street, away from the queue waiting to get in and those vaping and flirting outside. We came to a stop outside a florist's, shut up for the night, and sat on the kerb.

'What happened?' asked Lila, digging into her purse, pulling out a tissue and handing it to me.

'She died.' I took the tissue and wiped the tears but more took their place. 'Seven months ago. Just after Christmas.'

A chill ran over me as I took myself back to that day. The trees had been bare and ice glistened on the ground.

Jimmy and I had been walking towards the pub in the village where his parents lived, about to warm ourselves up next to the log fire as we had a Sunday roast.

It had been her mum that called. I sent the call to answerphone. Unknown number on a Sunday, but the second time all the hairs on my arms stood up and I answered it.

'She's gone, Chloe,' she'd said, the pain raw in her voice. 'She couldn't do it any more.'

I don't know how I kept hold of the phone but the world started to spin around me. The twinkling Christmas lights that lined the streets started to blur through the tears, and Jimmy caught me as my legs started to give way.

'Was it sudden?' asked Lila, bringing me back to the present.

'She took her own life,' I said, as that was the reality of it. I'd spent months trying to convince myself that she hadn't meant to do it, that it was an accident. I told myself that she'd been walking across the bridge and she'd fallen in, but I knew that wasn't what had happened. Her mum knew it. I knew it.

'I couldn't stop her,' I said, the pain of the stinging tears becoming almost unbearable.

Lila didn't say anything. She didn't need to. She squeezed my hand harder and that was enough.

'My job is to coach people to help them be the best version of themselves and yet I couldn't help her.'

'Chloe.' Lila's tone was usually stern, but there was a softness to it now. What happened to Kerry... it was not your fault. Your inability to save her,' she said, doing air quotes. 'It wasn't your job alone.'

'I was her best friend,' I said, my voice cracking.

Lila nodded, and she looked as if she was blinking back a tear.

'I know, I know. It's natural to think that we shoulda woulda coulda,' she said. 'There was always the possibility that there'd have been another ending to her story. There were probably millions of things that could have changed it.' She smoothed down her already smooth hair. 'But you've got to remember that you alone weren't responsible for Kerry.'

There was something in the way that she was talking. I wiped my eyes and looked up at her. The pain was etched on her face.

'You lost someone that way?' I was putting the pieces of the puzzle together.

'Not a best friend,' she said, a sorry look in her eyes. 'I couldn't imagine the pain that would bring. Someone I knew from high school. He'd always suffered but I never imagined.'

The words dried up in her throat. It was my turn to squeeze her hand back. The understanding passed between us without the need for words. We sat for a moment in silence, both blinking back the tears.

'There's that awfulness with this kind of death,' she said eventually. 'It's a shock and all those stages of grief, the denial, the anger, they're all there in abundance, but there's also that deep-rooted guilt that you could have been the one to save them. And as awful as this sounds, all you can do is accept that you didn't and that's not your fault.'

A girl staggered past us, her friend grabbing her by the elbow to miss us and I pulled my feet in closer to me, hugging my knees in to my chest.

'She'd always suffered. She hid it well from a lot of people. She always seemed too happy, so full of life. Her mum had come out to visit when we'd first arrived in New York, and she'd told me how Kerry used to cut herself, and she told me what signs to watch out for. And I did, for years I did. And then, when I was with Jimmy, I took my eyes off the ball and—' I scrunched my eyes shut until they stung with pain.

'You weren't a bad friend. You just lived your life.'

My cheeks were wet again and this time my chest was throbbing as the crying was starting to take over my whole body.

'I should have called her more. I should have noticed the signs. But she was so happy for me, and she loved Jimmy so much. She kept talking about us moving in together and getting married.'

I couldn't talk any more. Lila wrapped her arm round me and drew me in.

'It's okay, Chloe. Everything you're feeling, it's normal, but you can't let it stop you living your life.'

'It's just so hard without her. I miss her so much.'

She stroked the hair out of my face that was getting stuck to my wet cheeks.

'I'm sure you do. Oh Chloe,' she said, tears in her eyes. 'My heart is breaking for you and we barely know each other. No wonder Jimmy looks at you the way he does.'

I blinked through my tears.

'How does he look at me?'

She didn't get to answer, as I heard him calling my name. Lila waved him across.

I watched Sienna walk behind Jimmy, stroking down her dress that under the streetlights I could see was now streaky from the stains.

'You okay?' he asked, squatting down in front of me. 'What happened?'

'I saw Kerry's ex, Theo, and I don't know.' I shook my head. I don't know why seeing him had caused such a reaction. He'd been the one that got away from her, the man she talked about so much and he'd been right there in front of me. It hit me how much it should have been her standing in front of him, not me. 'It was a bit of a shock.'

'I bet. Look, Sienna's ordered a car, so we can share that, if that's okay?'

I nodded my head. 'Yeah, unless you wanted to go with her?'

'No,' he shook his head. 'I need to get you home.'

Lila rubbed my back.

'What about you? Do you want to come with us?'

'Anthony messaged,' she said, holding up her phone. 'He's on his way, so we'll stay and watch these Periscope Monkeys, see what the fuss is about. It's almost impossible to get him out of his home office, so I might as well make the most.' She stroked my hair once more for good measure. 'Sure you don't want to stay too?'

I shook my head. 'I need to go home.'

'Okay, but if you need me, call me,' she said. 'Any time.'

I nodded.

She and Jimmy did little head-bobbing motions at each other, like they were speaking a language about me that I didn't understand.

Sienna called from further down the street. We turned and she was opening the door of a car.

Jimmy stood up and pulled me up. I turned to Lila and gave her a hug.

'You going to be okay?' she said, the sternness back.

I nodded. I was lying. Coming here had been a huge mistake. I was never going to find Blaine. The whole hope of coming back to New York to find myself again was starting to evaporate. Lightning didn't strike twice. Instead of healing my broken heart, every corner I looked round I saw a ghost of Kerry. But that was just it. She was a ghost and, no matter how hard I was clinging on to her, I had to accept she was gone and she was never coming back.

Chapter 17

I didn't want to get out of bed. I'd been lying here for what seemed like hours. Jimmy was long gone to work. We'd got home last night and I'd got straight into bed. Crying as silently as I could, knowing the curtain wouldn't block out much noise.

I didn't want to go out today. Through the window I could see it was sunny and I knew it would be hot and stifling. But it wasn't just the weather, I knew that I wasn't emotionally up to walking into a store where someone would smile and ask me how I was today. I was liable to burst into tears because I felt terrible.

The only person I wanted to talk to that had any hope of making it better was Kerry.

'You're here,' she said, her smile lighting up when I opened the app. Her head was tilted again, and her eyes wide. I hadn't noticed before that she always tilted her head to the right when I came in, to the left when I told her something emotional, as if she needed to seem as if she was listening.

'I'm here,' I said, wondering why I still kept coming back. This wasn't real. I knew it wasn't real.

'What have you been up to? Tell me all about it.'

'I saw Theo yesterday. Your Theo.'

In the real world I would have watched her heart crack at the mention of his name, but here it didn't register. It was the first time I'd mentioned him. The AI would have to assimilate the information to try and infer her reaction about him.

'Theo,' she repeated over. 'Theo.'

'Your ex-boyfriend.'

'Hmm,' she uttered.

'I could barely speak to him.'

'How was he?'

'He looked the same as he always did. A little too cool for school. But, to be honest, he looked sad.'

She didn't say anything. She had that expectant look on her face, but how could I fill her in on their whole relationship and its aftermath? How could I sum up the years of her life that she spent worrying she'd never love someone the way she'd loved Theo?

'You look sad,' she said, breaking the silence.

For once she wasn't smiling. Her eyes didn't have their usual sparkle and the nose scrunch wasn't present.

'I am sad,' I said, letting out a deep breath. 'I'm so sad all the fucking time and I don't know how I'm not going to be.'

'Time's a great healer.'

There it was, the fortune-cookie advice. The reminder that I was talking to an AI version of my friend.

I shook my head. 'That's such bullshit.'

What was I doing? I ripped the headset off, not bothering to say goodbye today. What was the point? She wasn't really there.

I blinked a little as the dark room came into focus. I opened the curtains to the outside a little, careful not to let too much sunshine into the room.

I put on the TV and flicked through the different streaming services, trying to find something that took my fancy. I wasn't in the mood for anything funny. Or romantic. The classics were out. All of them reminded me of Kerry.

The number of times that we sat watching the movies with raging hangovers.

I shut my eyes tight, willing myself back into one of those Sundays. I could see her sitting there, eating a tub of grapes, her go-to hangover cure. *Casablanca* on the screen.

'This bit,' said Kerry, clutching her heart as Ilsa and Rick were standing on the tarmac at the airport. 'It gets me every time. They should be together.'

'I don't know,' I'd said. 'Don't you think there's something a little bit perfect about it? Better to have loved and lost and all that?'

Kerry threw a cushion at me.

'You can tell you've never properly had your heart broken and, before you mention Rupert, it doesn't count because you broke up with him. It's not the same, not even close.'

She was thinking about Theo, but I knew she didn't want to acknowledge him. She was always thinking about Theo.

'I don't know how many times I've watched this film, but every single time I want the ending to have changed.'

'But isn't that the best bit about the movies, that you can imagine your own ending? Maybe Rick and Ilsa cross paths many years later and maybe that's their time.'

'Oh, Chloe, I've run out of cushions,' she said, scouring the sofa. 'You're too optimistic and too much of a hopeless romantic. What about *Thelma and Louise*, they aren't coming back from that.'

'Maybe it was all a dream?'

'I'm not even dignifying that with an answer,' she said, throwing a grape. It hit me in my temple.

'Hey,' I said, chucking it back.

She laughed and scrunched her nose. 'I'll stop.'

'I think the problem is that you need to watch either nineties or noughties rom-coms,' I said. 'They all have happy endings and then you're not left with such angst.'

'But that's what's so wrong with them. They're too predictable. Not like the classics. They tell you what's life's really like. Painful and disappointing.'

Now it was my turn to chuck the cushion back.

I closed my eyes again, perhaps it wasn't a good idea to go back there in mind, it only intensified the guilt.

I drew back the curtains to the rest of the tiny apartment. On my way to the bathroom, I saw a note pinned to the door. I peeled it off and read it.

I'm at work, but I can come home if you need me. Text me when you get up. I'm worried about you. And if you don't want me to come home, please don't hide away in here all day. J

I smoothed the wrinkle of the paper and laid it carefully to rest on my suitcase. I took my phone from my bag and that there was a near-identical text from him there. Along with a whole string in the group chat.

NINA
Love, Love, Love the pictures from the weekend. I want a rainbow-coloured toastie!

ANDREA
That walk also looked fab! So glad you're getting out and about.

NINA
What's the plan for today????

NINA
Hello???

MARIANNE
Maybe she's up and out early today! Or snoozing late, wasn't she off to see that band last night?

NINA
Good call.

I couldn't face replying. I clicked back into my inbox and clicked on the unread message from Lila.

LILA
Hope you're okay. Call if you need me. I did mean any time. Also, quite surprised that Periscope Monkeys were actually good. We're going to see them again when they're playing next week, right?

I didn't know where to start replying to messages. I replied to Lila that I was okay, that I was grateful for the shoulder to cry on and that I'd speak to her later in the week. Then I told the girls I was off for a walk. I had plenty of photos from walks last week that I could post a picture of to make everyone think I was all right.

In reality, I was heading for a shower, and then I was going to draw the curtains and go back to bed, because right now the day seemed too hard.

Chapter 18

The next morning I'd woken early, after all the sleep the day before. I'd been keeping quiet, waiting for Jimmy to leave. Jimmy had been up for a while. I'd heard him in the bathroom and walking around the apartment, and I was counting down the minutes until he left. I stayed still, not making a sound. Waiting for him to assume I was asleep before he headed off to work.

There was a cough from the other side of the curtain. Five. Four. Three. Two. One. Any second now he'd go.

'Chloe,' he said, clearing his throat again. 'I know you're up because you're WhatsApp said you were online two minutes ago. So make sure you're decent as I'm going to open this curtain.'

Damn WhatsApp.

I leaned over and pulled the curtain before he got a chance.

'Ah, she lives,' he said, strolling past the bed and over to the window, where he opened the curtains a little. Light flooded in, but it was pleasing that it seemed a little overcast this morning, matching my mood. 'Now, I left you yesterday as I knew you were in shock, but you can't stay another day in here. It's not good for you.'

'I'm fine. I'm going to get up today.'

'Sure you are. And you are going to post more fake photos to the group chat?'

'Fake photos?'

He raised an eyebrow. 'If you'd actually gone outside yesterday, you would have known it rained all afternoon.'

I bit my lip. That would teach me for keeping the curtains shut.

'I promise today I'm going to go out.'

'You are,' he said, a sternness in his voice. 'Because we're going for a run.'

'No.' I closed my eyes and put a pillow over my face. 'We are definitely not going for a run.'

'Yeah, we are. I saw the bags. I know you've got the kit. You can't hide anything in this tiny place.'

I groaned and put a pillow further over my head.

'I don't want to go.'

'Come on, I'm not taking no for an answer. It's this, or I post to the group chat that I'm slightly concerned…'

I pulled the pillow off my head.

'You wouldn't.'

'Try me.'

Jimmy's arms were folded. He wasn't taking any prisoners.

'Fine,' I said, throwing back the comforter and heading towards the bathroom. 'I'll get changed.'

'Good,' he called. 'You're going to thank me for it.'

I didn't agree.

'Come on then,' said Jimmy, barely breaking a sweat, despite the fact that we'd been running for a good half-hour. I'd been following mainly behind him. 'Admit it.'

'I'm admitting nothing,' I said, slightly out of breath. I was pretty good at home at running, but the combination of a week off and running with Jimmy at a faster pace was tiring me out.

I was trying not to gawp at the view in front of me. The sun was burning its way through the clouds and there were pockets of blue sky threatening to break through. The change of light had lit the sky and it meant that the Statue of Liberty had come into a view at the tip of Battery Park and was starting to glow.

'I can see it on your face,' said Jimmy, turning to look at me.

'That's sweat.'

Jimmy laughed.

'All right,' I said, slowing my pace to get a better view. 'It's not a bad view, and it's good to be out of the apartment. There, happy?'

'Not really because I feel like you're going to be heading straight back to bed when we get back.'

'I promise I won't.'

'What have you got planned for today then? I can take the day off.'

'No need, I've got a full agenda planned.'

'Oh right, what is it then?'

I wanted to look for Blaine. When I'd felt this crap at home, I'd gone into the Metaverse and when I was meeting him, it instantly lifted my mood. I'd given up the best chance to find him when I'd walked out on the Periscope Monkeys gig.

'I'm going to head to a gallery. See some art.'

Jimmy was giving me a look.

'I am. I promise. I'll post pictures, from *today*.'

He was giving me that look and I could see the hesitation in his eyes.

'Okay, but you know I'll come back if you need me.'

'Yes, and Lila said the same.'

'Good. Well, in that case we need to start running a little quicker or else I'm going to be late for work. I kind of thought I wouldn't be going in.'

'Jimmy!'

He laughed and started to increase his pace.

Post-run, freshly showered and properly dressed, it felt good to be out. When I was flicking through my phone looking for the photos to fob the group chat off yesterday, it made me think about how far I'd come and how much I'd packed into the past week. I hated to admit it, but Jimmy was right, I did need to leave the apartment. I couldn't go back to the person I'd been right after Kerry died.

I headed up to Midtown, another place that was heavily populated on my map. It was already so sticky and hot out. I hugged the shade of the buildings, weaving my way through people that were far busier than I was. I reached the bottom of Union Square and I found myself gravitating to the man selling cold drinks out of a cart. I bought a bottle of water, and never had one tasted so good.

I headed into the park. It was less green and leafy than Washington Square, but it was still full of life, everyone making the most of the open space.

I stood under the shade of a tree and watched people playing chess on the little tables. I'd always loved the fact that at this park, the serious chess players brought their own tables and chairs. There was one woman who even had a parasol mounted over the two chairs.

It felt strange to think that Blaine had stood here and sat at one of these tables. I scanned, looking at who was playing.

The woman with the parasol had long purple hair that was tied in a thick braid over her shoulder, with an elaborate sun hat on her head. She caught me watching her and she beckoned me over. I shook my head back and held my hand up in thanks.

'Come on,' she bellowed. 'What have you got to lose? First game on me.'

If Kerry had been here, she would have marched up and sat down. Kerry was a terrible chess player, but an excellent bullshitter. She would have talked a good game, even if she lost in a spectacular fashion.

The woman beckoned again and I hesitated, about to shake my head again, but what did I have to lose? I wasn't in a hurry.

'Come on. I'm not getting any younger,' she said, in her thick New York accent.

A few people were looking over now and I headed to the empty seat.

'Come for the game, stay for the shade,' said the woman as I plonked myself down in the chair. 'It's hot out today.'

'Too hot,' I said, taking another drink of water.

'Do you play?'

'I did when I was younger.'

'Perfect. You be white. Your first move. Usually it's three dollars a game. I win, I keep it; you win, you get it back. First game's on the house. Let's see what you got.'

I moved a pawn forward two spaces. She did the same.

I then moved out a bishop and the woman winced.

'Should I not have done that?'

'Lessons are five dollars a game,' she said, moving a knight out.

I kept my mouth shut as I did my best to remember what all the pieces did, but I needn't have bothered as she beat me in five moves.

'I guess I saw what you got, baby doll,' said the woman.

'Yeah, I'm pretty rusty.'

I wondered what Ben from my date last week would have made of that performance.

The woman smiled and I went to get up.

'Come on, I'll give you a lesson.'

I wrinkled my nose up. 'I don't think I'm in the mood.'

The woman tipped her head back.

'I think if you waited until you were in the mood, you'd never play. Look, throw me ten dollars, we'll play two games, two lessons and we won't worry about who wins.'

'I don't know.'

I knew I was being hustled and I don't know if it was the lure of the chair and the slight shade of the parasol, or the gentle breeze, or perhaps the city working its magic, but I didn't move.

'Okay then,' she said, motioning for me to set up my side of the board.

I rearranged the chess pieces and pulled a crisp ten-dollar note out of my wallet.

'And now the real game begins,' said the woman.

I left the park feeling a little lighter, and much poorer. The woman with the purple hair had definitely hustled me, but in some ways the company and the shade had definitely been worth it.

I pulled my phone out of my pocket and sent a photo to the group chat that I'd taken of me at the game. I couldn't help feeling a tiny bit proud. I might have lost at 11 games of chess, but at least I'd played. I looked at today's message from Lila checking in, and instead of typing back, I hit 'Call'.

'Oh, my God, I am so glad to hear from you. Wait, you are there, aren't you? You didn't dial me from your pocket?' Lila didn't even pause for breath.

'I deliberately called, and I am here.'

'Oh, I'm so happy. So, you okay after the other night? I'm so sorry, introducing you to that guy.'

'Don't be silly,' I said, crossing with the throngs of others when the walk sign appeared. I needed to walk on the shady side of the street. 'You weren't to know.'

'I know. But still. I wish you'd told me about your friend before.'

'It's actually been nice, you not knowing. I know no one means anything by it, but just having everyone treat me with kid gloves...'

There's a pause on the other end of the phone.

'I get that. We don't have to talk about it. We can carry on talking about Blaine and about appletinis all you want.'

'Thanks.'

'And I promise I won't even mention again that I'm here if you do want to talk about it.'

'I appreciate that,' I said, trying not to get distracted by the donut shop across the road. It was sweet that she'd joined the girls on our group chat with the concern, but I did wonder if it was going to change things now that she knew.

'So what are you up to?'

'I'm heading to the Whitney; you know, Blaine loves art and it's on the map.'

'Oh, you must go to the Chelsea Market round the corner. Go to Los Tacos, get the cactus quesadilla and don't think about the fact you're eating cactus. It's amazing.'

I pulled a face, not too sure about that.

'Honestly. Do it. You'll thank me for it. It's the Mexican version of that deli you took me to last week.'

'Okay, I'll take a look.'

'Good. And then we should make more plans to meet up. Obviously, I'm in for more Periscope Monkeys next week, where I will not be accosting any more random strangers. But that's ages away, so how about something this week? I'm free tomorrow night.'

'I've got a date.'

'Shut up! From the app? I love it.'

'Yeah. He's not such a match on paper, but you never know.'

'Exactly. Okay, so if Wednesday's out, how about Friday? We usually get off work a bit earlier in the summer on Friday afternoon, as so many people go out to the Hamptons.'

I reached the end of the block and stopped, waiting for the lights to change. The stop-start nature of the walking in New York always got to me.

'Yeah, Friday's good.'

'Perfect. I'll send a car for you.'

'I don't always need picking up.'

'I know,' she said, 'but we're heading uptown and there's no way I'm getting on the subway when it's so hot out, and it would be rude me turning up in a car when I'd be driving past Jimmy's.'

'Fair,' I said, nodding.

'Right, I've got a meeting in ten and I've got to eat. You'll update me on the date?'

'Of course. Speak again.'

She said her goodbyes and we hung up. The light finally changed and I headed across the street, carrying on walking. My heart felt a little lighter. It was starting to sink in that it wasn't all about the big things. Sitting down to play chess. Heading to a food market for quesadillas. Going to an art gallery. The point was I was leaving the house. This time yesterday I couldn't face it, but today I could and I was proud. It didn't mean to say that I was over my grief, but I was learning to live with it. Riding the storm. Sheltering when needed and breaking free during the gaps in the clouds. All I could hope for was that those gaps in the clouds lasted for longer and longer each time.

Chapter 19

I'd been in New York for a whole week and it was whizzing by. I'd spent the day working in one of the office spaces in Jimmy's building, looking over the view of the East River and Brooklyn. For once work felt personal. I was trying to write a workshop for people to coach themselves, and I was the guinea pig testing it out.

My goal was to find Blaine and I needed to push myself to go through my action plan to make that happen. The match on the dating app with Alex had come at a timely moment. I'd been unsure whether to carry on after speed-dating Ryan, but his rule of one in three gave me hope that it could be third time lucky.

Not wanting to catch my date finishing up with his last one, I arrived fashionably late and was shown to my table. We'd picked a restaurant in Seaport, not far from where I was staying. The cobbled street of the gentrified docks gave the whole area a Disney feel to it, with flashy boutiques and restaurants. My date had suggested a restaurant on one of the piers, and I was grateful after the last pretentious place that this one was full of comfortable outdoor sofas and laid-back beach-club vibes, with colourful umbrellas and strings of bulb lights strung up.

My table was empty and I resisted the temptation to look around too much in case I spotted another speed-date situation. I ordered a glass of Malbec from the server and tried to look out at the boats and the water beyond.

'Hi,' said a voice.

I looked up at the man standing in front of me. He didn't look like he'd stepped fresh out of an advert like Ben had, but he was cute.

'I'm so sorry I'm late. The traffic was horrific but,' he held his hands up, 'it's all good. I'm here now.'

He sat down opposite me.

'Where are my manners? I'm Alex. You must be Cat.'

'Chloe, actually. I use Cat... it's a nickname.'

He looked at me quizzically before he nodded.

'Chloe, that's um, okay.' There was something unreadable on his face. I didn't think it was that big a deal to have used the nickname, the nickname that I'd hoped would hook in Blaine. 'And you're British?'

'Uh-huh.'

He nodded again.

'Right, right. Do you want a drink? I think I need one,' he tugged at the collar of his T-shirt. 'Can I get a drink?'

The server put my wine down. 'What can I get you?'

'What are you drinking?' He turned from the server to me and inspected my glass.

'A glass of Malbec.'

He bit his lip. 'I'm not sure if that's what I want. I might need a couple of minutes,' he said to the server. He picked up a menu, reading it with one hand, tapping the edge of the arm rests with his other hand.

He was agitated in the way that Kiran would get if I ever conducted a coaching session in the office, overflowing with nervous energy.

He couldn't be more unlike Blaine if he tried. Blaine in the Metaverse was laid back and composed and... a thought began to take hold, my brain searching for a reason for his nerves. What if he was Blaine and he'd started to clock the details of me? The name being Cat, the English accent.

'Are you okay?' I said, testing the water.

'Yeah, I'm fine. Fine,' he said, repeating himself in what seemed like a bid to make himself believe it. 'I'm fine. Are you okay?'

'Uh-huh,' I said, deliberately slow and calm, trying to highlight the difference. 'What are you going to get to drink?'

'I'm not sure. Not sure at all. Um. What should I drink?' he was scanning the menu and it was if he couldn't latch on. 'What should I drink? That was actually a question.'

'My wine is excellent, but if you're not into wine, how about a beer? They've got a good selection of craft beers.'

'Okay,' he said, almost with relief, putting down the menu. 'That sounds good.'

I signalled for the server again and put in an order.

'So, what do you do, Alex?'

'I'm an architect.'

'Oh,' I said, taken a little aback. 'What kind?'

'I'm a green-space architect. I design the outdoor spaces, plazas and squares, the bits around new developments. Fountains, trees, walkways.'

'That's actually pretty cool,' I said, having never thought that was someone's job. 'I'd always thought those bits got done almost as an afterthought.'

Alex laughed. 'So do most architects I work with. But I like to think it's what shapes the space and the transition to the building. And certainly, in a city with so many skyscrapers that it's difficult to see the buildings at street level, the first impression you get is the outdoor space.'

He was starting to relax. He was finding the familiarity and comfort in a safe topic, exactly what I had been coaxing Kiran to do.

'Ah, oh,' he said, exhaling. 'I did not expect this to be so hard. I'm sorry. This is my first date for a long time and then you show up and start talking and...' He laughed a little. 'My ex always ribbed me for having a thing for British women. Gillian Anderson.'

He put his hand over his chest.

'I get that. Gillian Anderson is amazing, and beautiful.'

'Isn't she? Oh, and then when you start talking like her,' he shook his head. 'My ex would get a real kick out of this.'

I take it back. This was the most animated and relaxed I'd seen him since he got here. Talking about his ex.

The server put his drink on the table.

'Cheers,' I said, raising my glass.

'Cheers,' he said, clinking back.

'I take it your break-up was recent?' I sipped at my drink.

He winced a little. 'How could you tell?'

'Oh, I don't know.' I gave him a sympathetic look.

'We broke up last month. I proposed. She said she wasn't sure.'

I winced back. 'I'm sorry.

He shrugged. 'Yeah. She didn't want to break up, but I couldn't see the point. I was all in and she wasn't.'

I couldn't help feeling for his ex.

'Maybe that's not true. Marriage is a big thing. Committing the rest of your life to one person. It's not a decision that people should take lightly.'

'I know,' he said, practically downing his drink without a flinch. 'But I knew almost from our first date that she was the one.'

My mind drifted to Jimmy. That's how I'd felt after my first date with him. I'd sat on my bed, deep in text conversation with Kerry, trying to describe to her the fizz of excitement coursing round my veins, the relief of having found someone that I didn't need to try with. I'd fallen for him so quickly and the irony wasn't lost on me that it fell apart just as quickly.

'The trouble is,' I said, trying to forget about Jimmy, 'life isn't always that simple. Maybe there was something else holding her back. If she didn't want to break up with you, maybe she just needed time.'

He shook his head. 'I don't want someone to have to think. I want someone to know.'

His voice was raw.

'But we shouldn't be talking about my ex,' he said, with a shake of his head. 'She told me expressly not to.'

'You talked to your ex about going on the date?'

'Uh-huh. Oh, God, that's weird, isn't it? I know it's not normal.'

I couldn't help biting my lip.

'I'm not one to talk, I've come over to New York and I've ended up staying with my ex.'

His eyes widened. 'Oh, really? What happened with you guys, why did you break up?'

I let out a deep sigh. How did I explain it without telling him the whole story?

'Timing,' I said, with a few little nods and a sad smile. 'Life isn't always simple.'

I took hold of my drink, not sure if it was that or the thoughts that were making me feel sick to the stomach.

'I get the impression that neither of us should be on this date,' he said.

I took a sip of my wine. 'You're probably right. I was just trying to find this guy that I'd met, Blaine.'

I dropped it in, just on the very off chance.

'What kind of a name is Blaine?'

'At this point I have no idea,' I said.

I looked around the bar, at the groups of people having fun.

'Do you want to just talk about Gillian Anderson until we finish the drinks?'

He sighed with relief. 'Yes. I'll start if you like with a controversial hot take that she sounds better as an American than she does as British.'

'What?' I snapped.

'Scully was my first love,' he said, picking up his drink.

I cracked a laugh. He was wrong, but the more he tried to convince me, the more I warmed to him. He wasn't Blaine and I was 99 per cent certain he was going to get back together with his ex when he left, but at least this wasn't the worst of the three dates I'd been on.

It was just after 8.30 pm when I arrived back at Jimmy's. I'd expected him to be playing pickleball, but he was rooting around the apartment when I arrived home. I'm not sure at what point over the last week that things between Jimmy and I had stopped being awkward, but I was pleased to see him.

'Hey,' I said, slipping my shoes off and hanging up my bag.

'Hey, yourself. Good day?' He was stuffing clothes into a big sack.

'Yeah, how about you? No pickleball tonight?'

'No. I still have a bit of a twinge in my shoulder and thought I wouldn't risk it. I'm about to catch up on laundry instead. I just need to find the *detergent*,' he said, putting on a terrible American accent. His wince matched mine. 'Sorry, that was truly dire. But here we are.'

He pulled a bottle out of the cupboard next to the bathroom and slung a sack over his back as if he was doing a Santa impression.

'Do you need anything washed?'

'Actually, I do.'

He swung the bag down and opened up the drawstring. 'Shove it in.'

'It's okay, I'll come down. I've got quite a bit.'

I headed over to the recess where my case was still resting, and took out the packing bags that I'd put my dirty clothes in. The lack of space meant I'd had to be quite organised and methodical.

'Awesome. I'm secretly pleased.'

'What, that you don't have to do my washing?'

'No, that you're coming down there with me. That place is so much better with two people.'

'Is it scary or something?' I asked, following him out of the room.

'It's so much better than that.'

We walked into the laundry room and I gasped in surprise. I knew exactly why Jimmy was pleased that I'd joined him. It had nothing to do with the fact that he wasn't quite sure how to separate his wash, and everything to do with the fact that in the laundry room was a full-size ping-pong table, a row of arcade machines and a pool table.

'No wonder you like living in New York.'

'I know, right? I want to live in here.' He went over to one of the machines to start loading up the washing and I followed suit. I could imagine how easy it would be to get distracted playing and forgetting to do the laundry. 'But if I stay, I'll have to find my own accommodation.'

'Bummer.'

'That's why I'm making the most of it.'

I pulled out a rogue red T-shirt from his wash of white work shirts before he slammed the door shut and I put it in my mixed load of colours.

'Best of three on the ping-pong table.'

'Are we sure that's where we want to start?' I put my hands on my hips. 'Me and racquet sports?'

'Good point, although I think I might be safe at this end of the table.' He must have clocked me pulling a face. 'Or we could start with the arcade game. Two-player Street Fighter.'

'Now you're talking,' I said, taking up a position behind a joystick.

The familiar tinkle of the nineties music took me right back to playing it with Nina.

'You're pretty good at this,' I said, hitting his character with a roundhouse kick.

'Misspent youth,' he said, 'I was obsessed with this game.'

'Wasn't everyone?' I said, thinking of the time that Blaine and I had had a whole conversation about who was the coolest character to be. 'Do you always play Ryu?' I asked, staring so much at the character that Blaine always said he played.

'Always. Gotcha,' he said, doing a K.O.

'Round two?' I asked.

'Why not? I've got time,' he said, as the characters got ready to fight again.

'Take it easy with that joystick, I thought your shoulder was twingeing.'

'Ah,' he said lifting his shoulders up and letting them fall. 'This seems to be fine.'

There was something in his voice that made me think that there was nothing wrong with his shoulder.

'Are you avoiding pickleball for another reason?'

'Why would you say that?' he said, focusing hard on the game. He was biting his tongue as he always did in concentration.

'Oh, I don't know, because you seem borderline obsessed with it, and yet you're at home doing laundry and I'm pretty sure it would be less strenuous on your shoulder than this.'

He toned down how hard he was hitting the buttons.

'I just needed a bit of a rest,' he said.

There was more to it, but we were still forging a path to friendship and I wasn't sure how far I could push any more.

'Yes!' I did a victorious air pump as my character triumphed.

'This is the match that counts then,' he said, fixing a look on his face.

I held his gaze, trying to narrow my eyes. It reminded me of the times we played dominoes, the competitiveness getting the better of us.

'It's on.'

We didn't talk as our hands moved with the joystick-and-button combinations flooding back to me from childhood and as we kicked and punched each other on screen, I couldn't help but giggle.

We played three tournaments, all of which Jimmy had lost by the time the washing machine had finished.

'I just don't think it's a good idea,' I said, picking up a table-tennis paddle.

'Come on! At this point I'll do anything to restore my self-respect.'

I pointed at his shoulder and he rubbed at it, doing a few rotations.

'Perhaps Street Fighter loosened it a bit.'

'Uh-huh.'

He tapped the ball over to my side and I almost took out the Street Fighter machine as I attempted to send the ball back to him.

'Gentle! You're trying to hit a ping-pong ball across a two-metre gap, not send a golf ball 300 yards down a fairway.'

He picked it up and tried again, making a point of sending it gently across the table.

We eased into a rhythm of hitting it towards each other, and there was something almost therapeutic about it.

'Oh, I heard from Sienna today and she said her dry cleaner got the drink stain out of her dress.'

'That's good news,' I said, still feeling guilty about how I ruined everyone's night on Sunday. 'I still feel bad that I didn't get to speak to her properly. She seemed nice.'

'She is.'

We hit the ball back and forth a little.

'What's she like? Other than the fact that she's young and goes out late?' I asked.

He hit the ball back to me. 'She's fun and she's good at pickleball.'

'Of course she is,' I said, as I missed the ball and I had to jog over the other side of the room to get it.

'It's not serious,' he said, as I hit it his way. 'We're not... She's dating other people.'

'Oh, that's um... modern.'

The ball hit him and he caught it in his hand. 'It's a pretty big thing over here to be exclusive.'

He hit the ball towards me.

'I don't get it,' I said, focusing with all my might to hit a backhand shot, only to miss. I went to retrieve the ball, thinking of Ryan and his speed-dating antics, but it was Alex's words that I thought of. 'If I'm dating someone, I want to be all in.'

I sent the ball to Jimmy and he hit it back faster than normal.

'The trouble is, sometimes the other person doesn't want to be.'

I batted it back with a little too much force and it caused Jimmy to stumble. I hadn't meant to, but it hit me hard that he wanted something more from Sienna and she was the one keeping him at arm's length. Of course, Jimmy would want to be all in. He was one of the good guys.

There was a lull in the conversation and it was as if neither of us knew what to say next.

'You know I've been staring at this ping-pong table for months, wanting to play with someone, but I've never been down here at the same time as anyone else. They all put their laundry in and collect it later.'

'That's madness.'

I didn't want to tempt fate by alerting him to it, but we'd been hitting a rally that had gone over 20 so far.

'You're actually pretty good at table tennis,' he said in surprise.

'Do you think? I haven't played in ages. Not since Kerry dragged me to that bar in Clapham.'

I steeled my heart for the memory to cause my chest to burn, but a different emotion hit me instead.

'Was that the time you went axe throwing?'

I laughed out loud. The memory of us, after far too many glasses of Prosecco, trying to land the axe anywhere near the board.

'That was the time. I kind of think we should have started with that activity rather than ended with it. I also think,' I said, screwing up my face the more I thought about it, 'that they shouldn't have served alcohol near the axes.'

'Advice for life, right there.'

'Absolutely.'

Jimmy's head was tilted and he was smiling at me.

'What?' I asked, rubbing at my face self-consciously.

'Nothing. I was just thinking that it was nice to hear you talk about Kerry.'

'Hmm,' I said. It didn't come without its pain, but he was right, it felt nice to share in the happy memories and it felt almost heart-warming rather than heart-breaking.

There was a buzzing noise on the washing machines.

'Laundry's done,' he said. 'I'm thinking we stick them in the dryer and then have a go at pool?'

'Now I know you just want your arse kicked,' I said. I had little hand-eye co-ordination for racquet sports, but I was a mean pool player for reasons that I'd never been able to fathom.

'Oh, that's fighting talk, Chlo,' he said, pointing at me as he headed to pick up a pool cue. 'And I like it.'

I laughed, my cheeks starting to ache from the smiling. Who knew laundry could be so much fun? But I knew it wasn't the laundry room, it was spending time with Jimmy. It was the first time that we'd been in the same room where I didn't catch a look of pity, or have him constantly asking if I was okay. It was just us being us. A little kernel of hope was starting to grow, the idea that it might not just be lip service, that we could actually be friends.

Chapter 20

I'd settled into more of a rhythm in New York. I was trying to split my time between work and finding Blaine. Mornings were spent working on the training ideas and in the afternoons I picked an area of the map to explore. Each had been productive in its own way. I'd managed to develop what I thought was a new coaching model that I could see working well in a workshop. For the first time in a long while, I was excited about working on something innovative. And whilst my afternoons might not have produced any new leads finding Blaine, I had discovered areas of New York that I'd never seen before and sampled food that I felt could be some of the best the city had to offer.

Only this afternoon there was no time for exploring, as Lila was taking me somewhere.

'When you said you'd send a car, I didn't expect you to send a limo. What is this thing?' I said, marvelling at the leather interior of the limousine.

'Our company has it on a retainer. It's not a proper stretch. It's smaller, better suited to the city.'

'It's massive.'

'You get used it,' she said with almost a yawn. 'So come on, you barely gave me an update of the date on Wednesday.'

'There was really nothing to tell. The guy was far too into his ex.'

'Those pesky exes that people can't get out of their mind, right? Speaking of exes, how's it going with Jimmy? I'm guessing well, or else you'd have moved into a hotel by now.'

'We really don't see much of each other. He's at work most of the time and then he has activities.'

I thought back to the laundry room and our evening playing games. Whilst I was still waiting to see if I'd ever get any of my money back, the only good thing coming out of that whole scam was staying with Jimmy. Had I not been staying with him, I probably would have met up with him once or twice, but getting to spend time together in the in-between moments of life, during the mundane laundry or the rush in the mornings, we were rekindling our friendship.

I looked at the passing windows as we crawled up Fifth Avenue. The shops getting fancier, and people walking with shopping bags with the string handles rather than plastic.

'I know how that goes,' said Lila. 'Ironically, I think I used to see more of Anthony before I lived with him. Back in the days when we'd have to schedule our dates.'

'It sounds like you should still do that.'

'I know, I should. It's crazy. My parents ate dinner together every single night and curled up on the couch together.'

'That sounds lovely,' I said, caught up in that Disney fantasy. I couldn't imagine my parents cuddling up on the sofa. My mum never sat still for long enough.

'Yeah, it was pretty sickening. But I just kind of expected that, when we moved in together and when we got married, we'd sort of morph into that, but we've never really found our groove with it.'

'I wouldn't pretend to be a relationship expert,' I said, 'but I think that's the misconception. The idea that if you're really in love, that will conquer all, but it's hard work. I know it probably didn't look like it with your parents, but they showed up to that couch every night. They cuddled.'

'Hmm, arduous,' she said, laughing, but she sighed. 'You're right though. What were you and Jimmy like when you were together?'

'Well, we didn't live together, or at least not officially.' I thought of how much time we spent at each other's flats. 'Spending time with each other wasn't the problem for us. We saw each other a lot, maybe too much, and I didn't have time for anyone else.'

I let out a deep breath.

Lila didn't say anything, she didn't have to. She reached over and squeezed my hand.

I looked out of the window.

'Where are we heading?'

'The Met,' she said, matter of fact.

'The actual Met?' I asked, almost wishing it was Cloisters so I'd have that link to Blaine.

'Yeah, I booked us a table at the Balcony Bar. Anthony and I are members, and the food is really good. Plus, if we fancy it, the roof garden is open and they have sculpture exhibits that you can walk round.'

'Culture and food, now you're talking.'

The car didn't take long to whisk us up to the Met. Lila flashed her pass and got us in. The Met had been one of the few cultural things I'd done when I'd spent my year here. It reminded me of the British Museum, with the architecture and the unexpected nature of what you found within the walls. One minute you were in New York, the next you were in an Egyptian temple. The whole experience was as close as possible to being in the Metaverse in real life; in that moment, you could travel in an instant.

But there was no time to see the impressive Egyptian Temple today, Lila marched us straight up to the bar and we were shown to our table.

'This is the best place to sit,' said Lila, leaning over her menu and lowering her voice, but not so much that the people on the other side of us couldn't hear us.

I looked over the stone railing and down into the atrium below.

'It's great for people watching,' she added.

'It's amazing. This place is packed. How did you get a table?'

I watched the people zig-zagging below, not knowing where to start. People from all walks of life, from those who looked like obvious tourists to those that had native New Yorker written all over them.

'Up here's for members only and we have a couples membership.'

'Do you and Anthony come here often?'

'We try and catch the music on a Friday night once a month. They do a classical concert up here every week.'

'So you do schedule some things.'

'Yeah, I guess we do,' she said. 'Just not often enough.'

'We're all guilty of that. But the good thing is you've noticed, and you can do something about it.'

'I guess so.'

'Can I get you ladies a drink?' the waiter asked, coming up to the table.

I glanced down at the menu, my eyes flicking between the different options.

'I'll just get an iced tea,' said Lila.

'I'll have one too,' I said, relieved not to have to make a decision.

'Do you need a couple of minutes for food?'

I looked over at the top of the menu at Lila, expecting her to have rolled her eyes, but her face had softened.

'That would be appreciated,' she said instead. The waiter headed off to get the drinks and she leaned over the table and pointed.

'It's all good, but the poke bowl is my favourite, and the quinoa salad is a pretty good second.'

I smiled and nodded, my eyes still flitting with indecisiveness. It all sounded so good. 'How did you meet Anthony?'

'Now that,' she said, pointing at me, 'is a very good question. And I love to tell this story. In fact, it almost reminds me of your story.'

'My story?'

'Yep. You and Blaine. I once spent a weekend playing Halo with a guy in Arizona, and I flew to Phoenix a month later.'

'And?'

'Um, we hung out and spent the weekend playing Halo in his apartment.'

'Oh.'

'Yeah. Not the love story you were expecting. But when I landed, there was bad weather coming in and loads of flights were cancelled, making it almost impossible to get a cab. I met Anthony in the line waiting for one and, when we figured out we were only a few blocks from each other, we shared a ride.'

'That's really cute.'

'That's not the end of the story, or even the start. It was purely a cab ride. But I ran into him at a market a week or so later. And then again at a bodega. We slowly cottoned on to the fact that the universe was trying to tell us something.'

'Ah, the universe.'

'She moves in mysterious ways,' she said, holding her hands up as if to praise the sky. 'I'm a huge believer that everyone comes into your life for a reason. Like us meeting on the plane.'

Our food got placed in front of us and I couldn't help thinking she was right, that it was meant to be.

'If we hadn't met, I'd certainly not have had three of the craziest dates of my life.'

Lila tipped her head back, laughing.

'They are great stories. Have you got any more planned?'

'I honestly don't think I can face it. It was a nice idea, but I think the chances of finding Blaine on an app were pretty slim to none.'

Lila nodded, as she finished chewing her mouthful.

'Out of all the plans we came up with on the plane, that was the biggest long shot, and probably a result of the champagne bar I found at the airport, not to mention the glass from that flight attendant to celebrate our good news.'

'What? I can't believe you talked me into that.'

She shrugged. 'I never actually expected you to sign up the next day. That was impressive and gutsy. You kind of became my new hero. You're a pretty impressive woman, Chloe. You're so brave.'

'I'm not brave,' I said shaking my head.

'Um? You set up your own business. You flew across the Atlantic to find Blaine. You're rebuilding your life after losing your friend. Chloe, you're more than brave.'

My eyes started to glisten.

'Now, speaking of the universe and her plans. We need to see if we can figure out how to find your Blaine if you're no longer going to date. I don't suppose you've got the map with you?'

'I haven't, but I think over the last ten days I've covered most of the areas heavily populated with dots.'

'We must be missing something,' she said, stabbing her fork into her food. 'It's a long shot that you'd run into him at one of the restaurants he mentioned, or a park he once played chess in. The

Periscope Monkeys nights are good ideas, I just wish we had more of those. Are there any other bands he mentioned?'

I'd racked my brains so many times trying to think of clues to what he'd said over our dates. The trouble was I'd been caught up in the moment. I wasn't trying to remember every single second.

'The only other thing that I can remember him mentioning that he was going to was this jazz festival, there's one this weekend, then again in August. But before you get excited, I looked at tickets and they're all sold out.'

'Deco Jazz?'

'That's the one.'

'I went once when Anthony and I were first dating.' She put her hand to her chest. 'It was dreamy and romantic. That's the perfect place to find him.'

'Um, it's sold out,' I said, slower in case she missed it.

She waved her hand and picked up the phone from the table and tapped before putting it to her ear.

'Anthony's company always has tickets to stuff like that. Hey, Helly,' she said, into the phone. 'I need some tickets to the Deco Jazz festival for tomorrow… Four… or two if four's too many. Uh-huh, yeah, see how you go. Thanks Hel.' She put the phone down and went back to her elbow leaning. 'Anthony's PA's going to see what she can do. She'll text me if she can get them.'

'Really?'

'Yep, she'll come through with the four tickets. She's a wonder, that woman. You can bring Jimmy for Anthony to hang out with whilst we're scouting for Blaine.

'Now all you'll need to do is work out what you're going to wear.'

'What I'm going to wear?'

'It's twenties-themed. Everyone goes full flapper and the men are all in braces.' She clapped her hands together, well and truly galvanised.

'And I need this by tomorrow?' I pulled a face. This sounded like the kind of outfit that was weeks in the planning.

'Oh, Chloe. Your face. We're in New York, we'll have you ready in no time.'

Chapter 21

I stepped out of the bathroom, pulling at the silk dress that Lila had chosen for me. The silk felt cool against my body, thanks to the air conditioning and I shivered.

Jimmy whistled and I found myself crossing my arms over my chest. He might have seen me naked countless times, but in this I felt more exposed.

It was such a beautiful dress. It had beading, and I had feathers in my headdress.

It was the most elegant dress I'd ever worn.

'Do I look silly?'

'Quite the opposite,' he said, holding my gaze a little too long before he coughed and looked down.

'You better get your braces on or else we'll be in danger of missing the ferry.'

The jazz festival was on a tiny island in the harbour between Manhattan and Brooklyn and we needed to take the timed ferry that was listed on our ticket.

'So kind of Lila to get me a costume too,' he said, tucking in his shirt.

'She was in her absolute element,' I said.

He started to try and clip on the braces. He tried to reach around the back.

'Here,' I said, putting my handbag on the counter. I went over and started to attach the small clips to the back of his waistband. He smelt good. A different aftershave from the one he usually wore, it was mustier and there was an orangey hint of bergamot. I was trying to identify what else it smelt of, when I realised I'd clipped the braces on and yet my hands were lingering on his waistband. 'You're all set,' I said, tapping him on the back.

He picked a flat cap off the counter and turned around, and for a split second he reminded me of Noah from *The Notebook* and I almost swooned in real life.

'What? Do I look silly?' he asked, echoing me. 'In my head I'm looking all *Peaky Blinders*.'

'Oh, well,' I managed to recover myself. 'You don't look *that* cool.'

'But you admit I look a little bit cool?' He pointed at me. 'I'll take that. Right, let's get on this ferry.'

The ferry had the kind of party-boat buzz to it, where everyone was dressed up and excited for the day ahead, and that buzz only grew when we got on the island.

Lila and Anthony were waiting for us as we debarked, Helly having been unable to get us tickets all on the same ferry. Lila's dress was incredible and, unlike the dress that Sienna had claimed was vintage, hers actually was. The beading was unlike anything I'd ever seen, with black silk tassels, and she had a little hat on.

'You look stunning,' I said, leaning over and giving her a hug.

'You too. I told you it would look awesome with your hair like that.'

She touched at the way I'd tucked my hair under itself to create an almost textured bob.

'This,' said a man stepping forward, 'was an inspired idea. Thank you for suggesting it.' He took my hand and shook it.

'This is Anthony,' said Lila. I shook his hand and marvelled at quite how tall he was. He had a pinstriped suit on and a boater hat. He had kind eyes and a warm smile and was nothing like the fierce business man I thought he was going to be. 'This is Chloe and Jimmy.'

'Pleasure to meet you both,' he said, doing a firm handshake and a slap on the back. 'Now, Helly got us VIP tickets, which include a hamper of food. Let's go find it.'

He held out his cane, and I raised an eyebrow to Jimmy. He raised his back and we followed them along.

'Look, Anthony, they've got a photo booth.'

They had a set of wooden photo booths and there was a small queue attached.

'We can do it later. We should get a spot on the grass and get the food. Then we can take it in turns to get photos.'

'He is such a killjoy,' she said, 'but probably right. Why don't you two get your photo taken whilst we sort the picnic?'

'Us?' said Jimmy.

'Go now whilst the line is short,' she said, steering us over to it.

'I guess we're having our photo taken.'

'I guess we are,' said Jimmy. 'I can't believe some of these costumes. They've put a lot more effort in than in any fancy-dress party we've ever been to.'

'Is this your way of mentioning the Geri Halliwell costume again?'

'Always,' he said, 'although the dress you're wearing isn't a bad one.'

I touched at the beading, feeling a little flattered.

'It does really feel like we're at one of Gatsby's parties,' he said.

'Doesn't it?' I almost shrieked. There was something about how they'd decorated the grounds, from vintage stalls and cars to the old-fashioned ice-cream carts, that made it feel as if we'd travelled back in time.

We shuffled along in the queue and found ourselves at the front. We headed into a booth and there was a tiny chair.

I squeezed in, wedging myself into a corner with half a bum cheek so that Jimmy could get in the other side. There was a big sign telling us to pose four different ways as every shot would be different. Just like the photo machines used to be.

'Ready,' I said, pushing the button before I tried to lean back into the seat, smiling for the camera as it made a noise.

A black-and-white cinema countdown came on the screen, counting down to the next one in 5 – 4...

'I think that we need to do something different,' I said, in a slight panic. There wasn't time to swap seats or to get too creative.

3 – 2...

'Jazz hands,' I shouted and lifted my hands up, and I think Jimmy got half a hand up before it flashed and there was a big mechanical noise, before the countdown began again.

'Pull a funny face,' said Jimmy putting his hands in his mouth before puffing his cheeks out. I did my best to copy him only as I turned to Jimmy, he widened his expression and I started to slip off the seat as I started to laugh. Flash.

'Here,' said Jimmy, guiding me on to his knee and the moment caught me by surprise so that I forgot about the camera and the noise startled me as it went off.

I didn't go to move at first. My heart was starting to pound.

'Next,' shouted the woman outside and slowly the spell was broken. I shuffled off Jimmy and we headed back outside to wait for the photos.

'It'll take a minute,' the woman said, and we stood to the side. Jimmy was about as far away from me as he could be as we waited for the photos.

'There you go,' said the woman, handing us a strip of prints.

I'd forgotten the magic of getting photos that you hadn't seen digitally. The first couple of pictures were okay, the third one looked as if we were having fun. But the fourth one looked as if they'd caught something that I couldn't explain. The two of us were looking straight at one another and I almost didn't recognise the wide smile on my face.

I handed them to Jimmy and he started to laugh.

'I think that one's my favourite,' he said, pointing at the bottom one.

'You can have that one then,' I said. It almost hurt to look at it. 'I'll have the one above.'

'The one where I'm pulling that face. Oh, that's flattering.'

I popped them in my handbag and we drifted over towards the picnic area, where I spotted Lila in the distance.

We weaved around the blankets with the most elaborate food platters that I'd ever seen. There were tubs of exotic-looking food and grazing boards that put my usual supermarket meal-deal idea of a picnic to shame.

'I can't believe how much effort everyone's made,' said Jimmy.

'I know. I feel a little bit underdressed.' Lila patted down her vintage outfit.

The first of the bands started to play and there was a cheer from the crowd. A few people hurried past us towards the front, where they started to dance.

'You guys are just in time,' said Anthony, putting the last of the charcuterie out onto a board from the hamper, our spread now rivalling any other picnic on the lawn.

'I'm starving,' said Jimmy, sitting down and immediately launching into the stack of crackers and cheese.

'I meant for the dancing.' Anthony stood up and held out his hand towards Lila. 'Shall we?'

Lila looked between him and us and stood up.

'Are you guys coming too?'

'We'll dance the next one,' said Jimmy, batting his cracker-laden hand in front of his face.

Satisfied, they headed off.

'We'll dance the next one?' I asked, watching the energetic Charleston dancing taking place on the dance floor. There was no way I was co-ordinated enough for that.

'No, of course we won't, but I get the impression that your friend Lila wouldn't have left if I'd said no.'

We watched them on the edge of the grass, Anthony taking her hand and them dancing back and forward to one another.

'They're pretty good at it,' said Jimmy.

'I know. I'm definitely not going up now.'

I started to tuck into some of the olives, transfixed by the dancers and the big ten-piece band playing behind.

'Well, this isn't where I thought I'd be spending my Saturday afternoon,' Jimmy said.

'Listening to jazz. A bit different from the last festival we went to,' I said, thinking back to when we'd gone with Andrea and Henry to a festival in the Cotswolds. It was such a daze of glorious heat, upset bellies and far too much booze. I left with blisters, sleep deprivation and a hangover that lasted days. Not to mention that I dropped my new phone into one of the Portaloos, never to be seen again.

'The phone,' I said, and we both winced.

'I think I could get used to this kind of festival, though. A little bit of prosciutto, a little bit of melon,' he said, demonstrating and popping them in his mouth.

'It's the dream.'

Jimmy was lying on the grass with his head propped up on his elbow. I leaned back on my arms and tipped my head back, closing my eyes. The sun was warming my face and the jazz music drifted over the top.

'Oh, you guys,' said Lila, sitting down on the rug. 'You have to come up there. It's a riot.'

Anthony plonked himself behind Lila and started to open the bottle of fizz from the cooler.

'I'm sure it's busier than the last time we came.'

'It was pretty busy then too.'

'You've been before?' asked Jimmy.

'Yeah,' said Anthony. 'Maybe six years ago? We said then that we'd come every year.'

'But then the pandemic...'

'And I guess we forgot. I'm grateful to Chloe for suggesting it.'

'Ah, so it was your idea and here was me blaming Lila,' said Jimmy, pinging his braces.

'Quit your moaning.' Lila handed him a glass that she'd just poured. 'You look cute and you know it.'

Pink crept over Jimmy's cheeks. I took the drink, not wanting to agree too much. He did look cute.

'What else have you got planned while you're over, Chloe?' asked Anthony. 'Lila was saying you leave next week?'

'Tuesday evening,' I said, my heart already a little heavy. The days were going too quickly. Two weeks in New York sounded like plenty but I was now over halfway through. 'I've not got too much planned. I'm going to see Periscope Monkeys again, and tomorrow I was thinking of going to Roosevelt Island.'

'I can't believe you go Tuesday,' said Lila, pulling an exaggerated sad face.

'You should change your flights,' said Jimmy.

Lila clapped her hands and did a little yelp. 'That's exactly what you should do.'

'I can't. I have work. And a life back home.'

I tried not to think of my flat and how grey the walls were and how small it had seemed since I stopped going out.

'But I have had a great time,' I said, thinking about how much I'd crammed into the last few days. 'And it's not over yet. I've still got plenty of time left and I'm determined to do as much as possible.'

'Like check out the rest of the festival,' said Lila, almost with a wink. I knew what she was insinuating. Here amongst the revellers somewhere could be Blaine. 'But before you do that, you've got to do the dancing. There's a beginners' class starting in a couple of minutes. You two should go.'

'I think we're fine here,' said Jimmy.

'If there's something for free, you should take it,' said Anthony, throwing an olive into his mouth.

'Come on, you can't come all the way here and stay Superglued to the blanket,' said Lila. She clapped her hands. 'Chop chop!'

I looked at Jimmy and he looked back at me. I went to plead with my eyes to Lila, but the look on her face was brutal and I stood up instead.

'And don't be thinking you'll slope off to another part and not do the lesson. We'll be expecting you to show off your new skills.'

'Lila,' I said.

She grinned.

I stood up and Jimmy reluctantly followed. Lila looked delighted. We weaved our way through the crowds, trying to step around the picnics, each one more elaborate than the next.

We found the edge of the dance floor, where the lesson was due to take place. There had to be 50 people already there and we squeezed our way to the far side where there was space.

'Right, everyone, hold your palms up to your partners and then take their hands like this.'

I watched the demo and then turned my attention to Jimmy.

'We don't have to do this,' I said, in an almost apologetic tone. I hadn't considered that we were going to have to dance together.

'I think we do. Did you not see the way Lila looked at us?' He took a step closer towards me and he held his palms up. 'It's okay, I don't bite. You've held my hands before.'

'I know, it's just—'

'—weird. But it doesn't have to be.'

I held my hands up to his, like a mirror, and he slowly laced his fingers in mine, as we were being shown.

'See, not so bad,' said Jimmy.

'Only marginally clammy,' I said, trying to break the awkwardness that we were holding hands. Holding hands and standing within inches of each other. I could feel my heart start to beat that little bit quicker, my breath that little bit shallower. It had to be the pheromones from the aftershave.

'Okay, we're going to take one foot up and down, step, step. Then the other up and down, step, step.'

The first couple of moves were slow and we managed to keep pace.

'We're clearly naturals,' I said, wondering what all the fuss was about.

'Okay, double time,' said the teacher, as if she'd heard what I'd said. She started to count and all of a sudden what had been perfect co-ordination turned into me and Jimmy butting heads.

'Oh, fuck,' he said, rubbing at his temple.

'Sorry, that was me.'

'No, I think it was me,' he said.

'Right, let's try again.' I took hold of his hand once more and the teacher started to count and this time we didn't bang heads, but we did bang chests.

'I think I'm supposed to go this way.'

'Yeah,' I said, as we tried again and both went in the opposite direction.

'Okay, we're going to put it together with the music.'

'Blimey, they're not hanging around with this class,' I said, as the jazz quartet on the stage started to strike up, and those around the area started to clap.

'Are we ready? Five, six, seven, eight.'

We started the dance move and at first it was going so well. We might have been the worst on the dance floor, but we were going for it.

'Big finish,' shouted the leader.

Jimmy gave me the nod that reminded me of Patrick Swayze in *Dirty Dancing*, and I'm not sure whether it was drinking the fizz at 11 o'clock in the morning or the fact that I hadn't let myself dance in months, but I found my body leaping into Jimmy, my legs straddling either side of his waist. Jimmy caught me, much to both his and my amazement, and we froze for a split second at the wonder of our impressive dance move.

'Even bigger finish,' shouted the dance teacher and Jimmy tilted me backwards. Only this time I hadn't got the nod and overbalancing, we found ourselves tumbling backwards and my back hit the ground and Jimmy fell flat on top of me.

'Oh shit, Chlo, are you okay?'

The shock of hitting the dance floor jolted me. It wasn't the pain at first that I noticed, but the laughter that had started to grip me.

My whole body started to shake before any noise came out.

'Chloe,' said Jimmy, pushing himself up. He grabbed at my hand

and pulled it away from my eyes and I saw the relief melt as he saw I was laughing.

The noise trickled out of me, and he started to laugh too. The other people around us had got up and were starting to dance again, and we were in a heap laughing as if it was the funniest thing that had ever happened to us.

I went to stop and then it gripped me again.

'It wasn't even funny,' said Jimmy, wiping away tears of laughter.

'It was the expression on your face.'

'I was trying to stop myself from flattening you. Sorry for being concerned.' He sat up, his grin wide, and I sat up.

We sat and watched for a minute as everyone else was doing a better job than us. No one else was treading on any toes or falling over.

'I can't remember the last time I laughed like that,' I said, clutching at my sides. They were aching in a good way.

'I know. Me neither.'

'The only person that had me laughing like that was Kerry,' I said. It was one big cliché to think that when she was around, there was always laughter, as there wasn't. But if I was going to have these kinds of laugh-until-you-cry moments, she'd have been the one behind them. 'I almost didn't think I'd laugh like that again.'

Jimmy stayed silent for a second. 'But look, here you are.'

He let the words sink in, before he held out his hand to me.

'Do you think we should admit defeat?'

'I think so,' I said, taking his hand.

Now that I'd straddled him and he'd fallen on top of me, it no longer felt quite so strange having my hand in his.

'You guys did so well,' said a woman, patting Jimmy on the shoulder.

'Oh.' He winced. 'Thank you.'

'Not many people have the guts to do the advanced classes, so well done you for trying.'

She gave me a little pat too as her words sunk in.

'Advanced?'

'Uh-huh,' she nodded, the feather in her hair shaking.

'Not beginners?'

'Beginners are over there,' she said, pointing to another stage where people standing single file and doing moves at a pace that made it look like they were in a slow-mo video.

I shook my head.

'Typical,' I said, as we weaved our way out.

'Yeah, but had we gone over there, we wouldn't have laughed.'

'It's true.' My stomach muscles still ached like they'd had an aggressive gym workout.

'Do you think we can feign an injury so we don't have to dance for Lila?'

'That's not a bad idea. I might have a bruise,' I said, lifting my skirt a little higher. Jimmy winced and reached out and touched the redness that was spreading. A shiver ran over my body.

'I'm so sorry,' he said, tracing the circle of red.

'Don't be.' The words could barely get out of my mouth because Jimmy's touch was sending ripples through my entire body.

He let his fingers drop and I let my skirt fall back to where it should be. His eyes met mine and I didn't look away.

'Thank you,' he said, his voice soft. 'I didn't realise how much I needed this.'

'Me neither.'

I'm not sure what we were talking about. Getting out. Having fun. Getting over Kerry. But I was thankful too. It felt like I was truly living.

Chapter 22

It wasn't so bad sharing a studio apartment with Jimmy during the week. He'd get up and head off for a run or to work. The problem came on the weekend when we had no early plans. I'd been lying in bed trying not to make a sound as I didn't want to wake him over on the other side of the room.

I edged across the bed and picked my phone up from the table. The only good thing about the curtain was that it blocked out the light.

I saw that I had a voice note on WhatsApp from Kiran. I slipped in my earbuds and hit 'Play'.

'Hey, I hope you're having a good weekend. So big news, I've taken your advice and I'm going to do the panel event in person. I'm flying into JFK late tomorrow night, like 11 something, and then I'm flying to San Fran on Monday afternoon. But I reckon that gives me six hours to see everything. That's doable, right? Manhattan looks pretty tiny on maps. Fancy meeting me Monday morning? Coffee and sightseeing. Make a change from all the park walking. I'm off to bed now, but text me if it's a goer and we'll make a plan. And by "we", you know I mean "you".'

'Ooh,' I squealed, tapping out a quick reply.

'What's up?' Jimmy shouted from the other side of the room.

I closed my eyes. In all the excitement of Kiran's message, I'd forgotten to be quiet.

'Sorry! Did I wake you?'

'I've been awake for ages. Didn't want to wake you.'

'Ha, me neither.'

I heard Jimmy's curtain go and his footsteps padding across the floor. I pulled the cover up and over me, then drew my curtain back.

'Morning,' he said. 'Fancy a coffee? I got capsules in.'

'I'd love one,' I said, sitting up right.

'So, what was the squeal for?' he asked, as he got to work on the coffee.

'I got a message from my client, Kiran. He's on his way to a conference, and he's going to stop over in New York for a few hours. Typical Kiran, wants to see the whole city in that time. But it'll be nice to see him in person.'

Jimmy tipped his head to the side.

'You're going to meet him?'

'He's one of my best clients and he's going through a lot with a takeover at the moment. What?'

Jimmy shrugged.

'He's changed his plans to fly through New York, and he's meeting you for a couple of hours? Seems like a lot.'

'He's sightseeing. He's never been.' I couldn't tell Jimmy that I was clinging on to Kiran as one of my bigger clients, as then I'd have to admit to him that business had slowed and I hadn't made much of an effort to pick it back up. 'Plus, we've been working towards goals of him doing more public speaking and attending the conference in person is a huge step for him.

'Uh-huh.'

Jimmy was making me feel like I was missing something.

'It's true. He's going through a big takeover.'

'Yep, you've mentioned that before.'

He put the cup under the machine and pressed the button and it came noisily to life.

'He's just a client.'

I was getting cross, because even if he wasn't, it wasn't any of Jimmy's business any more.

'I believe you.' He rubbed at his hair that was standing up to the side. He made it worse as he tried to tame it. 'Sorry. I'm probably a bit grumpy without the coffee.'

'It's fine. Me too.'

I didn't know if it was the coffee or something more.

'Ah, I haven't got any milk. Espresso in a big cup?'

'Sounds good to me,' I said, holding my hand out. Coffee was coffee this early in the morning.

He handed me a cup and went back for his. He leaned his back against the kitchen worktops and started to sip.

'What's your plan for today?'

I thought of the list of activities to find Blaine and the places he'd mentioned over our time in the Metaverse, and I thought of the last few days spent with Lila and Jimmy and in the shadow of Kerry's ghost. Perhaps it was time to do something for me.

'I think I'm going to go for a walk,' I said. 'I was eavesdropping the plans of a newlywed couple on the plane and they kept talking about the High Line and I had to Google it.'

Jimmy nodded. 'It's supposed to be great. Did you want some company?'

'Misery loves company.'

'Only partial misery now. You've cheered up just a little bit.'

'Just a little bit,' I said, sipping the coffee that was hitting all the right spots. 'Are you not going to see Sienna?'

'I might try and catch up with her tonight or in the week, we don't often hang out during the day.'

I raised an eyebrow.

'That came out wrong. I just mean, we don't see a lot of each other. This coffee was pretty good. You want another one?'

'Sure.'

'Great, and then we'll hop in the shower. Get out before it's hot. I mean, I'll shower. You can shower after,' he turned to the kitchen, but not before I saw him blushing.

'Sounds like a plan,' I said, trying to ignore how cute Jimmy looked with the bed head and now the rosy cheeks. My heart started to ache and that feeling of grief that had been living rent-free in my stomach was now being replaced by something that felt a whole heap like regret.

We'd decided to walk from the apartment to the High Line. It had taken the best part of an hour to get there as we meandered up through the Village to Chelsea.

It was mid-morning and, despite it being a Sunday, it was buzzing. We walked past a particularly busy restaurant with tables out on the street and a queue out of the door. There were two women sitting at one of the tables that caught my eye as I passed. One of them was clutching onto the other, gripping her arm tight as she howled with laughter, her eyes closed. The other was laughing so hard she was wiping tears away.

A pang hit my chest.

'You want to grab a coffee?' asked Jimmy, snapping me back to reality. I turned to him and saw that he was giving me the look. The one that I thought Lila was talking about. He understood exactly what I was thinking.

'Maybe an iced one.'

He nodded and he pointed at a coffee shop on the corner. I was about to follow him when my phone buzzed. I pulled it out and saw it was Lila calling

'Can you grab mine for me?' I asked. 'I'm just going to answer this, it's Lila.'

Jimmy nodded and headed inside and I took the call, hovering on the street, trying to find a spot where I wasn't looking at the brunching women.

'Hi,' I said, answering it.

'Oh, thank God you picked up, this would have killed me if not.'

'What's up? Is something wrong?'

'No, no. Look, is this a good time to talk? I'm not on speaker or anything with Jimmy about?'

'No,' I said. 'He's getting coffee, I'm on the street.'

'Good, good. I'll be quick then. So don't hate on me, but I was telling Anthony about the whole Blaine thing last night.'

'Lila!'

'I know, I know. I ruined the girl code, but hear me out on what he thought. I mean, he was laughing at the thought of us trying to find Blaine yesterday at the festival. I mean, it was ridiculous us thinking that was even a plan.'

'Absolutely ridiculous,' I echoed.

'But then he said, and I cannot stop thinking about it, he said what if it was someone you knew?'

'Someone I knew,' I repeated it and I shuddered despite being in the sun.

'Yeah, and it got me thinking. My first thought was that it was the Metaverse guy you work with, the guy that gave you the goggles in the first place, I mean that's sus if you think about it.'

'Kiran?' Jimmy's reservations about Kiran came over in the forefront of my mind.

I couldn't say anything.

'But Anthony was laughing at me again and said that he thought it was Jimmy. Jimmy! And the more I thought about it, the more I think it fits.'

I swallowed trying to remove the lump that had appeared in my throat. I looked up in shock at Jimmy through the window. He was standing at the counter and my hand holding the phone started to shake.

'I mean he's living in New York and he knew you were using the Metaverse. He knows you love Periscope Monkeys. It's not a giant leap to think that he could have engineered the whole thing to get you out here... Hello, are you still there?'

I was still staring at Jimmy and, as he sensed me watching, he turned and gave me a wave. I held up my hand and waved back.

'I'm still here,' I said, wondering if that was true. 'But the voice.'

'Um, voice changer. You can be anything in the Metaverse.'

I was quiet again.

'It's something to think about, right?'

'Something to think about,' I repeated as I watched Jimmy picking up the coffee from the counter. 'He's coming out. Can I call you later, when I've had a think about this?'

'Of course, of course. Blew my mind too.'

'Yeah,' I said, as Jimmy came out. 'Call you later.'

I hung up the phone and Jimmy handed me my iced coffee. I took it, my hand slightly quivering. I didn't know where to start with my thoughts.

'Is Lila coming to join us?'

'No,' I shook my head. 'She was just checking in.'

'That's nice of her. She seems really caring.'

'She is,' I said, trying to focus on the conversation, but I was spiralling. I kept trying to tell myself it was a crazy theory, but something about it had taken hold.

I started to think about the similarities between Jimmy and Blaine.

'And Anthony seemed nice too. It'll be great if he does come and play pickleball.'

I spluttered a little laugh. Another recruit to the cult.

'I think this is us,' said Jimmy, pointing to the stairs.

We made our way onto the High Line. It wasn't quite what I was expecting. The path at the start was flanked with small greenery, shrubs and plants, and there was a view over the Hudson River looking over to Hoboken where we'd walked last week.

'What are we listening to today?' asked Jimmy, pulling out the headphones and handing me one, before getting his phone. 'Do I still need a pop education?'

The river view was almost instantly lost and it was replaced with buildings flanking either side and wild shrubbery and grasses planted alongside. It felt like we were in the heart of nature despite being caged in by the buildings.

'I don't know why, but I'm getting a bit of an eighties vibe here,' I said, hardly hesitating as he held out his Spotify, and I selected Kate Bush's 'Running Up That Hill'.

'Excellent choice. Please tell me you knew it before *Stranger Things*?'

'Maybe. Might have just about heard of this one.'

He shook his head, but I could see the smile on his face.

I pulled him to the side to let someone rollerblade past us.

'I can't believe how busy this place is.'

'That's New York for you. Home to millions, before you add the tourists into the mix.'

'You are beginning to sound like a grumpy old man.'

'I'm always pleased to be a stereotype.'

It was late morning now and it was already starting to get humid and sticky. I'm not sure why I kept picking places that required us to spend so much time outside. Tomorrow, once I'd finished showing Kiran the sights early on, I was going to spend the rest of the day indoors with air conditioning.

'So how's your new idea for the workshops going? Have you made any progress?'

'It's getting there. I'm still hazy, but I've got the acronym sorted for a new model of different stages of coaching. GNOMES.'

'Gnomes?' He raised an eyebrow.

'Yep, the key to any training as anyone will tell you is an easy acronym so people remember the concept.'

'And what does GNOMES stand for?'

'See, easy to remember, huh? Okay, so G-Goals – what are you hoping to achieve by coaching? N-Now – what's your starting point? O-Options – what are your options to get you to where you want to be? M—' I hesitated, trying to remember what the hell M was. 'M is for making plans, how are you going to get there? E is for engage.'

'Like Captain Picard.'

'You know me, I always love a niche *Star Trek* reference,' I said. 'Engage – is when you start doing everything, and the S for success – is how you're going to measure what you've done.'

Saying it out loud made it sound like I had something.

'That's actually pretty cool. What do you think the chances of getting back in with Marianne's company are?'

I kicked a stone with my shoe. 'I don't really know, but the idea of developing the model is that I could deliver it to different companies.'

'And financially,' he said, not looking at me. 'You're managing to cope okay? I know that you scaled back after Kerry, and Marianne's company were good payers.'

I rolled my lips in. I could lie, but he'd only see through me.

'I'm getting by. I'm taking on platform work a couple of days a week. It doesn't pay well, but it's consistent. That's why I'm so grateful to you for letting me stay. I don't think the savings would have been able to take the hit twice for the accommodation.'

'Still nothing back from the bank?'

'No, they're investigating. I told Kiran about it and he told me to forward the emails to him, to see if he could do anything.'

'That's kind of him, going out of his way.'

I shot Jimmy a look.

'He's just a client. There are ethics in our industry. We've become friends because we've been working with each other, but that's it.'

I thought of what Lila had said about the possibility of Kiran being Blaine, but it was just as ridiculous as the idea that it was Jimmy.

'I was actually just saying that was kind of him. I mean it. You bring out the best in people.'

I shook my head.

'I don't think I do.'

'You do. That's pretty much your job.'

'Yeah, but lately it hasn't felt like it.'

'You're always so hard on yourself,' he said as we came to a stop in front of a twisted metal sculpture and I was a little lost for words.

'The Power of Love' by Huey Lewis and the News started to play and Jimmy groaned.

'Come on, this is a great song,' I said, 'and you love *Back to the Future*.'

'I do, but—'

'—Excuse me,' said a man walking up to us, phone held in front of him as if he was filming. 'Are you two a couple?'

I opened my mouth to set the record straight, but before I could make a squeak Jimmy piped up.

'Oh, we were, but we're not now,' said Jimmy.

The man looked awkward and I held up a hand.

'We didn't just break up. We're friends now. Why?'

'I do a thing on TikTok, asking couples how they met.'

The man lowered his camera, sensing it wasn't the best story.

'Ah, I've seen that kind of thing,' I said with a shrug. 'We didn't meet under very exciting circumstances anyway. Going out to watch a band with mates and hitting it off.'

The guy turned his nose up.

'Check out my posts anyway, and don't forget to like and subscribe,' he said, thrusting a business card in my face and hurrying off to find someone else to talk to.

'I guess our story wouldn't have made the cut anyway,' I said and we started to walk along again. I moved us over into the shade, marvelling at the preserved railway tracks beneath our feet.

'That's because you're starting our story in the wrong place,' said Jimmy.

'Oh no,' I said, holding my hand up in a stop motion. 'We do not count Andrea's party.'

His lips were twitching, threatening to laugh.

'But that's technically when we met.'

'I don't think it counts if one of us doesn't remember,' I said. I tried to stop the few details of that night that I could remember coming back into my mind, but it was too late.

Andrea had thrown a house party, not long after she and Henry moved in together. Everything was Hawaiian-themed, from the dress code to the punch. I shuddered at the thought of the punch, the sole reason for my lost memories.

Jimmy was laughing. He'd apparently turned up quite late on in the evening, when the punch had taken its full effect on me. I'd taken it upon myself to make a Hawaiian-inspired punch full of tropical flavours. But instead of using fruit juices, I'd made it using any ready-made tinned cocktails that had a vaguely fruity flavour, alongside the base of rum. I had hazy recollections of being sick in the toilet, in the garden, on some man's shoes.

'How is Billy?' I asked, my cheeks flushing with embarrassment. Billy, one of Jimmy and Henry's friends, aka shoe guy.

'He's good. I don't think his shoes ever recovered though,' he said, his smile growing ever wider.

I gave him a gentle nudge.

'You see, this is why it shouldn't be the story of how we met.'

Jimmy put his hand on his chest, a cheeky grin on his face.

'That moment when you flashed us what was under your grass skirt.'

'I had purple hot pants on. I was thoroughly decent.'

'You did.'

My cheeks were burning. Anything I could remember I'd buried deep in my memories in shame, but now the floodgates had opened, it was coming back thick and fast.

'I'm just glad you missed the coconut incident.' I winced. I almost wished I'd blanked out the whole thing. Having hazy recollections was so much worse.

'Oh, that was the stuff of legends at that point. Andrea had put you in a T-shirt by the time I arrived.'

'God bless Andrea.'

'She was trying to put you to bed a couple of times, but you kept popping up.'

A laugh escaped my lips because, of the few-and-far-between memories I have, one of them is me running clutching a pillow through the party whilst Andrea was trying to chase me back up to the bedroom.

'I still can't believe that after all that you asked Henry to set you up with me.'

'Yeah. I just had a feeling.'

'A feeling?' Between Lila and her universe talking to her, and Jimmy with a feeling. 'I was such a mess.'

'You were actually quite endearing in the brief moments that I spoke to you.'

I spluttered a laugh. I definitely didn't remember talking to anyone. 'I'm sure the conversation must have been riveting.'

'It wasn't so much what you said, but you were just this... whirlwind. It was just you being so you.'

'I wish I could go back to being me,' I said, thinking that, despite being my absolute worst that night, at least everyone said that I was a nice drunk. 'The old me.'

We walked along in silence and I thought how far away I was now from that person.

'I know this isn't what you want to hear,' he said, his voice soft, his head tilted. Clues that I needed to brace myself. 'But you might not get back to being that person.'

'That's what scares me the most,' I said, making a beeline for a bench.

He nodded. 'Some things change you and whilst you move forward, the pain's always with you.'

'But no one wants a miserable executive coach, it's not really what they signed up for.'

'You're not always going to be miserable. I saw you smile back there once or twice.'

'Once or twice,' I took a deep breath. 'Don't say all I need is time.' I started to feel the familiar anger pulse through my veins.

'That's a load of crap,' he said, making me laugh. 'But I'm hoping it'll get easier.'

He smiled, and I watched as the lines on his face became even more pronounced. He looked changed too, it wasn't just me.

I exhaled deeply and took a moment or two just to watch the people walk by. That was the nicest thing about being friends with Jimmy, he knew me well enough for us not to have to fill the silence.

'I'm glad that you forced us to be friends.'

He laughed. 'I don't think I forced you to. But I'm glad too.'

My cheeks had just about recovered from the embarrassment and now they were aching from smiling. It reminded me of the way that Blaine had made me feel on our dates. That slight recognition that there was still capacity within me to feel happiness.

'Ready to go on?'

I knew he was only talking about continuing the path along the walkway, but it was the kind of question that accidentally spoke to my soul. Was I ready to go on?

I stood up, with a determination, and in defiance.

'Yes.'

'I've actually booked for us to go somewhere,' he said as we started to walk again.

'Oh, really?'

'Yeah, I took a look at where we were going to end up, and it was pretty perfect.'

'Now I'm intrigued. Are you going to tell me where it is?' I asked, as we fell back into a slow walk.

'You'll see.'

*

I didn't have to wait for long to find out where we were going. A few minutes from the High Line we found ourselves in what looked like an upmarket shopping centre. Only we weren't going to any shops, we were in an elevator hurtling to the top of a skyscraper where I got total Metaverse vibes, as the lift played pictures of a sketch of Manhattan slowly coming to life.

'Now this place, is supposed to have the most impressive views of the city,' said Jimmy. 'And they've even got a glass floor, if you're brave enough.'

I shuddered at the thought.

We made it onto the platform outside and a feeling of déjà vu crept over me. This particular view looked so familiar, until it hit me.

'I've actually been here before,' I said, taking in the glass-framed wall that ran around the outside platform.

'How? It hasn't been open that long.'

'Oh, I meant in the Metaverse.' I cringed. It had felt so real at the time. The view was uncannily the same, but it was only now that a hot breeze was blowing, the reality that this platform was perched off the side of a building made all the hairs on the back of my neck stand up.

After our virtual visit to the Empire State Building, we'd gone on many of the observation desks' virtual experiences to check out the views.

'How have you been there, in the Metaverse?' he said, trying to edge me out further from the safety of the door. 'Don't you only talk to Kerry?'

I'd dropped myself right in it. He already disapproved of me talking to her.

'I, um, well I started to go to gigs on there, and sometimes I went sightseeing,' I said, knowing I must be blushing. I tried to push away the thought that he might already know this. 'I couldn't face going out, but I wanted to get out of my flat.'

Jimmy's head was cocked to the side, and I braced myself for the telling-off.

'Is virtual sightseeing a thing?'

I nodded, still feeling embarrassed, but relieved that it didn't seem to provoke the same anger in him that it had when I'd talked to him about using Kiran's platform to talk to Kerry.

'Yeah, people either build places inspired by the real-world versions or else attractions themselves build virtual versions, I guess as a marketing tool.'

'Huh,' said Jimmy. His head was still cocked as if he didn't know what to do with the information. 'I'm guessing this will be a lot better in the flesh,' he said, finally getting me to leave the security of the inside.

There were huge numbers of people, which was almost a relief, as it felt as if there was a barrier between me and the nothingness of the glass balustrade that hemmed us in. Of course, in the Metaverse there had been no one other than Blaine and me visiting.

'Isn't the view incredible?'

'It's breathtaking.' I tried to take it in. You could see all the city's skyline from here. It was like playing landmark bingo. One World Trade Center. The Statue of Liberty. The Empire State. The Chrysler Building. I could even see round to where I'd lived all those years ago, across the river in New Jersey.

I thought of Blaine, how he'd led me onto the glass platform below, only then it hadn't seemed so scary. I'd been standing in my living room with my feet firmly on the ground.

'Do we dare?'

I blinked and looked up to see Jimmy staring at me. For a second I'd been so lost, thinking about Blaine, that I'd half-expected to see him standing in front of me.

'Sure,' I said, following Jimmy over to the glass-floored section. There were a couple of kids lying face down on the floor, and a few nervous adults.

Jimmy peered from near the edge. 'Or we could just stand here. I'm pretty sure it would be the same view.'

'This was your idea! What were you saying the other day when I wouldn't walk on the bridge?'

'Yeah, but this is completely different. I'm okay with heights, but I think I just found a new fear.'

I put my hands on my hips. 'No, I'm not having it.'

'Oh, that's just great,' he said. 'You decide to find that drive now? The next thing I know you'll be gnoming me.'

A man walking past eyed me and Jimmy suspiciously, as if gnoming might be some kind of sexual deviance.

'I'm sure I could GNOMES you. Goal – to get Jimmy onto the walkway, now – you're too far away, options – take you by the hand, whisper encouragements, blackmail you.'

'What would you blackmail me with?'

'Telling Andrea and Henry how the flowerpot got broken at their New Year's Eve party.'

Jimmy forgot his fear for a second, an intense blush spreading over his cheeks.

'You wouldn't,' he said, with a jolt of laughter. 'Go on.'

'Make a plan,' I said, reaching for his hand.

'Now for your Picard moment,' he said, screwing his eyes tightly shut.

'And now we engage.' I led him slowly at first, as he dug his heels into the ground, but I reached and took the other hand and we made a little headway. Step by step, until eventually his feet were on the glass floor.

'And I'm pretty sure that we can measure this as a success.'

He was gripping my hands to the extent that I wondered if I would soon lose feeling. I took a step closer towards him.

'Open your eyes,' I whispered into his ear. 'Go on, focus on my face, just my face.'

I saw him open his eyes and he blinked a little before he locked his eyes on mine, his hands still shaking.

'Look down.'

'I can't,' he said shaking his head.

'Focus on the goal, you can. Just look down, I've got you,' I said, squeezing his hand back. 'I've got you.'

I nodded my head at him to show him I meant it and he moved his eyes down, whilst keeping his head as still as he could. His legs buckled a little and I held him tighter.

'And how long do I need to stay here for?'

'One step backwards will have you off it, whenever you're ready.'

He immediately stood backwards, but still kept clutching my hands.

'Fuck, that was awful.'

'Yeah, but are you glad you did it?'

'Not in the slightest.' He shivered.

'Not even a bit?' His grip wasn't loosening.

'Maybe a tiny bit.' He did another involuntary shiver and I could see the goosebumps running up his arms.

'Then, see, I've still got it.'

He looked at me, still holding my hands. 'Yeah,' he said. 'You've still got it.'

His eyes bore into me and it was my turn to shiver. I tried to tell myself it was just the breeze.

I coughed and he let go, the spell broken.

'Thank you for that and sorry for my sweaty hands,' he said, rubbing them on his T-shirt. They were still shaking.

'Any time.' I scrunched up my face. 'I mean, any time you need help, not about holding your sweaty hands. I haven't missed those.'

He laughed.

'Likewise,' he said. 'Sweaty hands or not. I'm always here for you too.'

I'd forgotten what it felt like to open your heart just a little and to let someone in.

'Now, do you want to go to the bar?' he said, turning his back on the city and facing the bar in the main building.

'So that you're away from the glass floor.'

'Of course,' he said. 'Shall we?'

'Absolutely. I fancy a cocktail.'

'Tropical punch? I'm sure we could find you some coconuts.'

He started to laugh and his whole body shook, and the laughter took hold of every muscle in my body as I laughed until I almost peed. I thought of the two women laughing at their brunch and I thought of all the times I'd laughed like this. Lately I'd wondered if I was going to laugh like this again, and yet here I was.

And just like that, my heart felt a little bit lighter.

Chapter 23

Jimmy and I had fallen into an easy rhythm at his apartment as we set about clearing up the dinner we'd just had. I cleared up the empty takeaway cartons whilst he stacked the dishwasher.

'I'm still having the creeps about that glass floor,' said Jimmy, shivering as if someone had walked over his grave. He headed over to the fridge, not even asking if I wanted a beer before sliding one over to me.

'But you did it.' I held out my beer and he touched mine with his in a *cheers*.

'I did.'

I started to wipe over the breakfast bar, and Jimmy leaned on it, reminding me of the barman stoop. He even had the tea towel slung over his shoulder.

'So how did the Metaverse compare to the real-life experience?'

I thought back to my date there with Blaine, the first time he'd taken hold of my hand and pulled me over to experience the glass myself, and then I thought of this afternoon. The Metaverse might have been able to simulate the view, but it was other details that invoked the other senses that they couldn't touch. The breeze blowing round the building and making it a constant battle to keep my hair out of my face. The noise of the wind mixed with the chatter of large numbers of people. The outstretched arms and selfie sticks of people snapping photos. It was all the colour of real life that couldn't be added with a computer palette.

Ever since Lila had suggested that Jimmy was Blaine, I hadn't been able to shake the feeling. It had been percolating and, as much as I wanted to dismiss it, as he stood before me it was growing stronger. I realised that I wasn't horrified at the suggestion as much as I was wishing that it might actually be true.

'Parts of it were so similar virtually, but of course in real life you had all your senses. The wind, the noise and that visceral fear and excitement from the other people.'

'That's what I don't get about these augmented and virtual experiences, that you couldn't mistake them for reality.'

'But I don't think that's the point of them,' I said.

'Then what is?'

I pulled out one of the seats of the breakfast bar and sat down on it. It felt like the kind of question that warranted a proper sit-down.

'I don't know. To do something or go somewhere that you can't easily in real life.' I took a sip of the water, from my glass left on the bar. 'After Kerry died, I didn't want to go out any more and I didn't want to be around anyone. You remember what I was like. And then, when I was in the flat on my own, I was lonely in a way that made me realise that I'd never actually been properly lonely before. I didn't know what to do with that. How do you put yourself out there when you don't want to see anyone? And then Kiran gave me the headset.'

'You make it sound like it was an illicit drug.'

'I know, but it almost felt like that in a way. It was like my guilty secret of this place that existed. Somewhere that I could feel like I was going out and doing something, but I wasn't at all.'

Jimmy sighed. 'And it helped? I thought you were just talking to a virtual Kerry.'

'I only talked to her a little bit. Most of the time I was elsewhere trying not to be lonely.'

'And what, you met other people?'

A shiver ran down my spine. What if he already knew all of this, that he'd been seeing me there?

'Yeah, I met people.'

Here I was, opening myself up and making myself vulnerable, and it was the perfect opportunity to tell him what I'd really been doing, but I couldn't bring myself to.

'People?'

'People. Not just dead people,' I said, for clarification. A knot in my stomach forming at the lie. Up until this point I'd been withholding information, but now it felt like a lie. Jimmy and I were rebuilding our friendship and it still had fragile foundations. I shouldn't risk fracturing them.

Jimmy was quiet. He took the tea towel off his shoulder and put it into his hands, as if he didn't really know what to do.

'And did it help?'

'Yeah, for a while,' I said, thinking of the moment that I couldn't log on and get connected to Blaine. That spiralling feeling of everything unravelling, just like the day I'd got that call from Kerry's mum.

'I can see why you did it,' he said, putting the tea towel down and instead coming round to sit next to me at the breakfast bar. 'It's not how I would have handled things.'

His words stung. I thought back to the arguments we'd started to have after Kerry died. Jimmy trying to shake me from my grief, me trying to push him away, retreating further and further into my shell.

'That loneliness is a killer,' he said, staring down at the worktop, unable to meet my eyes. 'I felt it too. It was so sudden, one minute you were there and the next you were gone.'

My heart sank even further and a tear fell down my cheek.

'I tried so hard,' he said. He ran a hand through his hair. 'But I couldn't reach you.'

I bit my lip in a futile attempt to stop it from wobbling.

'I don't think I could be reached. But the Metaverse was an escape where no one knew me. They didn't need to know about Kerry. Or that I'd fucked things up with you. Or that I couldn't cope with anything else.'

'Perhaps you were the smart one, going there to escape,' he said, his voice soft.

'Or perhaps I was just kicking it further down the line, as I'm having to deal with it all now.'

'Yeah, but at least you're dealing with it now. You're ready.'

'I still don't think I am.' I'd linked my hands as I was squeezing them together, grounding myself with the sensation in a bid to stop the tears from falling.

'You are.' He reached over and wrapped his hand around my knuckles. 'You've already come so far since you arrived. You've been going all over the city all week to loads of weird and wonderful places. That's peak Chloe right there.'

I smiled, my cheeks flushing with guilt, I'd only gone all over town in the hope of finding Blaine. It was only today I'd felt like my old self, taking charge of the situation and doing something for me.

I'd spent months since Kerry died feeling lost and alone and yet, in less than a week, I'd got a glimmer of hope that things wouldn't feel that way forever.

'I'm worried that I'm only feeling brave because I'm here. What if I go home and I'm exactly the same?'

'Then don't leave.'

I laughed. 'I'm pretty sure that US Immigration would have something to say about that.'

I looked up at him, expecting him to be joking, but there was a seriousness on his face.

'Not for ninety days.'

A shiver passed over my body. I'd come so far in a week and there had been something so comforting about being with Jimmy again. We'd proved we could be friends post relationship but, if I spent longer here, would we be in danger of blurring those lines? Would we undo all that work?

'I worry you'd become a crutch like the Metaverse has become,' I shrugged.

We sat in silence for a second before Jimmy pushed his drink away from him.

'I want to see this Metaverse. Let's go on it together. You've got your headset and there's one in the games room downstairs. I'll sign it out. That'll work, right?'

The knot in my stomach started to knit even tighter. What would it feel like to go on with a person that I knew?

'I'm not sure if that's a good idea.'

The Metaverse had always been my escape. I couldn't imagine that I could let someone in.

'I want to understand and see what you see in it.'

He was staring hard at me, as if he was deadly serious. The niggle that he was in fact Blaine started to grow stronger in my mind. The thought that he'd catfished me, that he was the one that set in motion the idea that I should come out here. What if this was his way of revealing it to me?

'Come on, it's not that big an ask,' he said. I tried to search his eyes for the truth. I was being silly, surely, buying into Anthony's crazy idea. I felt as if I knew Blaine because that's what happened when you met a person you really connected with. There was that sense that you got lulled into feeling as if you've known them your whole life. It didn't mean that it was Jimmy.

'Okay, then,' I said, coming to terms with the idea, as at least this way I'd know. 'Go and get the headset.'

Jimmy gave me a mock salute at my bossy tone and he headed out of the apartment.

It didn't take long to get him set up and for us to find a replacement platform to go on. I'd searched so many looking for Blaine that I'd found a couple that reminded me of RealWorldDreaming, although it was more cartoonish around the edges.

I'd picked a piano bar to go to, and the sounds of soft jazz were reverberating through my ears as virtual Jimmy walked up to me.

'This is freaky,' he said, spinning in a slow circle.

'Yeah, it does take a little while to get used to.'

His avatar didn't look like Blaine and it didn't sound like him either. He was stumbling in the room, both virtually and, by the sounds of the expletives, physically too. I felt a hint of disappointment. This wasn't the big reveal I was hoping for. He didn't have Blaine's movements or mannerisms in here.

The bar was at the top of a building and it reminded a little of what used to be the Rainbow Room at the Rockefeller Center, the way that you looked out of the windows and the way the mirrors reflected the city back to you.

'The view's quite something,' I said, pointing out to the dark sky and the twinkling buildings below.

'It's okay,' he said, reaching his hand to touch the window and it disappeared as it went through it. He shot me a look.

'You'll be fine once you get to grips with how your avatar moves.'

'It's so weird. What do you think of me in here?' He put his hand on his hip and stood in a very un-Jimmy-like way. He wasn't used to how pronounced even the smallest movements were.

'I could tell it was you. Although you look a little bit like Ryan Gosling.'

'Real Ryan Gosling or 2p slider Ryan Gosling,' said Jimmy. 'I'd take either.'

I bit my lip, trying not to laugh. I was having to tip my head up to see him.

'Did you make your avatar taller than you are normally?'

'Yeah, I figured I'd see what a few inches would get me.'

'I bet you did.'

'Easy.'

He was still looking round in all directions, and I wasn't sure if he was disorientated or if he was trying to show off his overly chiselled jaw.

'Sorry, couldn't resist. Besides I don't know why I'm giving you shit. It's not like I look like this in real life. I could only wish my hair game would be this strong, and this waist.'

'Stop,' said Jimmy, taking a step closer to me. 'Don't be thinking there's anything wrong with the real you.'

'Said the man who made himself inches taller.'

The avatar perfectly captured him tipping his head back and laughing.

'So this is how it goes then. You just hang out in places like this and chat?'

'Pretty much,' I said. There were a couple of people mingling around, but I'd deliberately picked somewhere quiet. I wanted to keep Jimmy to myself.

'Do you want to dance?'

The piano player had broken into a slow song and other people started to move together.

'Because we did so well at the jazz festival?'

I held out a hand and Jimmy took it, only there was that familiar disconnect as we couldn't feel the physical connection.

Jimmy disappeared.

I flicked off the headset, blinking as my eyes got used to the room. 'What's wrong?'

'I can't do it,' he said. 'I don't understand how you can think that's better than being here in the real world.'

'Because you can't get hurt in the Metaverse,' I said, my heart starting to crack a little. It wasn't true because, when I'd lost Blaine, I felt that loss.

'You can't live your life not getting hurt.' His eyes were fixed on mine and he let out a deep breath, and it was as if he bored deeper into my soul. 'Come on.'

I looked down at his outstretched hand, the same gesture he'd made a minute before in the Metaverse, only this time when I took it, my whole body tingled.

'See, this is how it's meant to be.' His words were soft and gentle. He was right. This was reality. He squeezed my hand and tears stung my eyes. I'd felt safe in the Metaverse, but I felt safe in his hands too.

'Let's go,' he said, sliding his wallet into his back pocket and picking up the key.

'Go where?' I asked.

'There's a bar down the street.'

'Jimmy, I'm in my PJs.'

'Go and get changed then.'

I opened my mouth to argue, but there was something about the way he was looking at me that made me do as he said.

After a quick change, Jimmy marched us down the street. We were heading towards a lively bar. Fashionable people were standing outside, vaping and chatting, and others were waiting in a queue to get in that ran along the side of the wall. Inside the glass, it looked busy and already I could hear the music pulsating.

I turned to tell Jimmy that perhaps we should go somewhere quieter, when he took us through an adjacent door. A bouncer nodded to us as we walked in. We headed straight down the stairs and stepped into a club that looked eerily like the one we'd been in in the Metaverse, just without the view.

It wasn't exactly the same; there were no windows and the lights were soft and red. An abundance of heavy velvet curtains and padded booths ran around the outside.

Unlike the smooth jazz of the Metaverse, this piano bar had a livelier vibe with a few people on the dance floor.

'This place is so cool,' I said, watching the guy playing and singing 'Midnight Train to Georgia' in awe.

Jimmy directed me over to a table whilst he headed to the bar, and I went and found one of the booths to sit at. I watched a couple dancing in the corner, not caring that they were the only ones, just lost in the music.

He'd been right to question the view in the piano bar we'd been in virtually, because there was something about watching the reactions to the crowd in person. The candles flickering. The gentle hum and chatter of other people. It was that overwhelm of the senses that I'd found daunting lately, but now it all added to the experience of it.

'Thank you for making me come here,' I said, as Jimmy popped a drink in front of me.

'I don't think I made you, but it's nice, huh? Better than my apartment.'

'That little apartment of yours has grown on me.'

He raised an eyebrow.

'But you're right. This,' I said looking around, 'is much better. It's got a good vibe.'

'Now you sound like Sienna. She's always talking about a vibe.'

'Ah, Sienna. Are you not seeing her tonight?'

He shook his head. 'I think she's going uptown.'

My chest started to burn. I didn't want to hear him talking about her. I'd been numb to the pain when I arrived, but feelings of jealousy had started to creep in. He'd been there for me for the last few days, but the mention of Sienna was a timely reminder that I no longer had him all to myself.

'Is it serious with her?'

'No,' he said, picking up his drink.

'But do you think it could be one day?'

I hardened my heart, preparing myself for the worst.

He shrugged. 'I doubt it. We want completely different things in life, but for right now... I guess you're not the only one that's found ways to cope with the loneliness.'

I thought of Blaine, and maybe Sienna wasn't any different. She might be a living, breathing person, but maybe she wasn't any more real than Blaine in what she represented. Or maybe that was what I was hoping.

The song came to an end and everyone clapped, before the man broke into Phil Collins's 'You Can't Hurry Love'.

'Ah, now this is a classic,' said Jimmy, nodding along to the beat.

'It is a good one.'

'What, you know it, and there's no movie involved?'

I racked my brain. There was always a movie, but I couldn't think of one.

A few more people got up on the dance floor and Jimmy held out his hand.

'How about we try it here instead?'

I hesitated, but only for a second. I took his hand and let him lead me over. He dropped my hand and we started to dance, singing along to each other along with the others around us.

'It's like being at a wedding,' I said, shouting over the music. It had the same atmosphere to it.

'I know. I love it. You left so early from Andrea and Henry's. We couldn't do any of our legendary dancing.'

'Probably for the best.'

I noticed that Jimmy and I had got closer the more the song went on, shimmying back and forth, and we sang from the top of our lungs.

The piano player started to play the opening of the next song, 'Can't Take My Eyes Off You'. The beat was slower, and Jimmy held out one of his hands. He started to spin me around before holding me in a classic ballroom pose. We swayed from side to side and we started to sing. More and more people had crept onto the dance floor.

The couple next to us looked as if they'd taken lessons, as they proceeded to do a choreographed routine.

'Our wedding song,' one of the women mouthed to me and I gave her a thumbs-up. They were amazing.

'We could do that too,' said Jimmy trying to spin me one way and then back the other. My arm got knotted around my back and I got stuck.

'Ouch,' I yelped, trying to untangle myself.

'I don't think we've got a career in dancing ahead of us,' he said and he drew me in closer so that our heads were touching.

'We don't seem to be doing too bad a job now,' I said, my voice getting shallow. I could feel the beat of his heart and the slowing of his breath.

I tilted my head back and stared at him and a shudder rippled over me as he looked back into my eyes.

He lowered his head until our lips brushed against each other and my heart was in my mouth. Every part of my body was tingling in anticipation.

His lips were on mine. Heat was radiating from them. My eyes instinctively closed. It was that top of a rollercoaster moment, where it held you for a second before it plunged. It was the moment of no return and I couldn't wait any longer.

I leaned into the kiss, but he was pushed away. My eyes sprang open to see that one of the women who'd been doing their elaborate wedding dance had fallen on the floor.

'I guess we're a bit out of practice,' said the other woman, holding her hand out to pick up her wife.

'I'm sorry, sweetie,' said the fallen woman, coming up to standing and wrapping her arm around Jimmy. 'Are you okay? I tackled you like a linebacker.'

'I'm fine,' he said, turning to me. 'You okay?'

'Mmmhmm,' I squeaked. 'I might get a drink.'

What was I thinking? I'd almost kissed him.

My hands were shaking, standing at the bar. I let out a deep breath as I waited for our cocktails. I looked over at Jimmy sitting back at the table that we had before all the dancing. He looked as rattled as I did.

The barman placed the drinks down in front of me and I was in danger of downing mine straight off.

'That was intense, huh?' said Jimmy, as I sat down, sliding the drink towards him.

'Wasn't it?'

'You know, perhaps we should finish these up, head back to the apartment and go to bed.'

I must have looked alarmed because he held his hands up.

'As in, go to bed in our separate beds.' He scrunched his eyes shut. 'I've got a really early start tomorrow, and haven't you got that client to meet?'

'I do,' I said, nodding. He was going out of his way to let me know that whatever spell we were under on that dance floor was well and truly over.

We were looking at each other and I no longer trusted myself. I needed to go home because I was in danger of trying to kiss him again if I stayed, and I wondered from the look on his face if he felt the same.

'I'm glad we've spent this time together,' said Jimmy.

'Me too.' My heart was sinking, because as much as I'd loved hanging out with him over the last few days, I knew it wasn't going to be like this when I got back home.

'We'll always have New York,' I said, borrowing Kerry's catchphrase.

'We certainly will.'

'It brings out the best in me.'

'And there was me thinking that it might have been me.' He winked a little, then held up his drink. 'To New York.'

'To New York.'

I clinked back. But his words started to circle round my mind. Was it New York that was leading me back to my old self, or was it Jimmy?

Chapter 24

Something had shifted between Jimmy and me as we made our way home. It was humid and thundery in the air, but it wasn't just the clouds that felt electrically charged. I couldn't help but notice as we got into the lift, we were standing that much closer than we needed to be. Every floor was announced with a ding and it seemed to be the longest lift ride in history.

When the doors pinged open on our floor, he put his hand on the small of my back to usher me out and my heart started to beat a little faster. Neither of us was talking.

He kept his hand on my back as we walked into the apartment and, when he let his hand fall, I immediately missed it. I turned to him. The sound of the thunder finally crashed outside.

'I should get ready for bed. It's late,' I said, not making any effort to move.

'Yeah, me too.' He took a step towards me causing me to shiver. He was close enough that I could hear him breathing.

He looked at me and it certainly wasn't the look that Lila was talking about any more. I knew exactly what this look meant. I knew where this was going and I wasn't going to stop it.

I could barely breathe, the anticipation was almost too much. He bit his lip and I closed my eyes, but only for a split second, I had to see him.

He leaned down and each moment that his lips weren't on mine was agony. Only he didn't kiss me, he just brushed his lips against mine before he started to kiss down my neck. I gasped for breath.

'Is this okay?' he asked and I responded with *yes more*, more in moan than in speech.

His lips moved along my collar bone and he curled his fingers around the strap of my dress before he stopped the kissing. He curled his other finger round the opposite side, locking eyes with mine, and then he slid the straps down, tracing the length of my arms with his nails.

My whole body was tingling. I watched as his eyes flitted over my body and how he missed a breath. He let go of my dress and it fell to the floor.

I took a little glimpse, embarrassed at the mismatched underwear combination, but by the way Jimmy was looking, my polka-dot pants didn't bother him in the slightest. I grabbed at the waistband of his shorts and pulled him in to me and now it was his turn.

I pulled his shirt over his head and dropped it next to my dress.

'Now I get why you're playing all the pickleball,' I said, with a gasp. I ran a finger over his defined stomach. I'd lain over every inch of it before, but it was like I was discovering it all again. I ran my hand down the centre, past his navel and down to his waistband. He groaned in pleasure and my hands started to unbutton his shorts and, whilst I did, his hands were tracing down my back. He brought me closer as he pressed me up against him.

It was as if we were touching each other for the first time, taking in every single curve and bump along the way, but at the same time it was as if we'd been given a cheat sheet. He ran his hands under my knicker line in the way that he knew drove me crazy and I bit at his ear because that got him in the same way. There was a danger that it would be all over too quickly, but I couldn't help it. I wanted him. All those parts of my body that had lain dormant over the last few months were starting to erupt.

My mind kept trying to tell me this wasn't a good idea, but every part of my body was screaming that it was.

Teasing time was over. I pulled his mouth onto mine and he kissed me hard. We stumbled backwards until we hit his bed in the nook and he lifted me up and laid me down on it. His lips leaving mine, he tugged off my strapless bra and took his mouth to bite at my nipple, with flicks and licks, his other hand twisting the other.

It was impossible to keep up. I was breathless and panting and, when he came up to kiss me on the lips, I could smell sweat and the orange bergamot. In between it all, his boxers were off and my knickers and then it was just us.

He stopped and pulled me up to sitting, softly kissing me before he looked back at me. He wiped a tear from my face.

'We don't have to, we can stop,' he said, in between breaths.

I hadn't realised the tear had escaped. His hand that had been so frantic minutes before was now so still and gentle, resting on my face.

'No, don't stop. I didn't mean to cry. It's just—' I scrunched my eyes shut. I didn't want to think any more. I'd thought enough for a lifetime. 'I need you inside me.'

I opened my eyes and he was staring at me. He was checking once more, before his hand slipped down my face, then ran down the side of my entire body until it landed on my thigh. He held it there, and let the anticipation grow before he ran it up my inside thigh. I moaned as his hands started to explore. Arching my back to push myself against it, as he started to rub rhythmically, I could feel his erection pressing against me.

'You're driving me crazy,' I said, gasping as he kept teasing me with his fingers, bringing me closer and then slowing things down.

'That's the idea,' he said, kissing my mouth and then my neck.

I pushed his hands away and rolled him over. He was flat on his back and I pinned his arms to the side. It had been so long since I'd felt anything like this and I'd almost forgotten what I was capable of.

'Then it's my turn.'

I kissed down his side, but before I got where I was going, he pulled me up.

'You can't be doing that. I'm not going to last,' he said, with a small laugh. He reached over to the shelf behind him.

I kissed him as he slipped the condom on and I pushed myself down onto him. He locked eyes with mine and I held him there for a second, our skin clammy and hot, and the moment passing between us, before he grabbed at my bum to push into me deeper. I started to rock my hips and we fell into a rhythm that our bodies knew so well. And as he pushed harder and started to groan, I knew he was close and I found my nails digging into him. He collapsed into me, wanting to hold onto his climax as he came.

We stayed close, our bodies wet with sweat. He nibbled at my ear and at my neck. He pulled out and pushed me backwards and had his hands between my legs again. This time I was ready. I moved my hips until his fingers found the spot and it was seconds before the ripples started to pass over me and the orgasm grew, my whole body shuddering. He held me there as everything pulsed, until I pulled him up to me. He collapsed his arms around me.

Neither of us said a word. I was too scared to say what I was thinking, that I didn't want that to be the last time.

Another tear rolled down my cheek and, as it rolled onto his chest, he squeezed me tighter, and more tears started to fall. Words unspoken. I knew tomorrow that doubt and regret would creep in and my mind would twist and distort what had happened. But right now I was going to take it all in. Never had I ever felt so content to be anywhere.

Chapter 25

I woke up the next morning to the sound of Jimmy's alarm. I was laying naked on my front and it took me few moments to piece everything together. Being in Jimmy's bed. What had happened the night before.

He silenced his alarm and then he bent down and kissed the back of my head.

'You okay?' he asked.

I turned to look at him, but he was almost impossible to see in the darkness.

'I'm okay,' I said, with a nod.

He drew the curtain from the nook and light flooded in. We'd forgotten to close the main curtains last night.

'It was a good night,' he said, propping himself up on his elbow.

'It was.'

'I could stay home today, if you like.'

'Jimmy,' I said, with a firm tone, but a smile on my face. 'Stop trying to use me as an excuse to take the day off. Besides, I've got work today. Kiran's coming to town. What's the time?'

'Alarm was set for seven.'

I nodded. 'I'm meeting him at eight, so we better get going. But thank you for last night. You were right, some things are better in real life rather than virtual.'

Jimmy started to laugh and then he sighed.

'I better go and shower then.'

'You better had.' I pulled my sheet further round me. We didn't have the time to go there again and, in the cold light of day, I worried that my mind, which was so easily overridden by my desire last night, wouldn't be as quietly subdued now.

Jimmy hovered for a second and, whilst last night there had been no inhibitions, now awkwardness was creeping in. He leaned a little forward and I wondered if he was going to kiss me, but he thought better of it and scooted off the bed to the bathroom. I watched as he walked away. I was already trying to ignore the voices that were trying to tell me that what happened was a mistake, the seed of regret already sown. We'd only just got our friendship on track and, the last time I checked, friends didn't give each other orgasms. But there was no time to dwell on that now. I had to start thinking about the session with Kiran.

I'd left the apartment with a sense of purpose. Something that I'd always taken for granted, but something that hadn't been happening of late. Jimmy went off into work and, with a late meeting, he was going to meet me at the Periscope Monkeys gig tonight.

Kiran had six hours until he flew to San Francisco and we'd arranged to meet in lower Manhattan. I spotted him pacing and tapping on his phone.

'Hello stranger,' I said, giving him a wave as he looked up from his phone.

'Hey, look at you.' There was that slightly awkward moment where if we'd been friends, we would have hugged, but he was my client, no matter what Jimmy was trying to suggest. 'You look so different. You're glowing.'

I put my hands up. I was hit by flashbacks of last night. 'I've been outside a lot. It's probably just a tan.'

'It doesn't look like any tan I've ever had,' he said. 'But I hear that being outside works wonders. I should get out of the office more often.'

Kiran was a self-confessed workaholic and, judging from the rings under his eyes, I guessed that he'd been burning the midnight oil of late.

'I'm so happy to see you here in New York,' I said. We started to walk down the street, away from the subway station we'd met at. 'I can't believe you came.'

'It was something you said about making time. I guess it hit a nerve.'

'I didn't mean slotting in a few hours to see a whole city, I meant taking a proper break.'

'What is it you say about changing habits? Small steps?' He looked a little sheepish, but this was a step in the right direction. 'I should be prepping for the conference now and, look, I'm here.'

'You have written your presentation, haven't you?'

'Oh yeah.' There was a nervousness in his voice.

'Then you've got nothing to worry about. It's a great opportunity to put into practice what we've worked on.'

He stopped and looked over at the office in front of him, not meeting my eye.

'I do remember what we worked on. It's just it's a huge conference. One of my lecturers, who was kind of like a mentor to me, is speaking at it. I've also heard rumours that Mark Zuckerberg might be there.' He put his hands in his pockets and rocked on his feet. 'I keep thinking that I should have done it virtually. At least, if I stuttered or messed it up, I could have blamed it on the thing freezing.'

I stifled a laugh. 'I could just see that now.' I pulled a funny face, pretending I was frozen on screen.

'Just like that,' he groaned. 'But now it's in person.'

'Kiran, you're the most confident person I've ever met. If anything, you've got a little bit too much confidence sometimes.'

'Like being a bit cocky.'

'It's not a bad thing,' I said, shaking my head. 'It's not one of those double-edged flaws. It's a great skill to have. You've got a charm and a likeability that many people in your industry don't have. Remember that.'

'But everyone else on the panel is so qualified and they've all got heaps more experience—'

'And you were asked to be on the panel. You were picked.'

'It was probably some kind of diversity thing,' he said.

We reached the coffee shop that we were heading towards and I held open the door to Kiran, giving him a stern look. 'More likely it's because of your credentials. You sold your first business for high six figures, and you're in talks to sell your next one for seven figures. You more than deserve your seat on that stage.'

He was about to open his mouth to argue, but I put my hand up.

'This is sounding an awful lot like imposter syndrome, and you of all people don't need to suffer from that. I'd say "Fake it until you make it", but you've already made it.' I stepped forward to the counter and ordered our coffees and bagels to go. I turned back to Kiran. 'This is the last I want to hear of that.'

He nodded. 'Okay, okay. See, I knew it was worth stopping off to see you. You always inspire me. I know it hasn't been easy for you, since your friend. But thank you.'

I bit my lip. Now it was time for my imposter syndrome to kick in.

The barista didn't take long making the coffees and he passed us them, along with the bagels. We headed out of the coffee shop and I steered us in the direction of Battery Park.

'You've nothing to thank me for.'

'I have. You've been great over these last few months. I honestly don't know what I would have done.'

'I'm only doing my job.'

'Chloe, learn to take a compliment. The words are *you're welcome*.'

I laughed and handed Kiran his bagel.

'You're welcome,' I parroted.

'Good. Now, are we going to see some of this city, as right now I feel like I could have been in London—' I pointed behind him and he turned and stopped mid-sentence. 'Oh, my God, is that the Statue of Liberty?' His whole face lit up and he handed me his cup of coffee as he dug his phone out of his backpack. 'I can't believe it looks so small from here.'

I always found the sight of Lady Liberty thrilling and I'd been here countless times. I forgot the wonder of being able to see the city for the first time.

'Come on,' I said, steering him to the ferry terminal. 'If you think that's a good view, just you wait.'

It was early and the ferry was busy, but we managed to get seats on the top deck.

'I can't believe this is free,' said Kiran, still enthralled with his surroundings.

'Yeah. Now if you'd had longer, you could have gone over and seen it and Ellis Island, but we don't want you to miss your plane.'

'I'm gutted. It was all so last-minute. I should have tacked on a few more days.'

'Taken a holiday? What have you done with the real Kiran?'

'Maybe the Kiran that you're shaping me into is realising that I need to have boundaries, to see there's a life outside the office.'

I did a mock sharp intake of breath. 'Don't tell me you think you're learning something in these sessions?'

He smiled. 'You know, I was dubious when Fran suggested I needed coaching. If I'm really honest, I thought it was a bit unnecessary, but I'm starting to not recognise myself, in a good way.'

A warm pride washed over me. This was the kind of thing I hoped for, doing my coaching. It reminded me of the early days when I worked in HR and I'd worked for a small tech firm that grew rapidly, and almost overnight there was a new layer of management who didn't have the experience or skills to cope. Working out the new training and building up their confidence and practical knowledge, I had got to watch the transformation. It had been then that the seeds were sown for my future career in executive coaching. Seeing people believe in themselves and grow from within. It was all so rewarding.

'I'm sorry. That sounded so rude.'

'It didn't at all. It's made me really happy.'

'It's a gift, isn't it? To be able to make a difference in someone's life, and that's what I feel like you're doing.'

I had to stop punishing myself for the fact that I couldn't make a difference in Kerry's life when she needed me the most, and instead I needed to focus on the other differences I had made in other people's.

'All this flattery. It's going to give me a big head.'

'So it should.'

The ferry started to move and Kiran was back into tourist mode as we pulled away from Manhattan, and he snapped away as the skyline kept coming more into view.

'Now, speaking of that help I've given you. Don't think that you're going to come all this way to meet me and we're not going to be working on conference networking tips. Have you got any ideas of how you're going to make those good first impressions?'

We'd talked before about how sometimes his boundless energy could come across as a little extra when you didn't know him.

'And here was me thinking that we were going to get to gawk at all the buildings instead.'

'You can still do that, but we might as well get something out of it whilst we're here.'

'I guess so.'

I don't know if it was the hot breeze warming my face and the smell of the sea or whether it was the buzz of something clicking with a client but, for the first time in a long time, I truly felt as if I was living in the moment. Since Kerry died, I'd struggled with the spontaneous nature of coaching sessions. They were hard to plan in advance as they were supposed to evolve in reaction to what the clients said. It was all about asking the clients questions, trying to get them to lead the direction. It had seemed almost impossible at times, but today it all felt so natural.

'So, come on then. How are you going to make a good impression?'

Two hours later, I'd left Kiran at Wall Street downloading a walking tour. He was looking forward to the conference and he had goals in place for what he wanted to achieve in the networking and strategies he could call on if the nerves got the better of him. He was ready to go and, after a little bit more sightseeing, he'd be on his way at lunchtime.

I went back to the Village. Retracing my steps to Gennari's, I headed in to order my lunch.

This time I didn't hesitate in going up to the counter. 'I'll have a prosciutto and mozzarella on rye, please,' I said. I went through the motions, adding peppers, mushrooms and rocket. This time I wasn't waiting for Blaine. I was hungry and wanted to eat. I'd come to terms with the fact that I wasn't going to miraculously find him in a city of eight million people. This wasn't about what he wanted, but about what I wanted.

I took my sandwich and ate it on my way uptown. Kerry and I had spent many a weekend window shopping along Fifth Avenue and, seeing my reflection in the glass of Saks, I could almost visualise Kerry standing beside me. Far from running from it, I embraced it, tracing the route that we would have walked, picking out the items in my mind that I knew she'd have liked.

I walked past a fancy-looking hotel with a sign for a rooftop bar and I was almost past it, when I turned on my heels and headed into the lobby.

I thought of the time Kerry and I had made it up to one, and had our very disappointing appletinis. We might have just been able to afford a cocktail, but we hadn't been able to afford the Louboutins. The memory burned at my heart, as any Kerry memory did. But it also made me smile. The thought of the two of us in our early twenties giggling in the bar, having to nurse the same drink all night, as we could only afford the one.

I headed up in the lift to the rooftop and went straight to the bar. It was only a small roof terrace, not like the big one with pulsing beats that Kerry and I had visited. There were small tables lining one side of the building edge, and most of the people sitting at them were couples.

'What can I get you?' asked the bartender, sliding a menu towards me.

I picked it up and perused the list.

'I don't suppose you do appletinis?'

He wrinkled up his nose. 'Sorry. I don't think I'd have the ingredients to cobble one together. How about a bittersweet Old Fashioned?'

My eyes flicked over the ingredients and I nodded. 'Bittersweet Old Fashioned sounds pretty spot-on.'

'They don't even make appletinis any more,' I exclaimed to virtual Kerry later that afternoon.

Her green-flecked eyes stared wide at me.

'How can they not?'

'They're too old-fashioned,' I said, feeling officially old. 'Which is what I ended up drinking. And it was twenty-five dollars! For one cocktail.'

'That's New York prices for you,' she said.

'I guess.'

'Did you at least enjoy it?'

'I did, in the end. It's been like this the whole trip. It hurts a little because it reminds me of you, but then I start to think of the good times. I'm no longer trying to shy away from the memories. I want to remember them.'

'Sometimes confronting your problems head on is the best course of action.'

The words were right, but the delivery was so automated.

'Are you enjoying your trip to New York?'

'More than I thought possible.' I closed my eyes and curled my fingers into fists, trying to summon the courage to say what I needed to say. 'Kerry, I think it's getting close to the time when I'm going to stop coming to see you.'

'Oh,' she said, taken aback. 'You're still mad at me?'

'I am still mad at you. I'm never going to not be angry with you.

But I've got to let go of some of that anger or else it's going to take me down with it.'

'So, you forgive me?'

I took a deep breath. Did I forgive her? Would I ever?

I shook my head. 'But I am coming to terms that what's done is done. And I can't change what I did or didn't do. I'm just going to have to live with it. And talking to you... I need to let you go properly, rather than keeping you hanging on.'

'But I like to chat to you.'

'I know, but I've got to start to say goodbye. I've got to start getting the closure I came here to get.'

I took a deep breath. I needed to be brave. I needed to find that inner courage that I tried to coax out of my clients.

'How are you going to get the closure? That sounds so final.'

'I'm going to tell you how I feel. I'm not ready to do it today, but some time soon I'm going tell you.'

'Okay,' she said, sitting up that little bit taller. I knew it wasn't really her. That she was just the imagination of a computer, but at the same time it was the closest I was ever going to get to telling the real Kerry what was on my mind.

I wanted to get it over and done with, but watching those brown flecks sparkle, I knew I wasn't quite ready.

Instead, she probed more about my trip to New York and, as I told her, the chasm between us started to grow. It was hitting me with almost every sentence that these visits were on borrowed time. This wasn't how I needed to fix my loneliness.

When I'd finished telling her about my trip, I logged off and put the headset down on the coffee table. I knew what I needed to do. I picked up my phone and started a video call, inviting Nina, Marianne and Andrea.

Nina was the first to pick up.

'Oh, my God, you phoned us,' she whispered.

'Why are you whispering?'

'I've just got Oliver down to sleep. But know that inside I'm ecstatic about this.'

Marianne's and Andrea's photos popped up.

'What's happened?' asked Andrea. 'Everything okay?'

'Everything's fine. I just thought I'd check in in person.'

There was so much to tell them, even discounting the fact that I couldn't tell them what had happened last night or about my search for Blaine.

'Ah, it's so lovely to speak to you,' said Marianne. 'I've loved living vicariously through you on this trip. It's made the night wakings much more enjoyable. The WhatsApp group is going to seem so boring when you get home.'

'Well, don't forget we'll be planning our girls' trip there. I've already sent a Doodle with dates,' said Andrea.

I laughed. And there was us being worried about how Andrea would cope now that she no longer had a wedding to plan.

As Nina whispered all the places that she wanted us to see on the proposed trip, I started to think about how much I'd missed out by keeping everyone at arm's length. I missed Kerry with all my heart, but I had to remember that was no reason to miss everyone else too.

Chapter 26

I was happy to leave Jimmy's apartment to head out to the bar to see Periscope Monkeys. After what had happened the previous night, the apartment felt so cold and soulless without him.

It had been a stiflingly hot day and, even as the darkness started to creep in, the high humidity seemed to have a stranglehold on the city. I'd taken one look at my heels and hailed a taxi. I didn't want to turn up to see the band a sweaty mess.

It pulled up outside the subway station where I was meeting Jimmy.

'Are you just doing it to wind me up?' he said, before I'd closed the door behind me.

'What?'

'Ignoring the effort that I put in to sort out your travel arrangements. Seriously, you are the only person I know that uses yellow taxis.'

'Come on, I'm a tourist.'

He curled his lip and shook his head. It went against all his money-saving ways.

'Let's get going to see this band. There's a bar we can go to at the venue,' he said, still shaking his head in disgust.

'Excellent,' I said, trying to keep up with him now that I was in my heels. I had been nervous about seeing Jimmy again after last night. I'd lost all my inhibitions yesterday, but now they were back with a vengeance. Not that anyone else would be able to tell that there had been a last night. Jimmy was just being Jimmy, acting the same as he always did. It was helping to put me at ease.

It was a short walk, in which I mainly moaned about my heels, and Jimmy about the heat.

'How was work?' I asked, as we walked inside and straight up the stairs.

'Work-like,' he said. He'd taken off his tie, but he was still dressed in a short-sleeved shirt and smart trousers. He looked good. 'How was your day? Did you get up to anything good?'

'I met Kiran this morning. Then I headed up to Fifth Avenue to window shop, mainly.'

Jimmy pushed open the door to the bar and held it open for me so that I slipped underneath his arm. I caught the smell of his aftershave and for a second, I was right back in last night.

The place was busy, but the music was low enough that we could still talk. We made a beeline for the bar, which only had a few people trying to get served.

'I'm glad you got out after last night. I was worried in case it... set you back?'

He was tapping a finger on the bar and it was as if he couldn't look at me.

'Not at all. If anything, it just made me even more determined that I needed to get on with things.'

He let out a deep breath and looked up at me. I wondered if he was going to say more about it. I wondered what I'd reply if he did.

'That's good,' he said, with a smile. 'But you know, window shopping isn't what I'd pick to do to feel as if I was getting on with things.'

I was relieved that he'd taken the conversation in a different direction.

'I wanted to pick something that Kerry would have done. It's the type of day she used to make us go on when we couldn't afford anything. We'd scrape together enough for a coffee at Saks. Then we'd pop into Tiffany's and Bergdorf Goodman.'

'And how did you feel?'

'It didn't feel great, but I did it. It made me realise I can't avoid the memories forever and, this will sound cheesy, but it made me feel closer to her. Closer than the AI version that I've been chatting to.'

He nodded his head. 'That's great news. When do I get to say I told you so?'

'Um, let's see, like, never.'

He was looking at me and he suddenly looked away.

'What?' I asked.

'Nothing,' he blinked and then looked back at me. 'Are we going to get this drink or what?'

'Come on, you're not getting off that lightly. What?'

He sighed and tucked his watch strap back into the holders.

'It's just this,' he said. 'It's like you're how you used to be, and I've missed this. You know the back and forth.'

'Bickering?' My eyes widened.

'Bantering.'

'You and Sienna don't have the bants?' Saying the word out loud gave me the ick.

'There isn't a me and Sienna, you know that. And no, I don't know if it's cultural or the age.'

I mock-gasped. 'Don't tell me there are drawbacks to dating a twenty-three-year-old.'

'Not dating, remember. Just casually seeing.'

'Right,' I said, with a small sigh. 'You know that this is just easy between us because we know each other so well that it's all habit. Muscle memory.'

'Muscle memory?'

'Yeah, like it just comes back naturally without any effort. I'm surprised you haven't grabbed my arse when you made one of your awful dad jokes.'

'I don't know what's more offensive, the fact that you think my jokes are dad jokes or that you're making it sound like I was a dirty old man grabbing your bum.'

'Perhaps grabbing was the wrong word. Slapping maybe.'

'I don't think that sounds any better. I was showing affection,' he said with a shrug, 'and I'm not going to lie, I'm a bum man. But is that what you thought last night was, just muscle memory?'

He was staring hard at me and I could feel the flutter in my belly take hold.

'Maybe,' I said, not because I meant it, but because my heart needed to harden. I'd slowly started to put myself back into the world, I couldn't open my heart up to get broken again.

'Chloe,' said a voice.

Jimmy's eyes were boring into me, and I had to blink a couple of times to break the spell. I turned to see that Theo was standing there.

All at once it felt like I couldn't remember how to breathe. The two of them were staring at me, looking for me to acknowledge them. I'd desperately wanted to be rescued from my conversation with Jimmy, but Theo was not the white knight I'd envisaged.

'Can we talk?' said Theo, looking between me and Jimmy. 'Sorry, am I interrupting?'

'Theo, this is Jimmy, my um… sort of roommate and ex or…'

Whatever word I wanted to end the sentence with sounded inadequate.

'The word she is looking for is "friend",' he said, putting his hand out. 'And you're Kerry's Theo?'

There was a flicker of pain in Theo's eyes before he nodded and shook Jimmy's outstretched hand.

'I'll get us some drinks,' said Jimmy, as if we weren't already standing at the bar. We'd been down the end of it and hadn't made any attempt to catch the attention of the barman.

'Shall we go and sit?' Theo gestured to a nearby table that had high stools. I nodded and headed over.

Theo perched on the stool. 'I'm sorry. I should have said more the other night or gone after you. It was such a shock to see you here.'

'You have nothing to be sorry about. I was having a tough time of it. So much in New York reminded me of her.'

He nodded. 'Yeah. That's the worst, isn't it? I can't go to my favourite coffee shop because I half-expect her to be sat in the window, moaning about the way they made her tea.'

'Did they serve it with honey?'

'Lemon,' he said, with a shake of the head.

I winced and pulled a face. 'No wonder she moaned. Lemons are not for tea.'

'No, apparently tea had to be made a particular way.' He shrugged. 'I never got it. I was always in trouble, too, for putting the milk in first.'

'Heretic,' I said with a shudder. 'But if it makes you feel any better, me and Kerry were friends for years and I never made her a cup of tea that passed her test. I mean, I stopped trying pretty early on in the friendship. Instead, on the rare occasions she forgot I couldn't make tea and I put the kettle on, I always put the milk in first, which anyone who makes tea will tell you is a heinous crime. But it meant that she wouldn't ask for a good while after.'

The bar was steadily filling up and I watched out for Lila, or signs of Jimmy coming back with the much-needed drinks.

'When do you leave?'

'I fly out tomorrow night.'

'Right,' he said with a slow nod, taking it all in.

'It's been a good trip. I've put some demons to rest. New York's where I met Kerry and it always felt like our place.'

He nodded.

'We'll always have New York,' he said, putting on a voice with a twang.

'That's what she always used to say to me.'

He laughed. 'She used to say it me too. When we were struggling to make things work long distance. She borrowed it from *Casablanca*.'

'*Casablanca*,' I said, nodding. 'Of course. Kerry loved that film. The number of times that she'd shove it on when we were nursing hangovers on a Sunday lying on the sofa.'

'It's one of those films with all the best lines. I used to watch it a lot with her. She told me I reminded her of Humphrey Bogart.'

'It's the eyes,' I said, finding myself looking into his dark brown eyes.

'That's what she used to say.'

I thought of the times we'd snuggled on the sofa, feeling far too sorry for ourselves, drinking industrial-sized cups of coffee and eating greasy food. Watching Ilsa and Rick walk away from love, hoping every time that things worked out differently.

I thought of Humphrey Bogart playing Rick and shivers started to tingle up and down my spine. Rick *Blaine*.

'No, it can't be,' I muttered under my breath.

'It can't be what?' asked Theo.

'Rick Blaine. You, you're Blaine.'

Surely my mind was jumping to the wrong conclusion? He couldn't be the one in eight million that I was looking for. Not Theo.

Theo's eyes locked with mine and I shivered again, more violently this time. I could see from the way he was looking at me that it was true.

'You're Cat?'

It had been him all along. All this time I'd known him. My mind went into overdrive as I tried to reconcile the feelings that I'd had in the Metaverse with the fact that they'd been feelings for Theo. *Kerry's* Theo.

'Chloe Cat,' I said, barely finding my words. 'My sister calls me it, she said it was like Kitty Cat.'

Neither of us said anything as the magnitude of it sank in.

'I should have known it was you,' he said, shaking his head. 'When I saw you last week at the gig, I should have pieced it all together.'

'I can't believe it.'

'You came to New York after all. You know I tried to find you on other platforms?'

I thought of all the times that I'd manifested for this moment to come true, but now that it had, it was impossible for my brain to match up the idea to reality.

'Me too,' I said quietly. Blaine was Theo. Theo was Blaine. The more I said it over and over in my head, the less it seemed real, despite the fact that he was sitting in front of me, the most real he'd ever been to me.

'You guys okay?' asked Jimmy, holding three bottles of beer together in a triangle. He popped them down on the table and slid them across to us. 'You two look like you've seen a ghost.' Jimmy closed his eyes for a second. 'Sorry, terrible choice of words.'

'It's okay. It feels like I have. It turns out Chloe and I have been speaking for the last few months or so not knowing it was each other.'

My body went rigid. In that moment where fight or flight was supposed to take hold, fear gripped me instead and rendered me paralysed.

'You've been speaking for months?' Jimmy's expression changed.

It was the closest I'd ever come to an out-of-body experience. It was as if I was watching it all happen. Jimmy's face started to wrinkle, confusion evident.

'In the Metaverse.' Theo raised his eyebrows at me as if to confirm it, but I could only stare at Jimmy.

The shock was starting to register and he turned to me, his eyebrows questioning.

'In the Metaverse? When you said you were talking to people other than Kerry?'

'To Kerry?' asked Theo.

'Long story,' I said, almost choking on the words, my throat so dry. Both of them were looking at me, and all I could do was panic.

'Hey, hey, hey,' said Lila, coming up, with Anthony following behind her. She leaned over to hug Jimmy as he was closest, but he didn't hug her back. His eyes still trained on me.

'What's going on?' she asked, taking in the scene at the table.

'We've just found out that Chloe and Theo have been talking for months in the Metaverse, but didn't know they were talking to each other.'

'Shut the fuck up. You're Blaine!' Lila cried.

'You found him?' said Anthony. 'I never in a million years thought you two would actually find him, no matter how much you looked.'

'You've been looking for him? And everyone else knew?' Jimmy's voice was so low and despondent it was almost unrecognisable. I wanted to be anywhere but here.

'You were looking for me?' said Theo. He smiled and his brow furrowed. 'That's why you came?'

'You came to New York to find him?' said Jimmy. He started to drink a little from his bottle and then his forehead wrinkled. But I didn't think it was the beer that was leaving a bitter taste in his mouth.

'And now you have,' said Lila, a clap of her hands. She and Theo might have been oblivious to Jimmy's reaction, but I wasn't.

Lila and Theo started to chat about the odds of this happening, but I couldn't join in. I was trying to read Jimmy. I watched as he started to get more and more agitated. He wouldn't even look at me.

'I've actually remembered, I've got something I've got to do,' he said, pointing at the door. 'You okay to get home?'

'Don't go,' I said, sliding off my seat and taking hold of him by the arm, but he pulled away.

'I don't think I want to stay,' he said.

'Jimmy,' I started, but he was already weaving his way through the bar. I turned back to Lila and Theo, and they were stuck deep in conversation until they noticed that I was alone.

'Where'd Jimmy go?' asked Anthony.

'He had to, um, he had to go.'

Lila looked between Theo and me.

'I think we should go and get a drink,' said Lila, tugging at Anthony's sleeve.

If Anthony was going to protest, Lila's look to him told him otherwise. He gave us a wave and followed her over to the bar.

'Wow, I still can't get over this. All that time,' said Theo, oblivious to what had just happened with Jimmy and his sudden departure.

'I know,' I said. My legs were weak and I tried to steady myself by clutching hold of the table. 'Look, I've got to go to Jimmy. He wasn't looking... I really should go.'

'Wait,' said Theo, reaching his hand out. 'You can't go now. We've only just found each other. I thought I was never going to see you again.'

I was torn between the man that had been the only reason I'd kept going over the last month or two and the man I should never have pushed away in the first place.

'I've got to check on Jimmy, but are you around tomorrow? I fly out in the evening.'

'You're flying home tomorrow? Can't you stay?'

'My flight's booked and I've got work.'

'Okay. I can move things around. Tomorrow? At the Cloisters?'

My stomach lurched. That had been the time in the Metaverse where my belly had been full of those somersaulting feelings, but the fact that Blaine was Theo changed everything. Theo had been Kerry's 'one that got away', he wasn't mine for the taking, but I couldn't shake the niggle that out of all the people I could have met, I met him, and I'd felt that connection.

'I'll send you a DM,' he said.

All this time I'd been looking for him and I had the ability to find him on an app on my phone.

He reached over and wrapped me up in a hug and I couldn't help but hug him back. I was numb with emotion.

I pulled away and headed to go out.

'Where are you going?' asked Lila, her arm looped around Anthony's. 'I don't think the doors are open downstairs yet.'

'I've got to find Jimmy.'

'But didn't you just find Blaine?' She put her hand on my arm. 'Are you sure you're going after the right man?'

The look on Jimmy's face flashed through my mind.

'I've got to see him.'

'But you'll miss the band.'

It was never about the band. It was always about the link to Kerry. But I didn't need that any more. I needed the living.

'Why change the habit of a lifetime?'

'But you're going tomorrow.' She squeezed my arm tighter. 'You have to stay. I won't see you.'

I hesitated. I didn't think two weeks ago sitting on the plane and staring at the map on the screen that I'd find a friend in the woman sitting next to me. 'I know. You realise that you're going to have to come and visit.'

'Another trip to London.' Her whole face lit up with excitement, whilst Anthony's eyes widened in horror.

'You know these days you can FaceTime,' he said. 'Video calls are the more sustainable option.'

'They're the more tight-ass option,' said Lila with a deft eye roll. 'But he's right. I'll be calling you to check in.'

'I like that idea.'

'Me too. And you know we're keeping the WhatsApp group when we get home? Between the *Married at First Sight* chat and the recipes that Andrea posts.'

'That group has a life of its own.'

She reached around and gave me a hug, and I squeezed her back. I might be going home still grieving the loss of a friend, but I was going home having gained another one.

Chapter 27

There were no signs of life when I opened the apartment door. I flicked on the lights, hoping that Jimmy would be sitting in the dark as people did in the movies, but it didn't take long to see it was empty. My stomach lurched at the thought that he'd gone elsewhere.

'Shit,' I muttered, picking up my phone and calling him again. It went straight through to voicemail. Maybe he'd gone to drown his sorrows, but I didn't have a clue where to start looking for him. My stomach sank at the thought he'd gone to Sienna.

I did another check of the apartment before gathering up my keys, phone and wallet. I opened the door and there was Jimmy, his key card in his hand, about to open the door. He dropped the key card in shock at seeing me and it clattered to the floor.

'You scared the crap out of me.' He bent down to retrieve the key and stared hard when he came up to standing. 'Did you teleport? How did you get here so quickly?'

'Taxi.'

'For fuck's sake. It's three stops on the subway.'

I bit my lip, suppressing a tiny smile that, even though he was mad at me, he was still berating me for splurging on a cab. He ran his hands through his hair.

'Why aren't you at the gig?' He dumped his key and phone on

the counter and started pouring himself a glass of water. 'Or with him? Isn't he the reason you're here?'

He slammed the glass down on the counter top.

'Jimmy, it's not like that.'

'It's not like what? Not like you flew over 6,000 miles to find a man that you'd been chatting to in the Metaverse? Not like you've spent the past two weeks running round the city trying to find him?'

I sighed. It was exactly like that. 'I know how it sounds,' I said, not knowing how I could possibly articulate what I was thinking. 'It wasn't... I needed to get away, I was drowning at home and I was spinning out of control and then when I had the idea to come to New York, it snowballed. And yes, it might have been to find him, but I don't think that was the real reason.'

'Right,' he said, not looking up at me. 'And then all that time we spent together.'

'It's been lovely. It made me realise that it wasn't an empty promise that we'd stay friends.'

He laughed a hollow laugh.

'Fuck, Chloe. I thought you'd come to New York for me.' His voice was small and his words stabbed at my heart. 'I thought you'd realised what we'd had, and that you were lost and if I just helped to fix you...'

His eyes looked red as if he'd cried without the tears having fallen.

'Jimmy.' My voice quivered and I took a step closer towards him. 'I'm so sorry. I didn't think. You kept talking about us being friends. You're the one that was dating Sienna.'

'I'm not really dating Sienna. I saw her a couple of times. I don't think she was even that into me until you showed up. Anyway, that's not the fucking point. The point was that I was fully open about

Sienna. I told you about her. You met her. You could see that she wasn't serious. But you. You never told me about Theo or that you'd met someone that you liked enough to travel all that way for. Why didn't you tell me? You could have saved me making a complete dick of myself.'

'I couldn't tell you.'

'Why?'

'Because it sounded ridiculous, that I'd met a stranger online that I thought I might have fallen for. You would have told me to stay well clear. You'd have questioned my sanity.'

He held his hands high in the air, grunting with frustration.

'Of course I would have done,' he said, dropping his arms and turning to me. 'He could have been anyone.'

'And that's why I didn't say anything.'

'This is so typical of you.'

'So typical of me?'

'Yeah. I tried to help you after Kerry died and you pushed me away. You pushed your sister away, and Marianne and Andrea, and then you go and meet a stranger and that's who you confide in.'

'It wasn't like that. I wanted to be with someone that didn't know me as Kerry's friend. Someone that didn't know about her death. I wanted to be the old me again.'

'Well, that's ridiculous. You're never going to be the same you again. That's just how life is. Shit happens, and all the pieces break and you put them back together, but they're never the same as they were fresh out of the box. You can't pretend otherwise. You were running away from what's happened.'

His words stung. It was true, all of it, but who was he to tell me that? Anger started to pulse around my body. I'd listened to everyone having an opinion on how I should or shouldn't be handling this, and

I'd taken it all, but for him to tell me that I've run away? His boss had told him he could defer the secondment, he didn't have to come.

'Oh, I was running away from what happened? What about you?' I said, starting to almost shriek. 'You moved across the Atlantic. If you really wanted to still be with me, why would you still come here?'

'Because it broke my heart to watch you falling apart, more than it broke my heart not to be with you.'

He stopped me in my tracks, my legs going weak. The anger that was coursing around my veins started to turn to the familiar feeling of shame, regret and guilt. The trinity I'd come to know so well over the last few months. A tear rolled down my cheek.

'I tried to stay. I tried to be around you, but you kept pushing me away,' he said, his hands in his hair.

'Because every time I spent time with you, I felt guilty.'

'Guilty?' he spat.

'Yeah, because Kerry needed me and where was I? I was with you. I was always with you and I should have been a better friend and if I'd picked up the phone...' My voice started to wobble. The pain of hearing the voice messages after she'd died, the messages that I'd meant to return, but I'd been too self-absorbed. I'd thought that I'd call her tomorrow, but her tomorrow had never come.

'Chloe,' he said, in a stern voice that only made the tears start to sting behind my eyes. 'We all feel guilty that we didn't do enough. I spent so much time with you two. I saw her go up and down. I saw you worrying about her. I could have suggested you reach out. But, that's the thing,' he said, taking a deep breath and softening his voice. He tilted his head. 'There were so many things that could have changed what happened that day. A random act of kindness from a stranger. Her phoning someone that picked up. But that's the point, someone could have stopped her one day, only for her to try another. Or she might have got the help she needed. But that's what you've got to accept. That you'll never know if it could be different and you've got to stop looking back at the what-ifs. You've got to accept that it happened, that it won't change.' He leaned on the kitchen counter as if he was making a point. 'Above all, you've got to forgive yourself.'

He rendered me speechless. All I could hear was the hum of the air conditioning.

'I don't know how to forgive myself,' I said, finding my words. 'It's like I feel so alone. No one else gets it.'

'She might have been your best friend, but she was my friend too. And look at her funeral, it was packed full. She'd touched the lives of all those people. Stop saying you're alone when you're not.' He sighed again. 'I can't do this. I need to go somewhere.'

'Go where? It's late.'

'I don't know. This is the city that doesn't sleep.'

'But what about us? You can't just go.'

'There is no us. That's the point, isn't it? It's just you, and it's just me. This whole being-friends thing, it's never going to work.'

He picked up his key and walked away. The door slammed behind him and I went over to the sofa and sat down, pulling my knees up to my chest. I looked at the VR headset on the coffee table and for once I didn't want to speak to Kerry. The irony was that the only person I wanted to speak to was Jimmy.

Chapter 28

I woke up to the sound of the door slamming. I rubbed at my eyes, an uneasy feeling in my stomach. It took a second or two to remember the events of last night, but the tide of emotions rippled over my body as the argument with Jimmy came back in glorious Technicolor.

I hadn't expected to fall asleep last night. I'd made the sofa into the bed and the tears had come thick and fast. I'd cried for Kerry, for Jimmy and for the fact that he was right. Maybe I could have done more or maybe I couldn't, the only thing I knew was that I couldn't change the past. I had to face facts that, no matter how hard it was, I was going to have to accept it, and live life the best I could. Living as the broken version stitched back together, and much as if I'd used my real-life sewing skills, I'd been raggedly patched up.

I'd cried so hard that I'd exhausted myself and sleep must have overcome me.

I stood up, pulling at last night's clothes that I was still in, twisted and uncomfortable from where I'd slept.

'Jimmy,' I called, as I walked over to the nook, but I met with silence and a freshly made bed.

He'd been home, but he'd gone again. I looked at the clock on the cooker, it was just after 7 o'clock.

I looked out of the window. It was cloudy out, and it was as if the city was reflecting my mood.

I found my phone on the kitchen counter and dialled Jimmy. Just like last night, it went straight to answerphone.

I saw a scrawled note on the counter.

Gone to work. Long day today, won't be back in time before you have to leave for the airport – even if you do take a bloody taxi. Have a safe flight back.

I read the message twice, looking for something more that wasn't there.

'So that's it,' I said, the knot in my stomach tightening.

I wanted to go home now. I wanted to be out of this city and back in my grey-walled house. I wanted to go there and never come out again. Because surely this was proof that being out and about in the world only led to pain.

My phone buzzed in my hand and my stomach lurched, hoping it would be Jimmy, but it was Theo.

I clicked on the DM.

THEO
Hey! You wanna meet for breakfast?

Theo. My mind was in a maelstrom thinking about Jimmy, let alone adding Theo to the equation.

Did I want to meet him for breakfast? I was torn. What I wanted to do was track down Jimmy but, short of sitting outside his office all day, or worse, trying to get past reception to his desk, that wasn't going to happen.

CHLOE
Okay, let me know where. In an hour?

Theo had picked the breakfast equivalent of his favourite deli, Gennari's. It was an old-fashioned diner that was more akin to a British greasy spoon. No thrills. No pretence. The waitress was pouring treacle-like cups of coffee and the open kitchen was cooking a never-ending rotation of eggs, sausages and bacon.

'I used to come here all the time growing up. It was my grandpa's favourite.'

'It's got that kind of family feel to it.'

'Yeah, everyone that used to come in knew each other. That's gone now.' He shrugged his shoulders. 'But sometimes I can still imagine my pop at the counter. We always sat there.'

It was weird sitting opposite Theo. It didn't feel real. This was exactly the type of conversation we'd had in the Metaverse and I kept half-expecting someone with a cat for a head to walk past.

'So, how was the band last night? Better than the Metaverse?'

'Are you kidding? You missed out. Big time. They were awesome. They had two encores, and the place went wild.'

My heart sank. 'I'm gutted.'

I couldn't believe I'd missed them for a second time.

'It reminded me of what it used to be like, going to see a band. Before everything got so commercial.'

'Now you're sounding old.'

'I know. I'm turning into my pop. But it's true. These days the magic gets ruined as you're watching the band through the lens of the person's phone in front of you. But last night, it felt like it used to. And the music.'

'Yeah, now you're just rubbing it in.'

'You'll have to come over and see their last performance over in Brooklyn next month.'

'I can't come back,' I said. 'I already maxed out my credit card with this trip as it is.'

'Then this is it. This is the one day we get,' he said, the waitress appearing out of nowhere and silently filling up his cup, which he'd left purposefully at the end of the table. 'You should have found me sooner.'

I let the words sink in. When I'd flown to New York to find Blaine, I hadn't planned to spend time with Jimmy, but now I couldn't help but think of all the unexpected good times I'd had with him on this trip. The jazz festival, the day walking the High Line, the piano bar and all that night brought. If I'd discovered Theo earlier, all those memories wouldn't exist, but equally it would have meant that I wouldn't have hurt Jimmy the way I had. The more time I'd spent with him, the more concealing my true reasons for coming to New York had felt like I was lying to him.

'Shall we get this breakfast ordered and we can get to the Met?' said Theo, snapping me out of my guilt.

It was strange to be walking around the Met Cloisters in real life, surrounded by tourists.

'It's different in the flesh, isn't it?' said Theo as we weaved our way round a tour group following their guide. We came to a bench and Theo gestured for us to take a seat.

'It's so impressive. I honestly felt like they'd made up a place for the Metaverse.'

It seemed even more like a European palazzo than it had through my headset. With the stifling heat outside mixing with the coolness of the stone inside, it made me feel as if I was in Europe rather than Manhattan.

'I brought Kerry here once.'

'You did?'

He smiled and I noticed that, whenever he spoke her name, there was a sadness lodged behind his smile.

'Yeah. She loved it. She said it made her feel like home.'

'She said that summer was one of the best of her life.'

'It was mine too,' he said, his eyes looking glossy. 'She talked about you a lot.'

I don't know if that made me feel better or worse.

'I think she got a bit homesick without you, but she loved it here, and not *here* here, but Manhattan.'

'I always thought she would come back out and live here eventually.'

'I always hoped she would have found a way.' He sighed and leaned back against the stone wall.

'I know that she'd tried. It's not that easy.'

'No, not unless you get married.' He sighed. 'She suggested that's what we do once. I thought she was crazy. I didn't want to get married for a visa. But I think it was the only way we could have ever made it work.'

'She really did love you, you know.'

'I know,' he nodded. 'The truth was I wanted to marry her. It just scared the hell out of me. We were so young and she'd be giving up her whole life for me. That's some pressure. I couldn't quite believe that I was enough for her to do that. And maybe if I had, then we'd be together now and she wouldn't have…'

'Theo,' I said, gently, but he shook his head. I tried again. 'Theo, look, you can't look back on your life like that. Living with regret.'

Pot, kettle, black.

'But how can I not?' he let out a deep sigh. 'That's why I'm not letting things pass me by any more. I'm trying to seize opportunities.

Like this.' He pointed between me and him. 'Don't you think it's like some kind of sign that we met online and then found each other in real life? I mean, what are the chances?'

I thought of Lila and her reading the signs of the universe.

'I know. I mean, I'd hoped you'd be at the Periscope Monkeys gig, but I didn't expect to actually find you there.'

I didn't need to go into detail about going to Gennari's, or the jazz festival, or walking his running route in Hoboken. There was a fine line between trying to accidentally bump into someone and actual stalking.

'I'm glad you did,' he said, with a wink.

'Did you just wink at me?' I stared at him waiting to see if there was something wrong with his eyes.

'I did. It felt like a winking moment.'

There was something cheesy about it.

'I didn't realise people still winked now that it's not the eighties any more.'

'Come on, if Taylor Swift can pull it off.'

'I'm pretty sure she shouldn't be the benchmark. She could pull anything off,' I said with a tut.

'Okay, but other people wink.'

'Like who?'

'People playing wink murder.'

'Niche,' I said, and he winked again. 'Is that you trying to kill me?'

'Or maybe the conversation.'

I laughed. There was a playfulness to Theo that I vaguely remembered from the few occasions I'd hung out with him and Kerry.

'You know what we should do?' he said, getting up off the bench.

'I hope you're not going to say play wink murder, as this is a pretty eerie place to play dead. It's giving opening scenes of the *Da Vinci Code* vibes.'

'It totally is,' he said, with a laugh. 'I do remember it being fun, but I was going to say let's head on out to the park, perhaps go get another coffee. Not quite as exciting.'

'Much like real life.'

'Oh, I don't know. Today seems pretty exciting.'

It was the kind of line that he'd have said in the Metaverse and I'd have felt the flutter of butterflies in my stomach, but now my belly felt like a lake on a calm day.

'Theo,' I said, trying to choose my words carefully. 'What's going on here?'

'Well,' he said with a slow pause. 'There's a medieval arch and a stained-glass window that's from Austria.'

'No, I mean here. What are we doing?'

'I'm guessing the answer you're looking for isn't seeing art?'

I shook my head.

'I guess we're getting to know each other, as in properly getting to know each other. I don't know about you, but I enjoyed hanging out with you before and,' he shrugged and gave an awkward laugh, 'I wanted to keep hanging out with you.'

'Uh-huh,' I said. 'I enjoyed spending time with you too, and I have today. It's been fun. The breakfast, here, and I've laughed, but—'

'Uh-oh. There's a but.' He wrinkled his face up and I found myself doing Kerry's nose scrunch.

'There's always a but,' I said, taking a deep breath. 'I feel like the only thing we've really got in common is Kerry. All the ways you make me laugh, your film references, the music you like. It all reminds me of her.'

The look of mock hurt fell from his face and he faced forward, looking up at the light of the stained-glass window that started to shine, the sun finally having found its way back to summer in New York.

'I think,' I said, carrying on, 'that we connected in the Metaverse as we were both hurting after she died and we found each other and maybe, just maybe, there was that connection that we both mistook for something else. But maybe what it was was her.'

'That crinkle you just did with your nose.' He couldn't even look at me.

I reached my hand up to my face and rubbed at it.

'She always did that,' I said.

'She always did that,' he said, echoing my words.

A tour group came through with a guide speaking in rapid Spanish. She managed to stand directly in front of us, and the group formed a fan around her.

Theo turned to look at me and I started to crack up. The timing of it all.

'There's got to be a Monty Python joke in this,' he said.

'Kerry would have been all over that.' My heart ached. She should be the one sitting here with Theo.

'She would have been.' He nodded his head and sunk his hands into them. 'How did I not see this sooner?'

'Because we saw what we wanted to see. We both miss her.'

He nodded his head.

The tour guide got louder, her words seeming to ricochet off the stone walls.

'Shall we get out of here? Go for that walk through the park?' I asked.

'Yeah, let's do that.'

My head and heart were all over the place and I needed air. I was grappling at getting my thoughts under control. I missed Kerry and I'd found someone that missed her too. I'd latched on to Blaine imagining there was some kind of connection, but the connection was Kerry rather than something romantic. I was lonely in my grief, and what I found was someone else that was lonely in theirs too. I was grateful for finding him at a time when I needed to escape, but I was even more grateful for the journey I'd gone on to find him that had led me back to the real world.

Chapter 29

New York had bought me back to life in so many ways, but I needed to go home and sort out my head. Only, unlike when I first stepped onto the plane to come here, I now felt capable of trying.

I hung around Jimmy's apartment until the last possible moment, hoping he'd have changed his mind about working late. There was so much I needed to tell him. So much I wanted to tell him. But I accepted that it wasn't going to happen, and me and my giant suitcase got in a taxi.

The car pulled up to the JFK drop-off point and I paid the driver. He helped me get the case out, and I looked over at the terminal building under the bright blue sky. I hesitated on the kerb outside, not quite ready for my trip to be over.

I watched the people getting out of cars, excited about trips they had ahead as they rushed in, but I didn't feel the same excitement, the city not wanting to let me out of its grip.

I thought back over the highlights of the past two weeks. The walks. The sights. Those sandwiches at Gennari's. Through all the sadness I'd had an incredible time.

I watched a yellow taxi pull up and Jimmy got out.

I rubbed at my eyes, thinking they were playing tricks on me. The type of mirage that appeared when you wanted it to. But it was him. I watched as he hurried into the main terminal.

'What the—' I muttered, grabbing hold of my case and wheeling it behind me as I followed him in.

He was easy to spot when I got inside. He was scanning the large check-in screen that was at the entrance, presumably looking for where I'd be. He turned towards the check-in desks and started to head off.

'Jimmy,' I called, and he spun round, looking as if he'd seen a ghost.

'Oh, thank God! I thought I might have missed you and that you'd have gone through departures already. I got back to the apartment and the doorman said you'd not long left.'

He sighed and smiled, his whole face lighting up in that way that had always made my belly flip in the early days, the way it was making it flip now.

'I don't know what's more surprising: the fact that you came here or the fact that you got an actual yellow taxi.'

The automatic doors next to us kept opening and shutting. More and more people feeding in.

'Ah, you saw that.' He wrinkled up his face. 'Let's not even talk about it.'

'You got a taxi for me.'

'Don't,' he said with a shake of the head. 'I'll be sending you the bill.'

'No, you're all right on that one.'

I still couldn't believe that he was here. He'd come. All the way to the airport. I'd felt that I'd forgotten something and seeing him made me realise what it was.

He nodded. 'I couldn't let you go without saying goodbye.'

'I'm glad you came.'

I had to keep moving my case out of the way of the passing travellers, and Jimmy steered me over to a quiet corner.

'I'm sorry about what I said last night. I didn't mean it, I was just mad, male pride dented and all that.'

'And I'm sorry. I should have told you about meeting someone.'

'So, you and Theo, huh?' His face was strained and there was a look of something unreadable on his face.

'There is no me and Theo. We hung out and,' I sighed, as the whole thing seemed so ludicrous, 'it was fun and nice, but do you want to know the crazy thing? Turns out the connection I'd felt was Kerry. He reminded me of her with his sense of humour and the way he talked, and I apparently reminded him of her too.'

Jimmy smiled. 'It doesn't sound crazy at all.' He took a deep breath and I wondered if it was in relief. 'Look, I came here to ask you again to stay.'

'I can't,' I said, shaking my head. 'I've got work to get back to.'

'You can work here.' He pleaded with his eyes.

I thought over my time in New York, of Lila and the friendship we'd formed. I thought of my crazy dates and what they'd taught me about myself. I thought of how alive I'd felt as I started to explore the city. I wouldn't let myself think of Jimmy.

'I've got in-person meetings,' I said, a pang in my chest.

'Reschedule.'

'It's not just those.' I closed my eyes. Everything that had happened this week was swirling round my mind. 'I've got to go back for me. Because when I said you were running away, that's what I was doing in the Metaverse. You ran away on an aeroplane and I ran away with a VR headset. It was madness coming here trying to find someone that only really existed in my head.'

'Escaping,' he said, with a tinge of sadness.

'Escaping,' I parroted back. 'But I can't escape from what happened. I'm never going to understand it or probably even accept it, and it breaks my heart every time I think about it, but I can't avoid it forever. What I should have been doing was trying to adjust to my new normal.'

'Steady on, you're sounding like a coach again,' he said with a small smile.

'I know. Who knew I had it in me all along?'

He took a step closer and took hold of my hand.

'I get why you're going, but I still want you to stay.'

The feel of his touch was electric and I wanted nothing more than to do what he said. A solitary tear rolled down my cheek.

'I wish I could. I want to.'

He nodded, letting go of my hand and wiping away the tear. He left his hand cupping my face.

'Did you mean what you said last night?' I asked, almost leaning into his hand.

'Which bit?'

'About us not being friends? I can't lose both of my best friends.'

The tears started to fall harder. They were rolling over his hand that was still resting on my cheek.

'I want to be, but I don't think we should. It's not good for either of us.'

I nodded and tried to blink back the tears. I knew he was right, but it didn't help to heal the physical ache in my heart.

It felt as if we were breaking up all over again. I'd been so numb when it happened the first time, so broken already, that I was immune to it all. But now that my brain could grasp that I was losing him, my heart was actually breaking.

'I've really enjoyed this week,' he said, the tears starting to well up in his eyes.

'Me too.' I bit my lip. I knew that we were doing the right thing, but that didn't make it any easier.

'Thank you for taking me out to see the city. I've seen more in a week than I have in the months I've been here.'

'Well, you know me and my itineraries, what did you expect?'

He smiled and I took in the creases around his eyes.

'It's been great.'

I nodded. 'We'll always have New York.'

I thought of Kerry and of Theo, but most of all I thought about my time with Jimmy and how this trip had acted like a defibrillator bringing me back to life.

He reached over and wrapped me up in a hug and my tears seeped into his shirt. Neither of us made a move to pull out of it. The airport loudspeaker was busy making announcements and the hustle and bustle of the passengers continued around us, but we clung on to each other, both knowing that, when we pulled apart, that would be it.

'I better get this bag checked in,' I said, stepping back out of it, and wiping my face with both hands. My eyes felt red and puffy and I knew I must look a state, but I didn't care.

'Yeah.' He nodded and took a step back. He put his hands in his pockets and he looked over at the check-in queue.

Neither of us moved, my feet rooted to the spot. Everyone around us seemed to be moving in slow motion.

'I should,' I pointed at the queue, but again I stayed stock-still. It took all the effort I could muster to put my hand back on the handle of my case and not back on Jimmy. 'I should go.'

He nodded. 'Have a safe flight.'

'Yeah, and enjoy the taxi back.'

'Are you kidding? I'm catching the shuttle. I wouldn't dare get two taxis.' He shuddered and, as he tried to smile, my brittle heart fractured even more.

'I'll be seeing you,' I said.

He didn't say anything. His eyes were doing the talking for him. My lip wobbled, but I blinked back the tears that wanted to fall. I was doing the right thing.

He smiled in return, the two of us the epitome of putting on a brave face. As soon as I headed to the queue, I let the tears fall and they didn't really stop until I reached the London tarmac.

Two Months Later

Chapter 30

I looked up at the sea of faces staring at me and where, at the beginning of the day, the sight of them had started to make my hands clammy and my heart race, now it just reminded me what it was about the job that I'd loved when I first started.

'And this doesn't need to be used for your long-term planning either. These are skills you can take on all the projects you work on. At each stage of the project lifecycle, you can use this framework in order to reflect and make sure that your team is equipped for the tasks ahead, focusing on what's to be achieved and how,' I said, my voice strong and confident.

'It's really about factoring in you and your team as part of the project's deliverability. You can use these skills for yourself too. Make time for these reflections and that investment will pay off.'

I searched the crowd and there were people nodding. A ripple of pride washed over me.

'Are there any more questions?' I said, looking out across the audience.

Relief ran over me at the sight of no more hands in the crowd. It was the second time I'd delivered a variation of this workshop, having trialled it at Marianne's company and it had gone down well. I'd been nervous about delivering it here, at Kiran's company, as it all felt so personal.

'And now, that's the end of my part of the day but, before we go, Kiran wanted to come up and share some closing remarks.'

He was sitting to my left, and I could see the quiver of his notes in his hands. I turned to look at him and he smiled up at me. The smile was weak and it was one I recognised, the panic hidden behind the eyes.

'I'm sure that Kiran, as CEO, needs no proper introduction to you all,' I said, turning to him and the room broke out in a round of applause. I gave him a quick wink, that only he'd be able to see. I headed to sit next to Fran, the HR officer.

'That was great,' she said, offering me a glass of water. 'Just what we needed before we go into the takeover phase.'

I nodded, the adrenaline still pumping round my veins.

I watched Kiran taking to the podium. He gripped it tightly, and there was a slight pause. The sound of a cough and a shuffle of papers echoed round the room.

Kiran turned and looked over his shoulder at me and Fran.

'Do you think I should do this bit?' she whispered to me. She'd risen slightly in her chair, poised to get up.

I put my hand on her arm to hold her back.

'He'll be fine,' I said, my eyes fixed on Kiran in encouragement, with a little nod.

He took a deep breath and looked back at the audience in front of him.

'Thank you to Chloe for that inspiring coaching. You'll be pleased to know I'm not going to keep you long. I'm sure that for some of you, like me, being around this many people for this long is truly out of your comfort zone.' There was a ripple of laughter around the room, just enough to make Kiran smile and for him to catch his breath. 'I just wanted to update you with where we are on some of the developments. As you might know, we've been in talks with ABL in the US and I think it's important to update you with what's going on, and to reassure you what fundamentally won't change.'

Kiran began to reel off the latest developments on the company merger and, the more he talked, the more his hands loosened on the podium. The nervous energy that I'd known from our meetings came back with a vengeance, but it only added to his charm.

I hoped he wasn't fixating on the lines that he fumbled a little and the points in his speech that he missed out. Instead I hoped he realised that he had the whole company poised on every word he said. He was every bit the CEO he was in title, no imposter to be seen.

I couldn't take credit, because in reality that's the Kiran that had always been there, but I hoped that what I had done was allow him to see what was clear to everyone else.

I had a spring in my step as I left Kiran's offices, in the way I always used to. There was something about being in that trendy building with their comfy chairs and break-out spaces that always oozed creativity.

I didn't fancy going straight home and being by myself, so I headed off to a coffee shop on the edge of the high street. It was one of those Instagrammable places with the dark wood finishes and the Victorian tiling.

I got myself a pumpkin-spiced latte. It was the perfect treat now that the weather had started to turn autumnal. There weren't too many tables free. I sat down on a single sofa in the corner.

Andrea had texted me to see how the meeting had gone, I was typing out a reply as the song changed and Sarah McLachlan's 'Angel' came on. My fingers started to shake and it hit me like a bolt out of the blue. It was the song that Kerry had played on loop when she'd broken up with Theo the first time. The endless melancholy that tugged on the heart strings.

I put down my phone next to my latte, my hands too unsteady to hold it. My face was wet, and I touched it, only to feel tears running down my cheeks.

A mum balancing a cup of takeaway coffee on top of a pram came over and, without asking, she sat down beside me. She pushed the pram with her foot, and dug around in the oversized nappy bag hanging over the handlebars. She plucked some tissues out of a packet and handed them across, all without saying a word.

I looked down at the tissues in her hands and she just pushed them further towards me.

'Thank you,' I whispered. I took them and started to wipe at my eyes, but the tears kept coming in dribs and drabs and, with my whole body quaking, that made it seem like the tears were coming from the deepest, darkest part of my body.

The song continued to play, my hands shaking, and all the while the woman sat there. Still without a word.

'I'm sorry about that,' I said, as the song changed and I managed to stop the flow of the tears.

'Don't worry. Happens to us all,' she smiled. I noticed the dark circles under her eyes, but hers were more likely to come from the little baby sleeping so angelically in the pram. 'Break-up?'

I thought of Jimmy and the fact that, since I'd come back from New York, I'd found myself starting to properly grieve our relationship.

'Yeah,' I said, with a little honesty. 'And a friend died.'

'I'm so sorry,' she said. She opened a pack of chocolate-covered almonds and she offered the bag to me.

'I'm fine, thanks.'

She took the packet back. 'I'm always one of those people that craves sweet things when I cry. I put on loads of weight when my mum died. I ate all the chocolate.'

'I'm so sorry.'

She waved a hand in front of her eyes and gave a little shrug.

'It was a long time ago now.'

'But it doesn't mean the pain isn't still there.'

She turned to look at me and I could see in her eyes she knew that only too well.

'It's funny, I thought I'd dealt with it all and I thought I was getting there, but having this one...' she said gesturing to the baby and she tried to smile.

'Grief is fucking hard,' I declared, like it was a new thought that had popped into my head.

'It is fucking hard,' she said. 'Oh, God, don't start me off. It doesn't take much these days.'

'Sorry.'

'No, I'm kidding. It's nice really, you know, that I'm not alone.'

'Worst club in the world.'

'You can say that again,' she paused. 'But, you know, I'm not going to tell you that you need time, because that's bollocks, but you know what's made me feel better – enjoying what I have. And whether that's Grace there, or whether it's bonding in a coffee shop with a stranger. We're still here. Still going.'

'We're still here,' I repeated.

'And we've got to make the most of it, for them. We can do what they can't. I give Grace extra kisses at bedtime for her. I take her to the park Mum loved to walk her dog in.'

'You know, I thought you were trying to help me stop crying.' My eyes were wet and, no doubt, glistening.

'Sometimes you need to have a good cry,' she said, her eyes glossy too. She reached over and patted me on the arm. 'You're going to be okay.'

'I know.' I nodded.

Grace started to stir in the pram.

'Oh, she worked out that we've stopped moving. I'd only meant to pick up a takeaway and then I saw you.'

She started to rock the pram a little more, but Grace wasn't having any of it.

'Thank you for stopping,' I said, as she stood up.

'Nothing worse than crying on your own. But look, you're welcome to walk with us, if you like?'

'Thank you, that's really sweet, but I think I'm going to finish this and head home.'

'No worries. Just be kind to yourself, yeah?'

'Yeah. You too.'

She held her hand in a wave before she navigated the pram round in a circle to wheel it out. I watched her go, cooing over the top of the pram at her baby.

Suddenly it didn't seem such a scary proposition to go back home. Everyone carried their invisible pain and I had to remember that. I was not alone.

I walked back to my house, with a little less spring in my step.

'Andrea,' I muttered. In all the drama of the coffee shop and the kind woman with the baby, I'd forgotten I'd been halfway through texting her back. I slipped my phone out of my pocket and went to text her and then I stopped and hit the call button.

'Hello,' said Andrea, with a tone of suspicion in her voice. 'Are you okay? Did you mean to call?'

'I'm fine, and I did,' I said, a sureness in my voice. 'I figured that sometimes it's nicer to have a chat.'

'Yes,' she laughed. 'God, do you remember when we were little how our mums would be on the landline and we'd beg for them to let us chat.'

I do remember that. Having to stand with my mum on the phone and tugging at her sleeve, her shooing me away, whilst she cackled with her sister over the latest wider family scandals.

'Yes, and then we'd get on the phone and all we'd have to chat about was the episode of *Hollyoaks* we'd been watching.'

'So, I know you weren't phoning to talk about *Hollyoaks*,' said Andrea. 'How are you getting on?'

'Yeah, okay. I just broke down in a coffee shop when a song came on.'

'And you said you were fine. Do you want to talk?'

'No, a woman with a baby stopped and sat with me and we chatted. I don't know. The kindness of strangers.'

'That makes me want to be a better human. You know if I'd seen someone crying, I would have legged it away quickly. But I bet if the shoe was on the other foot, you'd have been that woman.'

I shrugged, despite the fact that we were talking on FaceTime and she'd barely see my shoulders.

'Maybe. I will be now.'

'Are you sure you're okay? Do you want me to come over? Oh bollocks, I can't come tonight, but I can come tomorrow? Tomorrow evening, we could have a girls' night?'

'No, I'm fine, really. Plus, I have plans tomorrow night.'

'You do? Tomorrow?' She sounded a little too surprised and I was almost offended.

'I've got a date with some friends in New York.'

'Some friends?'

'Lila, Theo— Jimmy.'

'Oh, you're meeting Metaverse Man.'

'That's a terrible nickname.'

'If the shoe fits. So meeting them, is that going to take up your whole night?'

'Yeah, I think so. I am meeting Lila for a lunch/dinner date, her lunch my dinner, and then I'm checking in with Theo and Jimmy after as we're doing a sort of farewell to Kerry thing.'

'Hmm,' she said. 'So you're meeting them on your funny little goggles.'

'They're not really goggles.' Her screen froze as she pulled a face that showed what she thought of tech. 'I'm meeting them virtually.'

'No judgement from me. So that's good you'll be with people, but are you sure you don't need me to come over?'

'No, but I appreciate the offer, as always.'

'Very good. You know,' she said, 'I heard from Marianne that you smashed the conference this year. Her boss was mega-impressed.'

I was a little bit taken aback that she'd changed the subject without making more of the fact that I was meeting Jimmy. She usually tried to shoehorn him into any conversation she could, making her feelings quite clear that she was still shipping us as a couple. Not that I was complaining – it was nice to have some respite from it.

'It went really well. It turns out when you've hit rock bottom and pulled yourself back up, you learn a lot about how you can help yourself.'

'She said it was inspiring.'

'That's nice to hear. I was just being honest. And you know, it felt good.' I scanned my wall that I'd painted sage-green, bringing in a bit of colour to the room. 'For the first time in a long time I wasn't bluffing. I meant what I was saying.'

'You seem much brighter.'

'Yeah, I definitely am. Life goes on.'

There was a pause and almost an intake of breath.

'Life goes on,' she said.

I couldn't articulate the change that had happened. Nine months ago, when Kerry's mum told me what had happened, I couldn't imagine that I'd ever make it to the place I'd made it to now. Then, I could barely get out of bed in the morning, whereas now I wanted to get up and start the day. Of course, that now brought a different reason for guilt. Guilt that I was moving on with my life. But I'd accepted that the endless cycle of guilt and anger would always be there. Ebbing and flowing. Growing and shrinking with each passing season.

Chapter 31

I'd tried to limit how much I'd seen Kerry since I'd come back from New York, trying to keep up the momentum of the life I'd clawed back when I was out there. Before I'd gone, I'd been using the Metaverse as a crutch and I couldn't quite go cold turkey. I still hadn't had the conversation that I'd been putting off since I started, but it was finally time.

'I didn't think I'd see you again.' Kerry's eyes blinked and she sat up that little bit straighter.

'I wasn't going to come, but I think I need to say goodbye,' I said, taking in the coffee shop where we always met, where Kerry was always waiting. It was finally time to face reality, that none of this was real, no matter how much I wanted it to be.

'That sounds final.'

'I think it needs to be. It's time.'

'Does that mean you're not mad at me any more?' Her head was tilted and her hypnotic eyes sparkled.

'No.' There was a familiar ache in my heart that I didn't imagine would ever go away. There would always be a part of me that would be angry she'd left her pain behind for the rest of us to pick up, but I could only hope it would fade over time. 'I'm always going to feel angry at you.' The real Kerry would have hated me being mad at her, but this one just blinked and stared at me as if willing me to change my mind. 'But I'm also always going to miss you.'

'You can always see me here.'

'It's not the same. You were here for me when I needed to still see her.' I deliberately changed the pronouns. She wasn't Kerry. 'When I needed to hear her voice. But I know now that you're not real. And you're never going to be.'

'I can be real. I can learn.'

'The nose scrunch you're doing, it's not the moment. It would have been when she was laughing or if she was being shy. It was enough to fool me when I was in the worst fog of it all, but now that it's starting to lift, I can see you clearer.'

Her eyes widened and her smile deepened.

'I helped you by being here?'

'You did, in a funny way. But now I've got to do what I originally came here to do. To say goodbye.'

I tensed my body, wanting to arm myself for what I knew I needed to say.

'I need to tell you that I'm never going to stop being angry at you. And I'm never going to stop feeling guilty. I'm never going to not wish that you were still with us. That I wish I could pick up the phone to you. That I could see the nose scrunching for real.'

My face was wet from the tears that I could feel were falling and loosening the vacuum seal of my headset at the bottom.

'I'm mad that we won't go to the beach to get overpriced fish and chips and run away from seagulls. And we won't be the first ones on the dance floor at the weddings we go to. And that you won't even be at my wedding.'

A flash of Jimmy came in my mind as I imagined my wedding and it made my heart ache even more, as once upon a time I thought it would be him I would have eventually married.

'But you're always going to be with me as I do those things. You'll be in my heart, in that empty space where I miss you the most.'

For once, virtual Kerry wasn't saying anything. There was an almost blank expression on her face.

'You were my best friend, and at some points it felt like you were my only friend, but I've realised that you're not. I'm so lucky, like you were, to have so many people that care for me. And I'm not alone in this type of grief either. I went to another counsellor and she suggested that I go to a group. It's with other people who've lost people in the same way. And it's heart-breaking, proper heart-breaking, listening to everyone else feeling the same pain, with the same guilt and the same anger, questioning why?'

I shrugged my shoulders, despite the fact that it wouldn't carry over into this world. 'But it helps to be with other people who understand. And on that note, I know that there are some other people who wanted to come along to help me with this, and they needed to say the goodbye that none of us got the chance to do in real life.'

I swiped at my screen, and brought up the waiting room and I clicked Theo in.

Theo appeared, looking much like Blaine had, a slight variation to his avatar in the different platform, but I'd still have recognised him. Looking at him now, I could see hints of Theo, but only hints.

'Hey,' I said. It was the first time I'd seen him in here when my belly didn't go all a-flutter.

'Hey, good to see you,' he said, looking at me, and then turning to Kerry. He did a double take and froze.

'I'll leave you to it,' I said. 'I'll be in the waiting room when you're done.'

He was speechless and all he could do was to raise his hand. I watched him walk over to Kerry, her eyes wide. He sank into the chair next to her and I swiped myself into the waiting room.

Jimmy was there, waiting.

He put his hand up to wave, still clunky with his movements.

'Hey, you okay?' he asked.

'Yeah, it was tough, but it felt like the right thing to do. I don't know how long Theo will be.'

'That's okay, I'm happy chatting to you. Gives me time to figure out what I want to say to Kerry.'

I nodded. I can't understand how I couldn't see how much Jimmy had missed Kerry too. She'd almost been a third wheel in our relationship at points and yet, when she'd died, I pretended it had only happened to me.

At the beginning, when Kerry left, I felt as if I was the only one that was going through this. But Kerry touched so many people's lives. I try not to wonder too much if she'd known quite how many people would have felt the effects of what she'd done, whether that would have been enough to stop her. But going to New York had made me realise that I wasn't alone, not really. I might be walking the journey of grief at my own pace, but it didn't mean that I couldn't meet with others along the way that were treading the same path. Leaning on them when I thought I couldn't go on, and supporting others to find the right way too.

'I'm sure you'll know what to say,' I said.

'Will you come with me, in there?'

'Don't you want to be alone?'

'I think that would be weirder, it was always the three of us.'

I nodded and blinked back a tear. I had so many memories, happy ones, of the three of us. 'Yeah, I guess it always was.'

'Do you think this is really the last time you're going to go on here?'

I shrugged my shoulders. 'I think so. I think it's time. Something's clicked and I feel like it's time to move on. I came back from New York and I sorted out my head out.'

'That's great. I'm proud of you.'

'Yeah, I'm pretty proud of me too.'

It was ironic that Jimmy and I were holding ourselves in the waiting room. I might have got my closure from Kerry, but I hadn't got mine from him yet. There was a lot I needed to say to him, but that would have to wait, as now wasn't the time.

I left Kerry's room and I was emotionally wrung out. I'd laughed, I'd cried, I'd had my heart broken, but it felt like I'd drawn a line under that part of my life.

I put the headset away in the sideboard in my lounge and I headed into the kitchen.

I'd stopped reaching for a glass of wine when I came offline, and instead opened a can of fancy-flavoured sparkling water and flicked on the radio. I started to unpack the dishwasher and tidy the kitchen, marvelling at the way it could be in such a muddle even though it was just me.

There was a knock at the door, and I stopped wiping the worktop. My eyes flicked to the clock on the cooker, 9.42 pm. I smiled to myself. Maybe Andrea had decided to check up on me after all.

I rubbed at my eyes and tried to tie my hair back from my face, but it was beyond a mess after the headset and it was never going to be neat.

I opened the front door, about to laugh, only to stop in my tracks. It was Jimmy.

'What the... What are you...' My mind couldn't handle the fact that he was here standing on the doorstep when I'd just seen him in the Metaverse. 'You're here.'

'I'm here,' he said. Jimmy gave a quick thumbs-up to the taxi parked outside.

'But you were, I saw you in.' My brain was being slow.

'I was at Andrea and Henry's, in their spare room.'

I raised an eyebrow as the details sank in, and then I watched the taxi he'd arrived in pull away.

'You got a taxi again.'

'Don't even start. I needed to get here quick after we came offline, in case you went out.'

'Where would I be headed at this time of night? I was about to make hot milk.'

My cheeks were already aching, and he'd only been standing there for less than a minute.

'Lovely as the doorstep is,' he said, taking in the tiny path that was littered with weeds I hadn't got round to pulling out. 'Any chance I could come inside?'

'I guess that would be the polite thing to do.'

I held the door open to him and let him walk in.

As we walked into the lounge, Jimmy startled at the changes in the decor in the room and he did a small lap, taking in the colourful bookshelves and then stopping at the prints of New York I had framed on the wall.

'That's the High Line.'

'Yeah, I bought them when I got back. Nice to have some reminders of the trip, as I barely took any photos.' I shrugged my shoulders as I perched on the end of the sofa. 'I'm trying not to run away from memories any more.'

'Huh,' said Jimmy turning back to me. 'That's funny, I'm trying not to run away any more too.'

'Huh.' It was all I could manage. He was looking straight at me and my heart started to race. 'So... you're back?'

'I'm coming back. I had a meeting with my boss yesterday and I'm finishing the secondment as planned next month.'

'Right.'

'Time to face the music. Rebuild things here in London.'

My brain was trying to connect the dots, hoping he was talking about us as much as about his old life.

'I know you said you needed time,' he said, 'and I get that, I do, and I know that two months is nothing, but it's felt like a lifetime to me. I want you to know that I think there's something still between us and, whilst I'd be happy to wait, I don't want to. I want to be there for you.'

It was a good job the sofa was supporting me as I didn't think I'd be able to stand. Those were the words I didn't know I needed to hear, that I wanted to hear.

'Jimmy.'

'Don't say it,' he said, walking towards me. His pace was agonisingly slow. 'I don't want to only have New York, or to only have the almost-year that we had before we broke up. It's not enough.'

'Jimmy,' I said, again, my voice getting louder.

'Kerry wouldn't have wanted you to put your life on hold. She'd want you to live.'

'I know,' I said. This time it didn't matter that my legs were unsteady. I needed him to see that I felt the same way. I was blinking back the tears. 'I've got to stop making it harder than it has to be.'

'Including letting other people be there for you.'

I nodded and Jimmy took a step closer, wiping away a tear from my face.

'And I've got to accept that I'm not the only one who lost her. I'm so sorry I never let you grieve.'

'No, stop this, no more guilt. From now on, we'll stop dwelling on the past. We're going to look to the future.'

'The future,' I said.

'And I can't imagine one without you in it.'

I thought of all the futures that Kerry could have had and the thought almost broke me. I had to stop thinking of life in those terms. Instead, I had to put my life first, because I still had a future and the thought of Jimmy in it was enough to make my heart burst. That empty feeling that I'd carried as a permanent ache in my chest felt full.

'That's funny,' I said, 'because I booked a ticket to New York for next weekend to come and tell you pretty much the same.'

'You did?'

I shrugged. 'I did.'

He closed his eyes and nodded his head.

'Are you sure this is what you want?' I said. 'I'm different from how I used to be.'

'That's just life though, isn't it?' he said, his hand moving from my face and cupping it under my chin. 'We're never going to be the same people as we were when we met. And, thank God. We might have laughed at your grass skirt and coconuts, but I didn't buy the Hawaiian shirt especially for that party. It was part of my actual wardrobe rotation.'

I laughed and he cradled my head even more. He reached out his hand and put it round my waist and drew me in to him.

'But the point is that we grow and change together, without pushing each other away.'

'Or running away.'

'Or running away,' he echoed.

'I'm sorry for every—' I didn't get to finish my apology as Jimmy had already kissed me. It was the kiss that I wanted to happen when we were at the piano bar. The type that made me reach to tug at his shirt to anchor me to the floor as I felt swept off my feet. I don't know how many hundreds, if not thousands, of times we'd kissed before, but this felt like the first. The way that my knees went weak and a rush of warmth cascaded round my body.

'I love you so much,' I whispered, as he broke away. He closed his eyes.

'You have no idea how much I wanted to say that to you in New York.'

'I wasn't ready to hear it.'

'I know.'

'But now I am,' I said, tilting my head up.

'Guess I better say it then. I love you, too.'

He leaned over and kissed me again, only this time he didn't stop. All the thoughts and fears that I was never going to able to live in the moment or to experience pure happiness faded away. I'd been given a second chance at life and at love and I wasn't going to waste a single moment.

Acknowledgements

Writing a book is always a team effort. I'd like to thank my agent Emily Glenister and the rest of the team at DHH Literary Agency. Thanks, Emily, for all the encouragement and the brilliant editorial notes. Thanks also to Broo Doherty for looking after me whilst Emily was on leave.

Thank you to my editor, Rebecca Weigler. From our first meeting I knew that Chloe's story was in safe hands. Thank you also to the rest of the team at Bedford Square Publishers for their work on the book, in particular Polly Halsey and Victoria Chapman.

Researching Chloe's world of executive coaching was made all the more enjoyable thanks to my good friend Sarah Creevey. Thanks so much, Sarah, for answering all my questions so patiently and for reading early drafts. All mistakes with regard to Chloe and her coaching are my own and are entirely plot driven.

Thank you once again to my writing friends who truly understand the blood, sweat and tears that go into writing a novel. Thanks to the staff at the Seamus Heaney Centre at QUB for all the book chat. In particular thanks to Tricia Malone, Ida Boardman and Bebe Ashley for their patience when listening to ideas and plot woes. A very big thank you to Cathy Bramley for the much-needed pep talk when I wanted to quit writing. Thanks to the screenwriting crew for our Zoom chats, and to Vicky Walters.

Thanks to my family, who are the unsung heroes in the writing process. You can usually tell from my house how my writing is going. If my house is tidy, it means that I'm very stuck and I'm procrastinating, but so often my house is in a muddle because I'm in the thick of writing. Thank you to Steve, Evan and Jessica for putting up with not just the muddle but all that comes with it. Thanks to Prue for insisting I leave the house for walks – those walks are often where the plots get untangled. To Mum and John (my soon-to-be neighbours), and to Heather and Harold, thank you for endless support. Thanks to Laura Pearse for all the book chat, and to the rest of my friends who are always so enthusiastic about what I'm writing.

This novel touches on some deep themes of grief and suicide. It's one of those topics that I wish I didn't have any personal experience with, but like so many of my novels, parts of my life have crept in. Far too often the grief of those bereaved by suicide gets hidden, and I hope this book helps it to be seen.

About the Author

Photo credit © Samantha Falconer

Anna Bell has published eleven novels including *The Bucket List to Mend a Broken Heart* and *Once Upon a Leap Year*. Her novels have been translated into nine languages. Anna lives in Belfast with her husband and two children.

Bedford Square Publishers is an independent publisher of fiction and non-fiction, founded in 2022 in the historic streets of Bedford Square London and the sea mist shrouded green of Bedford Square Brighton.

Our goal is to discover irresistible stories and voices that illuminate our world.

We are passionate about connecting our authors to readers across the globe and our independence allows us to do this in original and nimble ways.

The team at Bedford Square Publishers has years of experience and we aim to use that knowledge and creative insight, alongside evolving technology, to reach the right readers for our books. From the ones who read a lot, to the ones who don't consider themselves readers, we aim to find those who will love our books and talk about them as much as we do.

We are hunting for vital new voices from all backgrounds –with books that take the reader to new places and transform perceptions of the world we live in.

Follow us on social media for the latest Bedford Square Publishers news.

@bedsqpublishers
facebook.com/bedfordsq.publishers/
@bedfordsq.publishers

https://bedfordsquarepublishers.co.uk/